S A V E D

S A V E D

K A T E   M O R G E N R O T H

HarperCollins*Publishers*

HarperCollins books may be purchased for educational,
business, or sales promotional use. For information, please write:
Special Markets Department, HarperCollins Publishers Inc.,
10 East 53rd Street, New York, NY 10022.

FIRST EDITION

Designed by Ann Gold

Printed on acid-free paper

Library of Congress Cataloging-in-Publication Data
is available upon request.

ISBN 0-06-019276-3

02   03   04   05   06   WB/RRD   10   9   8   7   6   5   4   3   2   1

For Jed

ACKNOWLEDGMENTS

This is a work of fiction, but I tried to get the facts right, where I could. The action in the book might seem farfetched, but it is actually far less dramatic than many of the real-life stories I heard during my research. There really is a Coast Guard air station at Sitka, and those helicopter crews go out when and where no one else will, day in and day out.

There were a number of people who were incredibly helpful in Sitka. At the Coast Guard airbase, Operations Officer Commander Karl Baldessari lent me his enormous breadth of knowledge, and with his abilities as a storyteller, Commander Baldessari could write a book himself. Lieutenant Commander Eric Riepe helped with the nuts and bolts of daily Coast Guard operations. Nurse Practitioner Bitsy Mosher shared her years of experience working with the personnel at the air station. And to Brenda and Pat Bean and their family, thank you for showing us around Sitka, one of the most beautiful places I have ever been. Thanks also for sharing your home, your hospitality, and the deer wrestling story.

My father-in-law, John Gore, introduced me to some fantastic people in the U.S. Navy who helped with the gritty technical details. Among these were Lieutenant Commander Peter Lento (USN Ret.), who happens to be a great editor and who came up with some creative ways to resolve the inevitable conflict between fact and fiction. Also, Rear Admiral Kirk Unruh put me in touch with Commodore Bill Elliot who gave me an overview of naval salvage operations. Commodore Elliot in turn pointed me to Commander Dave Davis, a giant in the field of salvage, who also has a rare knack for communicating technical issues to a layperson.

During the course of my research, I became truly fascinated with all things helicopter, and Jim Battle added his extensive knowledge of the Jayhawk design and told some great stories about the history of its development.

Those were the people who helped with the facts. There was also a whole team of people who aided me on the fiction side. Thanks to my family and friends, who provided invaluable support on the front lines of the editing process.

Lastly, my boundless appreciation for my husband (and part-time research assistant) who provided advice, encouragement, and ice cream.

What I got right is due to the assistance of all these people. The rest is a combination of creative license, unintentional errors, and plain old sea story. I hope you will allow the first, forgive the second, and enjoy the last.

SAVED

The thing is, helicopters are different from airplanes. An airplane by its nature wants to fly, and if it is not interfered with too strongly by unusual events or a deliberately incompetent pilot, it will fly. A helicopter does not want to fly. It is maintained in the air by a variety of forces and controls working in opposition to each other, and if there is any disturbance in this delicate balance, the helicopter stops flying, immediately and disastrously. There is no such thing as a gliding helicopter.

This is why being a helicopter pilot is so different from being an airplane pilot, and why, in generality, airplane pilots are open, clear-eyed, buoyant extroverts and helicopter pilots are brooders, introspective anticipators of trouble. They know if something bad has not happened it is about to.

—Harry Reasoner,
newscaster

 "If you want to hear a story about someone who really pulled some crazy shit, I should tell you about this fishing boat captain my father knew," Andy said. He dabbed at the trim of the long liner, the *Sea Smoke*, with a paintbrush. The water inside Crescent Harbor was calm, the wind ruffling the reflections of the boats. The air smelled of gas and oil and the fresh sharp scent of brine.

While Andy painted, his fellow crewman, Bill, sat on the side of the boat, smoking. Bill was staring out through the tangle of masts toward the twelve-foot breaker of moss-covered rocks and the fogbound peaks of Sugarloaf and Bear.

The buzz of a float plane cut through the quiet evening. Bill lifted his head to follow its invisible progress through the low clouds. "You want to talk crazy, we should be talking about those bush pilots," he said. "Who flies in this stuff? Can't see a damn thing."

"This skipper gives the bush pilots a run for their money," Andy said. "He'd sail through anything, this guy. It could be blowing forty, fifty knots, and it wouldn't faze him. And this was a while ago, back in the sixties, when you didn't have all this fancy equipment, and you couldn't call in the Coast Guard to pull your sorry ass out of the water if you were going down." He gestured with the paintbrush across the water to where the Coast Guard station was housed on the tip of Japonski Island.

"When he wasn't fishing, this skipper ran fresh fruit and vegetables to the towns up along the Inside Passage to make some money in the off-season. One trip, not long out of Vancouver, the weather turned funny. It was the kind of afternoon you just know a bad one's coming—kind of like today. Anyway, the skipper could have pulled into a cove and sheltered through the bad weather, but he decided to keep going. He didn't want his produce to go bad, and he was loaded down with stuff. He had potatoes, onions, squash, apples, everything you can think of, crammed into every square inch of space. So he sailed right into that storm. Turned out it was a doozy."

The float plane had landed, and it was quiet but for the strange, high-pitched squeak of the roosting eagles and the slap of a fish jumping and falling back into the water.

"The wind started gusting pretty strong, blowing the tops off the swells, and then the water started breaking over the bow. Well, that just happened to be where they had stored the squash, so with every wave a few dozen squash got washed out into the sound until the waves were filled with these squash. The crew is worried about making it through because the boat is near to rolling the rails, but this skipper, you know what he's doing? He's yelling at the crew to pick up the goddamn squashes. It's blowing near seventy, and they're chasing squashes— leaning out over the rails with fishnets, scooping them up and dumping them below. And you know what? They got every goddamned squash and got through the storm too. What do you think of that?"

"I think you missed a spot." Bill pointed to a place on the boat's trim with the end of his cigarette. Then he flicked the dangling ash into the water.

Andy went over the spot with his brush. "You don't think that's the craziest thing you ever heard?"

"I guess I heard crazier." Bill shrugged. "Seems like most guys around here have some story. Bound to happen if you spend enough time on the water—or enough time in Alaska."

The boats in Crescent Harbor bore names like *Stormy Sea, Lady Luck, Safe Harbor, Home Shore, Endurance, By the Grace of God,* suggesting that the men who sailed on those boats were aware of the edge of uncertainty on which they lived.

"Hey, Walt, you almost done messing with that engine?" Bill called out.

Andy paused, brush in the air, waiting for the reply, but Walt either didn't hear or didn't answer.

"It's time to go," Bill said.

"No argument here."

The harbor was deserted. Earlier in the day there had been several commercial fishing boat crews working to get ready for the season. They were easily recognizable in rubber boots, thick workingman's pants, and battered baseball caps. But half an hour ago, the last crew had turned off their Allman Brothers tape and headed to the P Bar for a beer.

The pleasure boaters, dressed in khakis and old sweaters, had left hours earlier. They had stowed their poles and tossed the unused bait— the tiny herring lying shoulder to shoulder in their Styrofoam beds— and had gone home early, shaking their heads over the chop out in the gulf. Even the traffic on Lincoln Street had fallen off, with the hum of a passing car infrequently breaking the silence.

Walt emerged from the cabin, his hands dark with grease from the engine. He was attempting to clean them with a gray rag.

"So you guys ready to go?" Walt said.

Bill and Andy were silent.

"Okay, I get the message. Just let me pack up." Walt disappeared back into the cabin. Andy bent to close the paint can and started cleaning the brush. Bill emptied his mug of coffee into the water and set it back inside the boat. The sound of footsteps made him glance up, and he watched idly as a man dressed in sneakers, jeans, and a T-shirt walked down the dock.

As the man passed by, he said a friendly hello. Bill nodded and stubbed his cigarette out on the planks of the dock. When he looked up again, at first he couldn't see where the man had gone. Then he spotted him jumping into a thirty-foot Bayliner a few slips down.

"Hey," Bill said. "Hey, there's some guy getting in Tom Leland's boat."

"What?" Andy wiped the damp brush on the leg of his pants and moved over to where Bill was sitting.

"Some stranger's in Tom's boat. Look at that, he's going into the cabin."

"Huh," Andy said.

Walt emerged from the cabin. "You guys ready?"

"Somebody's on Tom's boat," Andy told him.

"Oh yeah?" Walt said. "How about that? And I didn't believe him."

"Believe who?"

"Tom was talking about it last night at the P Bar. Said he sold his boat. Claimed he sold it to some chump who bought it for twice what it was worth. Guess this must be the chump."

"You don't think he's fixing to go out, do you?" Bill asked.

They heard the engine start up, roaring to life.

"Maybe he's just checking his new property," Andy suggested.

The stranger reappeared, climbed back out on the dock, and started uncleating the lines.

"Maybe not," Bill said. "Looks to me like he's getting ready to go out."

They all glanced up at the low clouds, and a smattering of raindrops hit the deck.

"Somebody better talk to him." Walt waited a moment before saying, "All right, fine. I'll do it." He stuffed his hands in his pockets, strolled down the dock, and stopped by Tom's boat.

The other men weren't near enough to hear what was said, but as they watched, they saw the stranger turn around. Walt pointed out to sea, and the man smiled and nodded. Walt said something else, and the man nodded again and said something in response. Then he bent to uncleat the last rope. Walt shook his head and started to walk back.

When he came up to where Andy and Bill were waiting on the dock, he stopped and turned to watch as the stranger climbed back into the boat and disappeared into the cabin.

"Guess he's going," Bill said.

"Yep. Said he wanted to go for a sail. See the sunset."

"Sunset?" Andy echoed. "Even if you could see it through those clouds, sun's not going to set till eight-thirty, nine o'clock."

"I told him that."

"Didn't you point out those clouds?" Bill said. "Does he know what they could turn into in a few hours?"

"Told him that."

"And the wind, did you tell him that when the flags are waving like that, they're trying to tell you to stay home?"

"Yep. Told him that too. Told him he could listen to the radio if he didn't believe me. But—" Walt broke off when they saw the Bayliner start to reverse out of the slip.

"There he goes," Walt said as the three stood and watched the stranger steer away from the dock and glide out past the breakwater.

"Think we should do something?" Andy said.

"You got something in mind?"

"Maybe he didn't realize how bad it can get, and how fast."

"I told him," Walt said.

"And?"

"He pretty much told me to mind my own business. He was real nice about it, though."

"What do you mean, real nice about it?"

"He said, 'Thanks for the advice, sir.' Then he went on doin' what he was doin'."

"Huh," Andy said. "Guess we did what we could."

"Yep."

"He might be fine. Especially if he sticks to the Inside Passage."

"He might," Walt allowed. "He also might get himself killed."

"Who knows," Bill said. "He might have some luck. The way the weather is around here, maybe we'll be wrong, it'll clear, and he'll get a nice sunset after all. You never know."

CHAPTER 2

Once he was beyond the breakwater at Crescent Harbor, the man steered his new boat to starboard, idling along the slow speed channel. As he passed the lighthouse, the boat rocked in the swells that rolled in from the ocean. White-caps bloomed at the peaks of the waves farther out to sea.

At his back, the town of Sitka looked ghostly, the steeple of the old Russian Orthodox church and the stately façade of the Pioneers' Home receding into the fog. The clouds stuck like wads of cotton between the mountains and the water where the buildings clung to the thin edge of coast.

From his vantage point on the boat, the man could almost see the end of the road to the north. It stretched only seven miles in either direction where it ended abruptly, Western hemlock and Sitka spruce rising suddenly from the hillside as if the road crew had left work one day and forgotten to return. If you wanted to get anywhere from Sitka, you needed a boat or a plane.

As the stranger headed out to sea, he rounded Japonski, a small island about a mile long, connected to the town by O'Connell Bridge. It housed three vital parts of the city: the hospital, the airport, and the Coast Guard station. The stranger glanced over as he passed by the Coast Guard's squat manila hangar, perched on the northern tip of the island. Then he pushed the throttle forward and the bow of the Bayliner lifted out of the water as it accelerated away, toward the open ocean.

The hangar that the stranger passed housed three H-60 Jayhawk helicopters. With those three aircraft, Air Station Sitka was responsible for the expanse of shoreline stretching from the Canadian border to the northern village of Yakutat, a span of twelve thousand tidal miles of mountainous terrain. It also presented some of the most difficult flying a Coast Guard pilot would ever see.

The weather in Southeast Alaska was famously changeable and powerful. Storms coming up from the south had thousands of miles of ocean to gather force. Occasionally, violent bursts of wind would flatten a whole mountainside of trees. Icing conditions—deadly to aircraft—were worse in the clean Alaskan air, and visibility was often nonexistent, especially in winter when it was dark twenty hours a day. No one but the Coast Guard flew after dark.

In the Lower Forty-eight, the Coast Guard's mission was restricted to emergencies over water, but in Sitka the air station did double duty, also covering all inland emergencies: lost hikers, stranded hunters, anyone injured or sick in any of the hundreds of remote villages that lined the Inside Passage. Sitka itself was remote enough to be considered an overseas posting, and to qualify for the assignment, a pilot needed at least one tour of duty—four years of flying.

But in other ways, the air station was like any other in the country. The helos were manned around the clock, with a four-man duty crew always on base and ready to go out. *Semper paratus* was the official motto of the Coast Guard; it meant "Always ready," but being "always ready" meant a lot of waiting.

That evening two members of the four-man duty crew—Teddy McDonald and Dave Lazure—were passing the time after dinner shooting pool. Teddy was losing, and now he started goofing, threading his stick behind his back to line up a shot. He was only five-foot-six, so he had to stretch up on his toes to manage it. He pulled back smoothly, but as he shot, the stick went wild and smacked the side of the cue ball. The cue ball careened off the bumper and into the four ball, which spun sideways into the corner pocket.

"Yes!" Teddy pumped his fists over his head. "I can't lose."

"Well, yes, actually, you can," Dave said. "I'm solids."

Teddy froze, his fists still in the air. "Oh." He dropped his hands. "Right. I forgot."

Struggling to hold back a smile, Dave moved around the table to line up his next shot. He bent over so his face was eye-level with the felt. Then he straightened, took a few steps back for a better view, and stood combing his moustache with his fingers while he studied the table.

Teddy positioned himself behind Dave to mimic him, raising his own hand to stroke his smooth upper lip and drawing a guffaw from Mike Hoffman, who was standing against the wall watching the game.

Teddy loved any audience, but his clowning was intended for the fourth person in the room—Ellie Somers. Ellie sat in one of the oversized leather recliners, trying to listen to the weather report on the radio, but Teddy, as usual, had managed to distract her, and she was shielding her face with one hand to keep Dave from seeing her silent laughter.

Outside, the wind blew the rain up against the window. It sounded like handfuls of sand thrown against the glass.

"What are you hearing on the radio?" Dave asked, and Ellie tried to compose herself to answer.

"Oh, the same," she said, though she hadn't heard the last report.

"This squall sure blew in fast."

"I could have told you it would," Mike said.

They all ignored him.

"You'd think that there'd be *someone* stupid enough to get caught out in it." Picking up the cube of blue chalk, Teddy ground it on his cue.

Dave wrinkled his nose in distaste. "What's wrong with you? We're here to get people out of trouble, not wish them into it."

"Excuse me, Lieutenant," Teddy said. "But I think that you feel exactly the same, you just won't admit it."

"You're disgusting," Dave responded.

"Somers?" Teddy appealed to Ellie. "Make him admit it."

She raised her arms over her head in a lazy stretch and shook her head. "No can do, Teddy."

"You could if you wanted to."

"Maybe," Ellie shrugged, "but I'm with Dave on this one. Sorry."

Teddy clutched at his heart. "Traitor. Turncoat. Two-timer. I can't believe you're agreeing with him."

"How can I not?" She smiled. "He's got a point—you are kinda disgusting. I mean, have you gotten a good whiff of your locker recently?"

Teddy grinned back. "Hey, but it's just gettin' good."

"Is there anything either of you wouldn't turn into a joke?" Dave wondered.

Teddy and Ellie looked at each other.

"No," they said at the same time.

"For Christ's sake," Dave said, but this time he couldn't hide the twitch of a smile. He tried to cover it by snapping, "Take your shot already, Teddy."

"Okay, okay, don't get your panties in a bunch." Teddy crouched in front of the table to line up his shot.

The door to the lounge opened and the CO, Commander Traub, stuck his head in. Teddy stopped just as he was drawing back the cue and straightened, Dave swung around on his heel, Mike pushed off the wall, and Ellie got up out of her chair.

"Good, you're all here," Commander Traub said, glancing around. Usually the enlisted officers, Teddy and Mike, would be in the crew's lounge, but he had asked them all to gather in the ward room—the officer's lounge—so he could talk to them together.

Traub stepped into the room and closed the door behind him. "That reporter who's doing the feature is here."

He looked at Ellie when he said it, but Teddy set aside his cue and dusted his hands against his chest, leaving streaks of light blue chalk on his flight suit. "Wants to talk to me, I imagine. I'm ready for the spotlight, Skipper. I won't deny my public."

Traub glanced over and said, "Be quiet, McDonald," then turned back to Ellie. "I don't know why I'm letting this go through after the last one. This time I don't want to be reading your little jokes about how, for practice, you fly blindfolded, or that if people aren't grateful enough when you rescue them, you toss them back in."

"That was pretty good, wasn't it?" Ellie said.

"The thing about throwing them back in, that part was me. I came up with that one, sir," Teddy said.

"All right, enough. Haven't I requested that you both be a little more professional?"

Traub wasn't only talking about their jokes; it was also a veiled reference to Teddy and Ellie's unusual friendship. It wasn't unheard of for officers and enlisted men to go fishing together, maybe have a beer—especially if they flew together—but there was usually a reserve, an acknowledgment of the barrier between them. However, Teddy had some trouble with the formality of rank to begin with, and Ellie didn't make any effort to maintain the distinction between officers and enlisted.

They'd hit it off the first week Teddy arrived. That was almost a year ago now, and although Traub occasionally mentioned something about their conduct, he mostly let it slide. Before Teddy came, Ellie had not been settling in well. On the surface she seemed to get along with her fellow officers, but they were almost all married with families, and she had made no real friends among them. In Traub's estimation, she had been disturbingly isolated. Teddy's arrival had changed all that.

"Lieutenant Lazure, will you try to keep these two in order?" Traub said to Dave.

"I'll try, sir. I can't say that I generally have much luck."

Dave had arrived a few months after Teddy, and he had become the incongruous third in a strange threesome. He had a high sense of propriety and responsibility, so his friendship with the other two was puzzled over. However, he did try to maintain a semblance of rank, and he usually managed to keep the other two from stepping too far over the line. For instance, Teddy never actually dared to use either Dave's or Ellie's first names, though he often called Dave "Lazure" instead of "Lieutenant Lazure," and Ellie was almost always just "Somers."

Traub said, "This reporter requested that he be able to speak to you all together while you were on duty, and I don't see the harm in it. I want everyone to help Lieutenant Commander Somers out."

"Always a bridesmaid, never a bride," Teddy sighed.

"He wants to talk to you too," Traub assured him.

"Really?" Teddy perked up, looking hopeful.

"He wants to know what it's like to fly with Somers."

Teddy's face was a comic picture of disappointment, but he recovered quickly. "That's an easy question to answer. Terrifying."

Traub pointed a stern finger at him. "None of that."

"You mean none of the truth," Dave muttered.

"How are all three of you on duty together, tonight of all nights? Did you rig the duty roster or something?" Traub said.

"Don't you believe in fate, sir?" Teddy asked.

"Then someone up there doesn't like me. At any rate, I think I've made myself clear. I'll go bring him in."

When the door shut behind the CO there was a moment of silence. Ellie sat back down by the radio, but she could feel Dave's stare without even looking. She tried ignoring it, but finally she turned and demanded, "What?"

"I was just wondering, why do you think this reporter wants to talk to you specifically?" Dave said.

Of course Ellie knew why, but it galled her—both the reason, and the fact that Dave felt the need to bring it up. Most of the time Dave's tirades didn't bother her—with the exception of this one subject: the special treatment she got because she was a woman. It was like getting a finger in the ribs in the exact place she'd been poked a million times before. It didn't hurt so much the first time or the second, but after the millionth it was sore as hell. If she'd thought about it she might have figured out that it had more to do with Dave than with her. They were the same age, had been in the service the same amount of time, and Ellie was a lieutenant commander while Dave was still a lieutenant. Dave was looking for excuses of his own, but all Ellie heard was the challenge to her ability, that old refrain she had been hearing ever since she could remember. She didn't show that it affected her; instead she did what she always did—she made a joke of it.

She said with a grin, "It's obvious why. 'Cause I can fly circles around all you boys."

Dave snorted. "Right."

"You think I can't? You don't want me to bring up what happened when we went down to Mobile for training last year, do you?"

"I didn't say *I* was better," he admitted, and Ellie felt a tinge of remorse for mentioning what she knew must be a painful subject. Dave had panicked during a test in the flight simulator. His confidence in his skills had suffered a blow, and he hadn't yet recovered.

However, Ellie didn't feel sorry for long because Dave said, "There's one man on this base that makes us all look like rookies. He's what I consider a real pilot, and don't pretend you don't know who I'm talking about."

Ellie glared at him. This was one thing she had trouble making a joke about. The base was too small, she thought. You couldn't leave behind your mistakes. However, even if she couldn't joke about it, at least she didn't have to show Dave that he had scored a hit. She merely acknowledged, "I know who you're referring to."

"*I* don't know," Mike put in. They all looked at him, and there was a short silence before Dave answered.

"Sam's the best. Sam Pantano."

"Shame on you," Teddy said. "You know better than to say that name."

Dave defended himself, saying, "I don't believe in coddling people's feelings. I tell it like it is."

"Like it is?" Ellie said. "Give me a break. The truth is that your hero, Sam, hasn't got any guts. He's a textbook pilot."

"He's got the Distinguished Flying Cross," Dave countered. "Where's yours? Oh, I'm sorry, I forgot. They don't give those out just because you happen to be a woman, do they?"

"Low blow," Teddy said, wincing in exaggerated pain.

But Ellie knew Dave had a point. They wouldn't show any favoritism in giving that medal out. It was the highest honor a Coast Guard pilot could be awarded. That's why she wanted it. If anything would prove that she was just as good as the boys, getting the DFC would do it.

"It's only a matter of time, Davey." She knew he hated it when she called him Davey. "I should have had it already for a couple of missions. The only reason I don't have one is that the stiffs up top love good little boys like Sam—sooo serious, sooo dedicated, do what they're told."

"No wonder they haven't given it to you," Teddy said. "You're not too good with that last part."

"Maybe you just haven't earned it," Dave suggested. "Ever think of that?"

She had thought of it, but she wasn't about to admit it. "Then why is this reporter coming across the country to talk to *me?*"

"You're right," Dave said. "As far as that reporter's concerned, you are the best pilot. The best *female* pilot." He didn't need to add that there wasn't a large supply to choose from.

Ellie gave him the finger and turned away, as if she were listening to the radio.

"You're pissed off because you know I'm right."

Ellie ignored him, but Teddy jumped into the fray. "Poor baby, nobody recognizes your genius and all because you have a—"

The door opened and Traub said, "Mr. Whalen, come in and meet the crew."

The reporter stepped into the room behind Traub. They sized him up. The reporter wore new hiking boots, faded jeans, and a North Face jacket that cost as much as they made in a week. He reminded them of a world where you had more clothing choices than a flight suit, where work was done behind a desk, and where the biggest risk you took on a regular day was maybe switching phone companies.

As they studied him, the reporter stared back. He saw two men with pool cues. One looked like a young Mickey Rooney. The other had a bushy moustache and lantern jaw and was good-looking in the style of a seventies' movie star. There was a husky, corn-fed kid with a blond crew cut against the wall, and then, in the armchair beyond the pool table, the only woman. He had expected a stern, masculine woman, square-faced, short-haired, and thin-lipped to match the fact that she had what was usually a man's job. She wasn't very feminine in the sense that she wore no makeup and her shoulder length hair was raked back in a ponytail that looked a bit limp and greasy, but she had a wide heart-shaped face, and her features were almost delicate—an impression strengthened by the contrast between her dark hair and pale skin. However, there was nothing delicate about the broad grin he'd glimpsed briefly as he entered the room.

Traub made the introductions, pointing each crewman out as he named them. "This is Petty Officer McDonald. He's a flight mechanic. And this here is Lieutenant Lazure, pilot. Over against the wall is a new addition to the team, Petty Officer Hoffman. He's a rescue swimmer. And finally, Lieutenant Commander Somers, pilot." He paused. "Well . . ." he clapped his hands together. "I guess I'll leave you all to talk. Let me know if you need anything else."

As he was leaving, Traub glanced at Ellie sitting by the radio, still listening to the broadcast. He frowned, caught her eye, and drew a finger across his throat. Reluctantly, she reached over and turned the radio off. Traub nodded approval and closed the door behind him.

The reporter fit his hands casually in his pockets and looked around the room. He had ten years of hard-core news reporting behind him, and even some wartime coverage. It was only recently he'd switched to magazines. He was getting more money, but he'd found that feature-writing bored him. He missed the rush of the on-the-scene news, the deadlines, the immediacy of tragedy. Now he was doing feel-good fluff about some woman pilot out in the Middle of Nowhere, Alaska, who, it looked like, spent most of her time sitting around.

"You guys play a lot of pool?" he asked.

Teddy answered him, confessing, "I'm thinking of switching over to the professional circuit."

Dave explained. "We do a lot of waiting to get called out."

"How about you?" Whalen asked Ellie. "Do you play?"

"Only for money," Ellie said. "I'm not going to strike it rich in this job, so I need to supplement my income somehow."

"She could retire on the money she's won from me," Teddy said.

"I've beaten her," Dave told the reporter.

"Yeah, like once," Teddy added.

"Three times," Dave corrected.

"Out of how many?" Teddy asked.

Dave didn't answer.

"And you?" the reporter asked Mike, who stood silent against the wall.

"I just got transferred," Mike said. "But I could probably beat them if I wanted to."

"Oh really?" Teddy turned to look at him. "Is that why you've been here a month and haven't asked for winners? Because you didn't want to embarrass us? Do you want to humiliate him, or should I?" Teddy asked Dave.

"I'll flip you for it," Dave said.

"What about me?" Ellie demanded.

"You only play for money, remember?" Teddy said.

"I sometimes make an exception when there's an opportunity for extreme embarrassment."

"I'll take you all on," Mike said.

"There we go." Teddy clapped in appreciation. "Those are the qualities we like in a rescue swimmer."

"And what are those?" Whalen asked, dutifully taking out his notepad.

"A little bit of bravery and a big serving of stupidity," Teddy replied.

"Stupidity?" Whalen said. "Why stupidity? Where does that get you?"

"Dead," Dave interrupted. "Don't listen to Teddy. He likes to run off at the mouth."

The reporter was interested in this line of discussion. "Does that happen often?" he ventured. "I mean, do you lose a lot of people in your line of work?"

"More than we'd like," Dave answered evasively.

The reporter tried again. "One is more than anyone would like," he pointed out, trying to elicit more information.

But Dave simply said, "Exactly."

Whalen figured he wasn't getting much out of the guy with the moustache. He turned to the new kid. "Have you been on an S.A.R.?" When he asked the question, he spelled out the three letters that stood for "search and rescue."

"You don't spell it out. You say 'SAR,' like it's a word," Mike told him. "And no, not yet. There've been a few calls, but they've mostly been medevacs. We also had to deliver some pumps to a fishing boat that'd grounded, causing flooding in the ship's lazarette, but you don't need a rescue swimmer for any of those."

"So do you think you'll be going out tonight?"

All four looked toward the window, the rain still beating against the glass. He'd asked the question that had been on all their minds since the storm blew in.

"Maybe," Mike said.

"And when you get called out, do you ever think that this time might be the time that you don't come back?"

There was another uncomfortable silence, but Ellie saved them this time. She said, "Doesn't make a difference. You have to go out . . ."

The other three joined in to finish the sentence with her, ". . . but you don't have to come back." They all shared grins, even Dave.

"Sort of a motto," Dave said. "Unofficial, of course."

"Sounds more like a death wish than a motto," Whalen observed. "What actually happens when you get called out? I mean, how do you know that there's an emergency?"

The reporter was looking at Ellie, hoping she would answer, but it was Dave who spoke again. "Well, the distress call comes into the command center in Juneau, and they check the position. If it's in our area, they call our operations center and—"

They heard the click of the speaker systems switching on. Their ears had become so attuned that they were all moving toward the door before the first rising note of the whoopee. Just as the first wail was dying away, the announcement came over the intercom, "Put the ready helo on the line. Put the ready helo on the line."

"That's how," Teddy said over his shoulder as he headed out.

"Wait, where . . ." but they were out of the room before the reporter could finish his question, and not one of them, despite their unofficial motto, considered the possibility they might not come back.

"Mayday, Mayday." The stranger, who had set out so confidently, gripped the handset of the VHF radio in one hand while he struggled to hold the Bayliner steady into the waves with the other. The bow of the boat was lifted by one of the mountainous breakers, and he laid on the power, the engine revving to climb the steep wall of water. The rain was slashing against the glass, and the blackness was so complete it was like trying to see through a blindfold. The wind was howling down over the tops of the waves, and the waves themselves, rolling on without end, sounded like the heavy crash of thunder. He found that his imagination hadn't come close to preparing him for the sensation of plunging through a storm at sea. The sheer raging power of the elements was so fierce he found it hard to believe they were merely indifferent. The wind and water had a viciousness that seemed personal.

He had tuned the radio to channel 16, and he spoke again into the handset, "Mayday, Mayday. This is the *Black Rose*, requesting assistance from any possible source. Mayday. Mayday."

And then, miraculously, he heard a voice respond.

"This is the U.S. Coast Guard. What is your exact position and the nature of your distress? Over."

His fist loosened and he almost dropped the radio. He took a better grip, and keyed the handset to talk. "I am taking on water, and with both bilge pumps running, I'm still losing ground. My location is approximately thirty miles north of Sitka, about five miles offshore. That is not an exact position."

Here was another unforeseen difficulty. He hadn't done much sailing on his own, and what he'd thought was a navigation system had turned out to be a depth radar, or "fishfinder." He was approximating the distance by calculating the speed and the time, but that didn't take into account the current.

"How many people on board, and do you have survival suits or a life raft? Over."

"One person. I'm alone. I have a survival suit, and . . ." he glanced over his shoulder to double check if there was an inflatable raft, and as people are apt to do, turned the wheel just slightly as he turned his head. When the next wave hit, the water caught the bow of the boat and tossed it sideways. The revving motor only made it worse, and suddenly the boat was broadside to the wave. He lost his grip on the wheel and went tumbling to the other side of the cabin, smashing into the ceiling as the wave rocked the Bayliner, nearly rolling it, but the boat bobbed up through the water, and the man was dumped on the floor of the cabin.

It was with a sense of relief that he picked himself up and reached again for the wheel—until he realized that he had kept his grip on the handset of the radio, the severed cord now dangling uselessly.

As the duty crew hurried down the path to the locker room to change into their aircrew dry coveralls, or ADCs, Ellie dropped back behind the others. Then she called to Teddy. She had to call twice before he stopped and waited for her, shifting from one foot to the other impatiently.

When she caught up with him, she draped an arm around his shoulder, as much to slow him down as to give her an excuse to talk quietly in his ear.

"I want you to do me a favor. I want you to use that silver tongue of yours tonight for a good cause."

"You've finally realized that I'm the man for you," he said, snaking his arm around her waist. "I knew you were saving the best for last."

With her free hand, she peeled his arm away. "Not quite, Romeo. On the flight out I want you to chat up Mikey there."

"Sorry, he's not my type."

"I want you to distract him, dummy. Like, you know when the doctor gives you a shot?"

"I hate shots."

"Right, so the doctor starts asking you about what you did last night, or where you took your last vacation, to get your mind off the fact he's about to stick a huge needle in your arm."

"Or the fact that for the first time you're about to leap into the ocean to save some stranger in the middle of a bitch of a storm," Teddy added.

"I knew you were smarter than you look."

"Yes, ma'am. I can do that," he agreed. "But where did this soft side come from? What happened to the hardass I know and love? You sweet on this kid or something? Does he bring out the maternal side you've been repressing?"

"Shut up," she said, a little too sharply. She knew Teddy was just kidding, but she found it hard to take, even from him. Either she was accused of being a "hardass" or she was teased for acting "maternal"—she was always either too much like a man, or too much of a woman.

"It's just that it's a tough night for his first time," she explained more mildly. "I thought he might need some help."

"Are we talking about the same kid? The one with the big mouth? The way he talks, he could rescue a whole cruise liner."

"Sure, he talks a big game," Ellie said. "But that's what makes me nervous."

"I don't want my pilot nervous. Don't you worry. I'll keep him entertained with the stories of your discarded boyfriends."

"You try that, and you'll be joining him in the water."

"Don't mean to hurry you," Dave called from the doorway of the hangar. "Anytime you're ready."

Ellie and Teddy both quickened their pace.

When they were finished changing into their ADCs, they hurried over to the operations center where they were briefed on the mission. The briefings at Air Station Sitka were often long, compared to other postings. At air stations in the Lower Forty-eight all the crew needed was a run-down on the nature of the distress, the coordinates, and whether or not the victim was in the water. At Sitka, since they were responsible for missions over land as well as emergencies over water, the flying was often more complicated. Combine the mountainous terrain with a hundred-foot ceiling and bad icing conditions—a familiar scenario in the area, especially in winter—and they would have to circumnavigate, some-

times doubling the mileage. The ops center was where they would plan
the route.

This time the flight planning was comparatively easy; it was a straight
shot up the coast. However, the crew soon discovered that nothing else
about it was easy. They didn't have exact coordinates, and the information was minimal. Radio contact had been broken off abruptly, but the
command center at Juneau hadn't gotten any notice of EPIRB—the
emergency signal that was triggered by a boat's sinking. They didn't
know if they would be looking for a boat, or a man in the water . . . or if
there was even anything to find.

Twenty-three minutes after the alarm sounded, Ellie eased the H-60 off
the tarmac. She pulled the collective up, which changed the pitch on the
blades of the rotor and lifted the helo. While still on the ground, they
had run through the preflight checklist, but now that she was in the air,
Ellie tested the controls in a low hover. With her feet she pressed first the
left, then the right pedal, and the nose of the helo swung slightly in one
direction, then the other. Then she put a feather-light pressure on the
cyclic, testing left, right, and forward. The helo moved left, right, then
forward.

"Everything looks good," Ellie announced.

"So let's go," Dave said.

"Your wish, my command." She eased forward on the cyclic and
lifted the collective, and the helo moved into the wind, the rain hammering on the windshield. In seconds they were over the water, the
waves running hard toward shore.

Ellie couldn't hear Teddy or Mike over the internal communications
system, and from that she knew Teddy must have switched to conference 2 on the ICS so that he and Mike could chat without disturbing
Ellie and Dave as they flew. Teddy was probably talking Mike's ear off,
Ellie thought. Mike wouldn't have a moment's peace to think about
anything.

With that problem solved, Ellie turned her attention to flying. From
the moment they lifted off, she felt like a fish thrown back into water. As
she turned north and the crosswind made the helo yaw right, she
adjusted with the left pedal. When she banked back into the wind, she

had to ease up on the collective to lessen the pitch of the blades, but she did it automatically, almost as if she felt the stiff wind on her own arms. It was as natural to her as walking. That level of unconscious ability was called "feel," and even Dave would have admitted that Ellie had it.

At a cruising speed of 150 miles per hour, even with a headwind, it took less than twenty minutes to reach the approximate position of the boat. If they'd had a specific position, they would have instituted a Victor Sierra search, flying radials out from a specific point in a clover-leaf pattern. A VS search was designed for smaller search areas in which there was a high probability of finding the target, but since the position they had received was an approximation, they decided on a grid pattern search instead.

As they started flying the grid, Dave asked, "Everything ready back there in case we find him? You put the chem sticks on the basket so you'll be able to see it? It's black as pitch out there."

"I know it," Teddy acknowledged. "Summertime, six hours of dark out of twenty-four, and this is when we get called out."

"But we have the night-vision goggles," Mike said.

"Yes, but those only enhance ambient light," Dave explained. "If there's no light to enhance, then there's only so much they can do. There's nothing light in an Alaska night. Doesn't get much blacker than here."

"I knew that," Mike replied. He *had* known how the goggles worked; he had simply forgotten. Not having flown at night in Alaska, he'd had no reason to remember. "So how are we gonna find the guy?"

"He might still be with the boat," Ellie offered. "If he's not with the boat, we'll just have to hope he's got a survival suit with lots of reflective tape. Then we'll have a decent chance of spotting him. If I were floating around at sea, I'd want to be mummified in the stuff."

"Even so, we'll need some serious luck if we're going to find him," Teddy said.

They all quieted for a few minutes then and concentrated on the water below. They were just able to make out the whitecaps of the waves, peaking and curling before collapsing back into the sea.

"Those swells look like they're a decent size," Mike said after a while. "What would you say, thirty, forty feet?"

"About that," Teddy agreed.

As they looked down, each wave seemed to be climbing successively higher, as if rising up to claim them from where they hovered in the sky.

At that second, they were all considering the possibility that Mike would have to go down into that heaving ocean. Ellie was thinking that it was a hell of a night to send down a rookie, Dave was wondering if they might lose Mike as well as the survivor, and Teddy was trying to think of something to say to distract Mike from the sight.

Mike stared out the window. Finally he sat back in his seat. "Damn," he said, "I wish one of you guys had told me to bring my surfboard."

There was a moment of surprised silence before they all laughed.

"I'm surrounded by comedians," Dave groaned.

"This is a kid after my own heart," Teddy said.

"I think he'll do just fine," Ellie added.

What they didn't know was that even as Mike joked, he was thinking to himself, Please don't let us find him.

The man blinked and rubbed his eyes with one fist. They felt hot and dry in their sockets from peering through the windshield into the night, trying to see the waves before they lifted and tossed the small boat like a cork. It had been hours since he had called in the Mayday, but he suspected he knew what the problem was. They couldn't find him. He had probably been off on his estimate of his location, and the storm wasn't slackening. If anything, it was worse, and he was almost out of gas. No gas, no power. Before, when he had been tossed broadside, he had been able to wrestle the boat back into position. Without power he wouldn't be able to keep the bow into the waves. One really big one and the Bayliner would roll, fill with water, and founder.

In the last few hours, he hadn't left the wheel for fear of that one big breaker, but with the gas running out, he figured it was time for last-ditch measures. He waited for a swell to go by before he let go of the wheel, jumped down the few steps into the cabin, and started searching.

Without someone to hold her straight into the waves, the Bayliner turned slowly. The next rush of water hit, and the boat was slammed sideways. He was knocked down, and as he landed, he felt a sharp pain in his side; the corner of a countertop had struck him in the ribs.

When he scrambled back to his feet, he was careful to hold on as he worked his way around the cabin, searching the cupboards and the storage space beneath the seats. He managed to stay upright when the next wave hit, but the third one threw him, and this time he struck his head. Blackness hovered at the edge of his vision and he was dizzy enough that he had to stay down for a moment. Then, when he got up, he felt a dangerous weakness in his knees.

He was worried about the damage to the boat—and to himself—but he kept looking. One more wave and a bruised elbow, and he found it: a flare gun with four spare charges.

Four charges, four chances.

■

After several intense and empty hours of searching, Ellie was the most played-out of the four. The entire time she'd been tracking the grid, she'd had to battle the wind. It buffeted the helo like it was a kite on the end of a string and not 22,000 pounds of machine, fuel, and equipment. But at least Ellie had something to struggle with—the others were exhausted from sheer inactivity. They'd spent the time staring out the windows, their eyes straining uselessly against the black carpet of ocean.

They should have had the help of a second helo, but ten minutes after the second crew had taken off, they had been diverted to a medevac mission. A man in the small village of Angoon had an acute appendicitis, and he needed to be transported to the nearest hospital for emergency surgery. The third helo was in the middle of a six hundred hour overhaul, its guts scattered on the floor of the hangar. There was a cutter steaming its way up from the south, but it would be several hours before it reached the area.

They didn't speak much in the cabin of the H-60. There was the occasional "Is that something?" Then Ellie would swing down closer, but there was only more empty ocean. Finally Dave voiced the worry that was in the back of all their minds. He said, "We're approaching bingo fuel. Soon we'll be low enough we'll have to think about heading back."

"We have time to go a little longer," Ellie said. "We have at least three-quarters of an hour."

"That would be cutting it close," Dave replied. "That would almost put us into mama's time." In calculating bingo fuel, Dave considered the number of miles as well as how the wind would affect the helo, and then he threw in fifteen or twenty extra minutes—for "mama."

"We have time. We can go a little longer," Ellie insisted.

"Going longer might not be the issue," Teddy said. "We might have flown right over him and not even seen him."

"And maybe we haven't," Ellie countered.

No one voiced that other possibility: that they might be searching for a body and not a survivor.

"Do we really have time?" Teddy asked. On the ground he was Ellie's firm ally, but in the helo he tended to side with Dave's caution.

"We have some," Dave said. "But it's not infinite. At some point soon we'll need to assess—" he broke off abruptly, saying, "Did anyone see that?"

Ellie jumped on it. "See what?"

"I thought I saw something out of the corner of my eye. Like a flash of light. It was probably lightning, but I thought it might have been . . ."

". . . a flare," Teddy finished. "I think I might have seen something too."

"Where?" Ellie demanded.

"West of us. Farther out to sea."

Ellie banked the helo, and they flew for a few tense minutes, scanning the dark, heaving ocean below.

Nothing.

Ellie started to wonder whether she was headed in the right direction.

The others must have been thinking the same because Dave said, "I don't know, Ellie. Maybe—"

"What?" Ellie said.

"Hold on a second."

"What is it?"

"I've got something on the radar," he told her.

The boat, when they finally found it, was dead in the water, broadside to the waves. Teddy switched on the Nitesun. It was their most powerful searchlight, but against the expanse of the ocean, it looked no bigger than the beam of a flashlight.

"He's getting pounded," Teddy said.

"If he's there," Dave replied, but at that moment a man in a survival suit appeared on the deck.

"Do we try to retrieve him from the deck, or do we want him in the water?" As Ellie posed the question, they all saw him raise his hand in a salute. He was looking up at the helicopter, so he didn't see the curl of the wave. As soon as it started swelling under the boat, he turned to grab onto something, but it was too late. The wave broke over the boat, and when it bobbed back up from beneath the water the deck was bare.

"Where'd he go?" Ellie said.

Teddy swept the light over the ocean, finding nothing. "Come on, come on," he muttered, circling the empty boat.

"Wait, there," Mike said. "Back up. Yes, there."

"Good eyes," Teddy praised him.

"I can be ready to go down in three minutes," Mike said.

"What do you think, Teddy?" Ellie asked for Teddy's assessment because he was the one who would be responsible for getting Mike back in the aircraft.

"This guy hasn't been in the water long. Let's see if we can put the basket down near him, and maybe he can climb in himself."

"I'm ready to go in," Mike reported.

"I know you are, but if we can get him in without your going down, it will also be quicker."

"We'll try that first," Ellie determined, ending the argument.

They ran through the hoist checklist, and then they were ready to go into the hover. Hovering over the ocean at night during a storm was the hardest maneuver a pilot could attempt. The wind battered the helo, and it took a complicated dance with both hands and feet to maintain position. The greatest danger was that a hard gust would force the nose up and the tail down. With its belly presented to the wind, the helo would be driven back, possibly burying the tail rotor in a wave. If that happened, they'd be in need of rescue as well.

The wind wasn't the only difficulty. With a sideways driving rain and the running waves, it was difficult to judge what was moving—the water, the rain, or the aircraft. A pilot sometimes experienced "the leans"—a three dimensional version of a common sensation. Anyone who has ever been stopped in a car and had the sudden feeling they were moving backward when, in fact, the vehicle next to theirs was moving forward, has experienced a form of the leans.

Teddy dropped several magnesium flares to help assess the drift and provide reference points in the black expanse of ocean. As the flares hit the salt water, they ignited, casting a pale yellow glow as Ellie made her approach and established a hover above the survivor.

From there, she depended on Teddy to be her eyes. She couldn't see beneath the helo to maneuver, so it was Teddy's job as the flight mechanic to talk her into position. It was a job that seemed simple, but which carried with it incredible responsibility and required steely self-control. No matter how tense or dangerous a SAR got, the flight mechanic needed to keep his voice calm and even. Not only could excitement, tension, or panic interfere with the flight mechanic's ability to direct the pilot, it could also affect the pilot's flying. With just a voice in their ear to go by, tone and inflection took on supreme importance to the person at the controls. Teddy might act like a clown on the ground, but once he was in the air he was known around the air station as the flight mech with a voice you could fall asleep to.

"Easy right," Teddy said. "A little more . . . good. We're above him, but bring it forward ten to allow for the wind drift. Hold, hold, hold. Ready to hoist."

"Begin the hoist," Ellie replied.

"Basket's going out the door . . . basket's going down."

But it didn't go down. Below the helo the wind caught it and sent it twisting back toward the tail rotor. Teddy brought the basket back up and tried again. This time, just before it reached the water, it was caught by the wind driving over the top of a huge swell. The basket tossed violently at the end of the cable, sweeping aft once again. Teddy was forced to reel it in again. And again. And again. Finally Teddy said, "I'm worried about the cable—it's really chafing on the rails. I think I might have a better chance from a lower hover. Can we try that?"

"Mike, would you keep an eye on that altimeter for me?" Ellie said as she brought the helo down.

"Okay, ma'am. I think that's enough," Mike called from the back. "That last wave just about broke over the wheels."

Teddy sent the basket down once more, and this time it landed in the water only fifteen feet away from the survivor, on the uphill side of a rising wave. The man struck out swimming. From the helo Teddy could see him cutting through the water and simultaneously rising with the swell, so he seemed to be swimming toward the belly of the helo.

At the hoist controls, Teddy was making sure that, as the wave lifted the basket, he retracted the line so there wouldn't be too much slack. If a man was caught in a loop, the cable could slice right through him.

The survivor reached the basket as the wave crested. With the spotlight trained on him, Teddy could see him grab it and pull himself inside.

"He's in," Teddy said, but even as he spoke, the wave broke. When the survivor surfaced, he was still in the basket, but the basket itself had been wrenched off the line. The hook was now swinging loose over the water.

Teddy bit his tongue on the curse.

"Are you bringing him up?" Dave asked.

"The basket's come loose from the cable," Teddy said.

There was a grim silence inside the helo.

Then Mike spoke. "Send me down. I'm ready." He gestured at his gear, but he also meant something else. Before, he'd been nervous—more than nervous—but as he'd watched Teddy lower the basket to the man in the water, he had started to feel like a player who'd been benched on the sideline. He started thinking that this was, after all, what he had trained for. This was what it was all about, and SARs like this didn't come along very often. Coasties sometimes waited years for a mission like this.

"How are we doing for fuel?" Ellie asked.

"We're low," Dave said. "But we can stretch it out a little longer, I think."

"Send me down," Mike repeated.

"What do you say, Teddy?" Ellie said.

Teddy glanced down at the water and then back at Mike. "We can try it."

Mike already had his dry suit on, and now he slipped into his fins, hood, mask, snorkel, and gloves.

Teddy brought the cable back up, attached it to Mike's harness, and then directed Ellie, repositioning the helo. "Forward fifty . . . forward ten . . . hold . . . hold."

Mike stood in the doorway.

"Left five . . . hold . . . hold."

Teddy signaled Mike with three taps on the chest, and Mike responded with a thumbs-up.

"Deploying the swimmer," Teddy said. "Swimmer going down."

Mike swung out the door as Teddy reeled out the line. It looked good—he was headed right for a trough close to the man in the water . . . and then the line jerked to a halt. Mike found himself dangling between helicopter and water. He craned his head back to look up, but he couldn't see Teddy in the doorway.

"Hold, hold, hold—the cable's birdcaged," Teddy called. This was the situation Teddy had been afraid of when he saw the cable rubbing the rails. Birdcaging occurred when the cable frayed, and the frayed portion was wound back into the drum, disturbing the alignment. But, though Teddy had been worried, he could never have foreseen that this would happen with Mike dangling from the line.

"Could anything else go wrong?" Dave exclaimed.

"Is Mike in the water?" Ellie asked, almost at the same time.

Teddy replied to Ellie's question. "No, ma'am. Not yet."

Underneath the helo, the wind gusted and blew Mike sideways. He was caught in a wild pendulum swing, a wall of water rushing toward him. The view from above had been deceiving. Looking down on the waves, he hadn't been able to judge their true size. Now he was staring straight into one, and it was about to swamp him.

At that moment, Teddy sheared the hoist cable and Mike fell almost gently into the water that boiled around his legs. He was lifted with the wave, and as he reached the peak, he dove to avoid the blowing chop.

"I sheared the hoist and Mike's in the water," Teddy reported calmly. "His location is only about twenty feet away from the survivor. It shouldn't take long for Mike to reach him."

"We can't get them up without the hoist," Dave pointed out. "We're going to have to leave them for the next team to pick up."

"No." Ellie's answer was immediate and uncompromising.

"What do you mean, 'No'?" Dave said.

"I'm not leaving Mike down there alone. Not in that mess. Not on his first trip."

"We don't have a choice," Dave told her.

"He's right, ma'am. I don't see that there's anything we can do," Teddy agreed. "We're out of it. Game over."

Ellie laughed, and the sound of it sent a shiver of unease through the two men. "Now there's where you're both wrong," she said. "It's not even close to over. In fact, this is where it gets interesting."

The noise of the main rotor was deep, like the beat of a pulse. The wind swirled through the open side door of the helo, and rain drummed against the windshield. Over the headphones there was silence.

After a moment, Dave said, "Interesting? I don't think I like the sound of that."

"What are you suggesting we do?" Teddy asked.

"We've got the ERD, don't we?" Ellie said. "This is exactly what it was designed for."

ERD was short for "emergency rescue device," and it consisted of a simple metal plate with a standard marine winch mounted on it. It was developed in response to a similar situation—during a SAR 175 miles off the North Carolina coast, the cable to the hoist had frayed and bird-caged in the drum with the rescue swimmer still in the water. With no way of retrieving him, they had to leave him on scene with a raft, in fifty-foot seas, in the middle of the night. They returned to retrieve him later that morning, but that incident led the Coast Guard to develop an alternative device that could act as a backup for the hoist. However, there were difficulties with the ERD—the main one being that to get someone back into the helo you needed to manually winch them up.

For once Teddy lost his cool. "Think about this a second. Mike weighs over two hundred pounds, and the other guy's survival suit is probably half filled with water, and we're hovering at about fifty, sixty feet. I can't crank both of them up in the time we have."

"Could you crank them from ten feet?" Ellie said.

"Maybe . . . probably, but it doesn't matter if I could or not. There's no way to get down that low in seas like this. That would take some serious flying."

"And?" Ellie said.

"I know you're the ranking officer," Dave said. "But if we're going to die with you, don't you think we should share in the decision?"

"So decide, but you better say yes quick. We're getting low on gas."

"Teddy?" Dave asked.

"What the hell," Teddy said. "What the hell."

"This is crazy," Dave said. "I can't believe we're doing this."

"I knew there was a reason I liked you boys," Ellie told them.

"I'm flying with a lunatic," Dave muttered.

It took Teddy only a few minutes, working at full speed, to mount the ERD. He fitted the metal plate to tie-down rings on the deck of the aircraft, and then it was just a matter of running the line—a regular climbing rope—to a pre-positioned pulley. Finally he said, "Ready back here."

"I'm not ready," Dave said, staring through the windshield at the surging water beneath.

"Relax, Dave," Ellie laughed. "When this is all over, you'll realize that we're having a good time."

"Right."

"Trust me."

"What the hell do you think I'm doing already?"

Ellie had to circle back to make her approach into the wind. Teddy found Mike and the survivor with the Nitesun light.

"The helo won't be as maneuverable down there, with all the turbulence. If we overshoot them, we'll have to start from scratch," Ellie said.

"We don't have enough fuel to start from scratch," Dave informed them. "We only have this one shot, thank God, because I don't think I can do this again."

"How about we position a little downwind, and let the current bring them to us? It will give us some leeway," Teddy suggested.

"Sounds like a plan," Ellie said.

"Not much of one," Dave added.

Ellie ignored him, and asked Teddy to conn her in.

"Forward thirty . . . right ten . . . easy right . . . easy forward," Teddy said. "Hold. Okay, we're close enough. Take it down."

Now it was Dave's turn. He was watching the altimeter and eyeing the coming waves through the front windshield. "All right," Dave said. "Let's do it."

Ellie brought them down, making constant tiny corrections with her feet and hands, reacting to the wind as it pounded the helo with the same force it whipped up the forty-foot waves beneath them. Keeping the helo stable as she went down in that wind was like trying to pour water into a glass from the height of a hundred feet.

"Thirty feet," Dave announced. "Twenty . . . fifteen." Then, under his breath, "Sweet Jesus."

They were no longer hovering above the waves but among them. Teddy reported that he had lost sight of Mike and the survivor, but he thought they were just over the next swell.

"Here it comes," Dave said. "Altitude."

Ellie saw the wave through the glass in front of her and brought them up, but she had to be careful when they crested the wave because that's when they hit the wind. If she wasn't careful, a gust could catch the nose and toss it up. In recovering from that, she would lose position . . . if she was able to recover.

As the wave passed beneath them, Teddy said, "I can't see them yet. They must be coming over the next one."

Ellie eased the helo back down in the next trough.

They hovered, waiting for the swell to rise in the windshield.

"Here it comes," Dave said. Then, almost blankly, "Oh my God."

Ellie looked through the glass to a solid wall of water. The wave towered over the helo, at least twice the height of the others. Impossibly, she saw Mike and the other man at the crest of it, looking down at them, their faces pale blank ovals.

"Rogue wave. Up," Dave cried. "Up, up, UP!"

It all seemed to happen very slowly. She hauled back on the cyclic and yanked the collective nearly into her armpit, and the helo's nose tipped up. They climbed the face of the wave as it curled higher and higher. The engine revved, fighting against the downdraft that tried to suck them under with the crashing water. Then they were at the top, the water tickling the underbelly of the helo. She could hear Teddy yelling into the headset. She was half expecting to fall out of the sky, to tumble back with the wave, but the water fell away beneath them, and they were still in the air. Then she finally made out what Teddy was yelling. It was "We got 'em! We got 'em!"

"What?" she demanded. "What are you talking about?"

"Mike's on the line, and the other guy's holding on to one of the wheels. That last wave swept them right into us."

Teddy tugged on his gunner's belt to make sure it would hold him, then leaned out the doorway. There was Mike, only an arm's-length away, gripping the thin rope with both hands. He had somehow kicked off one of his fins and made a loop around one foot to take some of the weight off his hands. The other man, unbelievably, was clinging to the wheel strut.

They had them, but now Teddy had to get them inside. He glanced down and saw that they had maintained the altitude they had reached when climbing the rogue wave. The water suddenly looked very far away.

"Bring us down," Teddy said. "If they fall, I want it to feel like water and not concrete."

"Right," Ellie agreed.

Teddy looked back out at Mike. A crank or two would bring him within reach of the doorway. He just hoped that Mike had a firm enough grip and the movement wouldn't cause him to slip.

Teddy crouched over the ERD and, remembering the drill they had done and how hard it had been to turn the crank, he threw his weight into it. That's when he discovered the power of adrenaline. He'd heard stories of women lifting cars when their children were trapped underneath, and now he experienced a little of that strength. The crank turned almost easily. Leaning out, he saw Mike's hands, still gripping the rope, appear just under the lip of the doorway.

Teddy released the crank and knelt at the edge. Reaching down, he grabbed the harness that Mike wore over his suit, and yelled into the wind and the noise of the chopper. "Mike!"

Mike looked up, his face screwed into intense concentration, all his effort going into holding on.

"You've got to let go of the line!" Teddy yelled, nearly in his ear. "One hand at a time, grab the doorway here."

Mike stared up at him but maintained his grip.

"Come on, you can do it. I've got you. I won't let you fall."

Mike looked down, and Teddy thought he'd lost him. Then one

hand loosened and reached up to the doorway, then the other. But he hadn't yet transferred all his weight to his hands—some of it was still supported by the foot wrapped in the cord. At that moment, the loop around his foot unwound, and he slipped. He was hanging from the doorway of the helo by his clutching fingers.

Teddy felt him falling and, because of his grip on the harness, felt himself almost pulled out of the helo. But his gunner's belt held, and Teddy gave a panicked heave. Mike came up, and once he was chest-high, Teddy pulled him in.

Mike scrabbled forward on his hands and knees as far inside the door as he could get. Once he reached the opposite wall, he rolled over on his back and gave Teddy a shaky thumbs-up.

Teddy leaned over, hands on his knees, breathing hard, but he hadn't forgotten that there was still another man clinging to the wheel strut. When Teddy straightened, he saw to his surprise that Mike was already on his feet, stripping off his gear. The kid had seemed iffy going out, but there was no doubt now that he had risen to the occasion.

Teddy leaned out the doorway again, and he saw the survivor still hanging from the strut, just out of reach. The question was, How was he going to get him inside?

Mike joined him in the doorway, also strapped into a gunner's belt. They both saw the man let go with one hand and reach toward them. At first Teddy thought he was holding his hand out for them to grab, but then he saw that the man wasn't looking at them. He had his eyes fixed on the swinging line from the ERD.

"The line," Teddy said. He hadn't considered that the man might voluntarily try to transfer himself from wheel to rope. It certainly wasn't ideal, but was better than anything Teddy had come up with in the last few minutes, so he leaned out the door and set the rope swinging.

When it neared the man, he reached out to try to grab it, but he missed and it looked like he was about to pitch out into space. Teddy closed his eyes for a second, not wanting to see the man as he fell, but when he opened his eyes, the man was still there and reaching for the rope again. This time, as it swung near him, his fist closed around it.

Even as Teddy wondered how he was going to transfer his weight, the man tightened his hold around the wheel with his legs and reached out with his other hand. He was stretched out alongside the helo, his legs around the wheel strut, his hands on the line. Then, like an acrobat, he carefully unwound one leg, and then the other, and the rope swung back toward Teddy and Mike, both standing ready in the doorway.

Simultaneously they leaned out and reached for him. The survivor was looking up at them, and in the back of his mind Teddy thought the man's face looked strange, but before he could think why, the man had let go of the rope and grasped first Teddy's hand, then Mike's with a powerful grip. As they heaved, he pulled as well, and he swung himself up and in, landing in a crouch on his feet just inside the doorway.

The man stood up, but both Teddy and Mike kept a hold on his hands because he stood so close to the opening. Mike ushered him in, and Teddy let go of his other hand, giving him a questioning thumbs-up. The man returned it.

Then Teddy became aware of Dave's voice through the ICS, calling urgently, "Teddy? Teddy, are you there? Teddy, can you hear me?"

"I'm here," Teddy said.

"Teddy!" Ellie almost shouted. "What happened to you? Did we lose them?"

"Lose them? Come on, who you think you're talkin' to? Hey, Mikey, why don't you say hi to Lieutenant Commander Somers?"

In a low, rasping voice that she wouldn't have recognized, Mike said, "Hey, ma'am."

"We've also got a guest over here," Teddy went on.

As Teddy turned to the survivor, he suddenly realized what was strange about his face. The man was smiling. Not just smiling, he was grinning.

Teddy spoke into the man's ear, "You want to say anything to our pilot?"

"Sure." He bent to speak into the mike, and Teddy heard him say, "I was wondering, can we do it again tomorrow?"

"He said what?" The reporter shook his head. "No way. I don't believe it."

Teddy raised his right hand. "I swear, it's the truth, the whole truth, and nothing but. I know I have been known to exaggerate in the past—"

The Coasties standing around the table, eavesdropping on the story, laughed at that.

After getting back from the SAR, the duty crew and a ground crew just getting off after working mids had gone over to the Eagle's Nest to celebrate. The Eagle's Nest was a bar a couple hundred yards down the road from the hangar. It was housed in a low white building, its trim painted the bright blue of the Coast Guard insignia, with a sign that read MORALE outside the entrance.

"Okay, enough," Teddy said. "These guys exaggerate too. I'm not *that* bad."

That raised another howl from the small crowd.

Whalen had waited outside the hangar in his car for Ellie and the crew to return from the SAR. He'd sat there so long he'd gotten cramps in his legs, but he hadn't minded. It brought back memories from his reporting days, before he'd switched to features, when there was an urgency to getting the story. And the wait had been worth it. The crew had returned high as kites, pumped full of adrenaline from the night's activities, and without a moment's hesitation, they had invited him out.

"So I like to tell a good story," Teddy said. "I admit, I'll sacrifice a bit of veracity to liven it up for my listeners, but this story doesn't need any help from me. If you don't believe me, ask Lieutenant Lazure. Will you guys believe it if he backs me up?"

There was a general assent.

Teddy confided to Whalen, "Lazure's such a boring bastard, he won't even give the truth a little legroom, but he does come in handy in these types of situations. He's better than a notary." Teddy lifted his head and called out, "Hey, Lieutenant."

Dave was over at the bar buying another round.

"Hey, Lieutenant," Teddy bellowed.

"I'm coming," Dave yelled back, tucking a beer bottle under each arm, and corraling three pints between his hands. He made his way over to the table and, still pinching the bottles against his sides, awkwardly set the pints down, then retrieved the two beers from under each arm. "That's all right, don't help or anything," he said.

"I need you to back me up on something," Teddy said, ignoring the rebuke. "The guy we picked up tonight, did he or did he not say, 'Can we do it again tomorrow?'"

"That's what it sounded like," Dave admitted.

"See," Teddy crowed. "I told you."

Whalen took that opportunity to get verification on another detail. "And is it true that a wave swept your rescue swimmer and the survivor right into you, and the survivor was hanging off the wheel?"

"You don't believe me?" Teddy pretended to be outraged.

"Well, I didn't actually see him," Dave said, but then he relented. "But Mike said it was true, and get this." Dave leaned toward Whalen. "I don't know if Teddy told you, but at one point Mike and the survivor were at the crest of a wave, and they were looking *down* on us in the helo. If Ellie hadn't climbed up the face of it, the crest would have broken over us, and they might have been washed into the rotor."

"Just like that scene in *Indiana Jones,* when the guy backs up into the propeller," Teddy put in.

"I wouldn't say this in front of her because she's got a big enough ego as it is," Dave threw a glance over his shoulder to where Ellie was deeply involved in a fooseball game across the room, "but she did all right tonight."

"Sure," Whalen said. "But it seems to me like the rescue swimmer—Mike, right?—it seems like he had the hardest job. All Lieutenant Commander Somers did was maintain a hover over the survivor."

"All?" Dave said. "All! My old instructor used to say that hovering at night over the ocean was like standing in a pitch-black room, on one foot, juggling."

Whalen didn't try to hide his skepticism.

"You don't know much about flying a helicopter, do you?" Dave said.

"Not much."

"Go ahead," Teddy urged. "Tell him, Lazure."

"You want a short lesson? Flying Helos 101?"

The reporter shrugged. "Sure."

"All right, I'll keep it real simple. Or as simple as I can make it."

"How hard can it be?"

"You can judge for yourself in a minute," Dave replied. "I'll start with the controls. First you've got the collective. That's the lever to the left of the seat that kind of looks like a long emergency brake. The collective changes the pitch of the main rotor blades. When it's all the way down, then all the blades are flat, or parallel to the ground. The more you raise the collective, the greater the pitch on the blades. The steeper the pitch, the more lift is created. That makes the helo go up or down. Got that so far?"

"It's simple," Whalen said. "That's basic aerodynamics. I think I learned about that in second grade—when they tell you to stick your hand out the window of a car while it's moving. The more you tilt it, the more the moving air forces your hand up. That's lift."

"Now that you've got that down, let's move on. Next we have the cyclic. It's like an oversized joystick between your knees, and that does pretty much what you expect it would do. You push the cyclic forward, the helo moves forward. Same with backward and sideways. When you're flying forward, you also use it to bank into turns. The cyclic changes the pitch on the blades on only one portion of the rotor disk, but I don't want to confuse you—you don't need to understand how it works."

"I get it," Whalen assured him. "So far it seems straightforward."

"That's what the cyclic does on its own. It's also used in conjunction with the collective to climb, descend, and adjust the airspeed, though you can also use the cyclic alone to climb and descend."

"Okay." Whalen hesitated. "But I thought the collective was what made you go up and down."

"If you're not moving forward. If you're in forward flight, the best

way to go up is to use both, but I haven't finished with the flight controls. You also have the tail rotor pedals. Those control the pitch of the
blades on the tail rotor. One pedal increases the pitch, the other
decreases it, but all you really need to know is that the pedals move the
nose of the helo. To move the nose to the right, you press the right
pedal, to move the nose left, you press the left pedal. Still with me?"

With this explanation, the reporter nodded. "Makes perfect sense."

"There's one other thing I have to tell you about the pedals. It's true
that what happens when you push one or the other is that the nose
moves, but that's not their main function. Their main function has to
do with the design of the helo. The helo flies because the main rotor
turns the blades and the blades create lift, but in addition to lift, you
have another force called 'torque.' Because of torque, when the main
rotor turns in one direction, the body of the helo wants to spin in the
other direction, and it would if you didn't do something to counteract
it. That's what the pedals are for. When torque starts to spin the helo's
nose to the right, you use the left pedal to keep the nose pointed straight.
The more power you use, the more left pedal you need to counteract the
torque."

The reporter was frowning in concentration, and everyone in the
crowd around him was grinning.

"Are you ready to put it all together?" Dave asked.

"Sure," Whalen said, pretending more confidence than he felt.

"We'll start with something easy. Say you want to move to the right.
What do you do?"

"You move the cycle to the right," Whalen said.

"All right, then what?" Dave prompted.

"Then the helo moves to the right."

"It's not so simple. When you move the cyclic to the right, you're
using some of your lift to move the helo sideways, so if you want to
maintain the same altitude, what do you have to do?"

"I guess you'd need to increase the collective," Whalen said.

"Yes," Dave allowed, "but when you increase the collective, you also
increase the torque, so what do you need?"

"More left pedal?" Whalen replied, but it was more of a question than
a statement.

"Not bad. Now you're moving to the right. Everything's fine . . . that
is until you want to stop turning. Then you need to adjust everything all

over again, and that's just a simple turn. Let me put it this way. When you're flying a helo straight and level, you need to adjust something, on average, every eight seconds. That should tell you how much coordination and skill it takes to fly one of these machines even on a clear sunny day. Most helicopter pilots would never go out in the weather we had tonight. That's what we're trained to do here in the Coast Guard. We're expected to be able to fly in those conditions, and what Ellie did at the end—well, that's why she's flying here in Sitka."

From behind him, Ellie said, "What shit are you talking about me now?"

Dave jumped at the sound of her voice. "I was giving a lesson in how to fly helicopters."

"Was he using me as an example of what not to do?" she asked the reporter.

"Not exactly . . ." Whalen replied, not wanting to betray Dave, but Teddy had no such compunctions.

"Not exactly—try not even close. He's spent the last ten minutes explaining how to fly helicopters so this guy could maybe begin to understand how tough that little stunt you pulled tonight was."

"Yeah, right," Ellie laughed. "Next you're going to try to sell me a bridge."

"Ask him yourself," Teddy said, jerking his head at Dave.

Ellie turned to Dave.

"Well, it wasn't easy," Dave grumbled, not quite meeting Ellie's eyes.

She was caught off guard. It was about the closest thing to a compliment she had ever gotten from Dave.

"But you can't take all the credit," Teddy said. "We deserve some recognition for agreeing to go along with your ridiculous scheme. Especially when I didn't think there was any way you were going to pull it off."

"So why did you go along with it?" Whalen asked him.

"I shoulda known to be more careful around a reporter. Okay, you got me," he held up his hands as if surrendering. "I have to admit, I only agreed because I was sure that Lieutenant Lazure would veto it. What the hell were you thinking?" Teddy said, turning toward Dave and pretending indignation.

"I was listening to you, you idiot," Dave said.

"Listening to *me?* Who's the idiot?"

"So neither of you really wanted to do it?" the reporter said.

"It was a crazy thing to do," Teddy said. "I know there have been worse SARs, but it was the craziest night of my life. Also happens to be the best night of my life." He raised his beer and took a long drink.

"Better than your first lay?" someone called out.

"Yeah, well, I heard his mother isn't very good in the sack," Ellie said before Teddy could swallow his gulp of beer and answer.

Everyone hooted with laughter.

"That's because she didn't get as much practice as you do," he shot back.

The hoots changed to catcalls.

"Truce?" Teddy offered.

"Sure, you want to call a truce when you've got the last shot off," Ellie said.

"Fire away, then. I won't defend myself. You're the man of the hour. And," Teddy turned to Dave, wagging his finger, "I want the lieutenant to admit it for once."

Even Dave was still high from the events of the night. He laughed and gave in easily. "All right, Teddy. Whatever you say."

"That's right. Anyone else need convincing?" Teddy held up his fists as if ready to fight.

"I do." The voice came from over by the bar. Everyone swiveled to look.

"Didn't see you over there, Commander Pantano, sir," Teddy said. As he spoke, he snuck a glance at Ellie. The smile had slipped from her face, and she was staring down into her pint as if it were a bottomless pit.

Though the air station wasn't a big place, it wasn't often that Ellie and Sam were together in the same room. Their feud wasn't long—Sam had only been on base five months—but it was bitter. All the more so because of the way it had started.

After Sam's comment, there was an awkward pause. Then Teddy said, "You know, normally I'd fight to the death to defend Lieutenant Commander Somers's honor, but I hate to ruin a pretty face."

Even Sam smiled at that. The idea of Teddy fighting anyone was funny, his chance of beating them was laughable, and in a match against Sam it was ridiculous. Sam was a solid six-two—a good eight inches taller than Teddy—and even if Teddy had the slightest chance of landing a blow to Sam's face, Sam's nose was already twisted and he had a scar that cut across one eyebrow. There were rumors that he used to be a boxer. Sam's explanation was that he used to have a hot temper, but no one on base had ever known him to even raise his voice.

"I can see you're scared," Teddy said. "And I'm not an unfeeling man, so I'll let you off this time, sir—but only if you take it back."

Ellie looked up from her beer, and she and Sam locked stares. Ellie was the first to look away. A moment later she heard Sam answer Teddy, "All right. I take it back." He was playing along, but his voice was hard and caustic as he added, "You're right. I don't want to fight—not all of us can be as brave as you."

He stood and dug in his pocket for some money. He counted out a few bills and placed them on the bar, saying, "I'll leave you to your celebration," then turned and walked out.

"Guess I scared him off," Teddy remarked after the door had closed, but after Sam's sharp sarcasm it fell a little flat. After a second, he tried again. "Hey, Somers, you're almost dry, lemme buy you another." He raised his voice to the bartender. "Another round for the cowards over here," he said, and this time everyone laughed.

The evening deepened into early morning, and the crowd around the bar thinned. The later it got, the drunker everyone became. A few of the Coasties tried to get Ellie to join in a drinking contest, but she fended them off, saying, "No thanks. I'm not a guy, so I can get drunk without making it a competition." And she proved her point by sitting with them and getting just as bombed.

Teddy was in his element, surrounded by a small audience. At that moment, he was holding forth, rather louder than necessary, on the health benefits of beer. He held up his glass to illustrate and discovered that it was empty. "Emergency, emergency," he called out, working his way over to the bar.

The reporter had been watching for this opportunity. He followed and leaned in over Teddy's shoulder to ask, "Can I buy you another?"

"You trying to loosen me up?" Teddy said. "Because it won't work—I'm already about as loose as they come. I feel like I have to warn you because I know I hate it when I spend money on something I could have gotten free. Happened to me once with this woman in Juneau . . . but that's another story." He waved his hand and swayed a bit on his feet.

"Thanks for the warning, but I'm on an expense account," Whalen said.

"In that case, I'll take two," Teddy replied.

"Why don't you get a table. I'll get the drinks." Whalen ordered from the bartender and carried three beers over to where Teddy had taken a table back against the wall. He was sitting there, yelling insults at a friend across the room.

"Ah, there you are. Thank God, I was dying of thirst." Teddy took a long draught and when he surfaced, he said, "So what do you want to know, Mr. Reporter?"

"I was wondering, who was that guy?" Whalen asked.

"What guy? The one I was just yelling at?"

"No, not that one," the reporter said, and Teddy seemed to catch on. "You mean Commander Pantano."

"Yes. Him. Who is he?"

"He's another pilot," was Teddy's unusually brief answer.

"What's his deal with Lieutenant Commander Somers?"

"Deal?" Teddy echoed, feigning ignorance.

"Why was he attacking her like that tonight?"

"It's not just tonight. He's been pretty critical of her flying in general. Thinks she's got a cowboy attitude."

"Cowboy?"

"You know," Teddy said. "Thinks she's a little reckless, wild, that sort of thing."

"But it doesn't matter what he thinks, does it?"

"He has the ear of a lot of higher-ups, and he's close with the CO."

"Does he do this kind of thing to other pilots?"

"No," Teddy admitted.

"Then why Lieutenant Commander Somers? Is he jealous or something?"

"Commander Pantano doesn't need to be jealous—at least not of her flying. He's a great pilot. Even the people who don't like him much admit that."

Whalen had caught the incongruous phrase "at least not of her flying" so his next question was, "What is he jealous of, if not her flying?"

"That's a whole 'nother story," Teddy mumbled into his beer.

"That's the story I want to hear."

"I shouldn't talk about that," Teddy said, shaking his head.

"I won't use it for the article," Whalen promised.

"Weeell . . . I don't know . . ." But Teddy was too much of a gossip to resist. He leaned in and lowered his voice. "Okay. I'll tell you. Commander Pantano was posted here five months ago. When someone first arrives, if they're not married, we invite them out—I mean me and Lieutenant Lazure and Lieutenant Commander Somers—to sort of welcome them to the air station. Commander Pantano came out with us a few times, but he didn't drink, never stayed out very late, and he always called me 'Petty Officer McDonald,'" Teddy made a face. "You know, real by-the-book kind of guy. Somers seemed to like him, though. They'd sit at the bar and blab on for hours about pilot stuff. She'd be so busy talking, she'd barely get through a beer. She was getting to be as dull as he was."

Whalen suspected that the truth was that Teddy might have been a little jealous himself.

"I could tell he liked her," Teddy went on, "but I figured his chances with Somers were slim to none."

"Why's that?"

"I don't know. She just isn't interested in that stuff."

The reporter nodded. In the course of his reporting, he had met a good number of people like Ellie—who were seemingly without fear in situations where most normal people would be terrified, but who were scared to death of any kind of commitment. "So Commander Pantano made a pass at her, she turned him down, and now he's bitter?" Whalen guessed.

"Not quite. He'd only been here a month or so before he got word that he was being offered a spot promotion, and you know where they were sending him? Hawaii. Can you believe this guy's luck? He gets a spot promotion to a place where there's sun, sand, and lots of beautiful women wearing bikinis."

"And?" Whalen said. He still didn't get the connection.

"All of a sudden, Somers and Commander Pantano are the new hot item. Don't know exactly how that happened, but they were a couple. I barely saw Somers for the next month; they were practically inseparable. I have to admit, I was a little worried. I thought that she might even have been falling for the guy, so I started ragging her about it, and I got the real story. She was just dating him because he was leaving at the end of the month. That meant no messy breakups, no awkward encounters— they'd have some fun, and then he'd be gone."

"She must have liked him a little too," Whalen suggested.

"I guess," Teddy said grudgingly. "But Pantano sure cured her of that."

"What happened? What did he do?"

"That's the best part of the story. The night before he was supposed to leave, Somers made a big deal out of it, romantic dinner for two, then back to her place, where she had planned a surprise party. It turned out that Commander Pantano had a little surprise for her as well. I actually found out about it before she did. I ran into him the next morning down at the hangar, right before he was supposed to be leaving, so I say to him, 'Commander Pantano, I can't lie and say everyone's gonna miss you, or that I'm sad to see you go, but I want to wish you good luck.' You know what he said to me?" Teddy paused for effect.

"What did he say?"

"He said, 'Thank you, Petty Officer McDonald. I won't miss you either.' I was a bit offended by that, so I said to him, 'How could you not miss me?' Then he said—and I have to admit it was a pretty good reason—'Because I'm not going anywhere.'

"He'd fallen head over heels for Somers, poor guy. He'd turned down the spot promotion, committed possible career suicide to stay in Sitka . . . to be with her. Only he hadn't told her yet. He swore me to secrecy. He thought it was to be this big surprise." Teddy shook his head. "I almost felt sorry for him. He was trying to be romantic. He'd kept the fact he was staying a secret, and he was going to show up at her door when she thought he was on a plane for Hawaii."

"Oh no."

" 'Oh no' is right. Apparently you could hear them yelling three doors down."

"Could you hear what they were saying?" Whalen asked.

"She was saying that he should have asked her before making a decision like that."

"She had a point," the reporter acknowledged.

"Yeah, but he was saying that she shouldn't have led him on. My guess is that she let him think she was more into it than she was, and said something like, 'If only you didn't have to leave . . . ' that sort of thing."

"Ouch."

At that moment, Dave called out from across the room, "Teddy, come over here and help me." He was trying to get Ellie out of her chair, but she wanted to go to sleep on the table.

Teddy looked back at the reporter and grinned. "My second rescue of the night."

■

About the time Ellie was tossing back her last shot, it was midnight in Vladivostok. The mist drifted between the masts of the small boats, parting over the dull bows of the metal tankers. The big ships creaked and sighed in their moorings, but their decks were deserted. There was no one to notice the gentle slap of the wake from the 130-foot freighter against the huge steel hulls as the smaller boat slipped through the water and out of Golden Horn Bay. The freighter pointed east, heading toward the Alaskan coast.

When Ellie dragged herself into the office the next day, the paperwork was waiting. Not only did she have to complete an incident report, but she was also responsible for keying in the operational logs for the helos. She couldn't afford to get further behind than she already was, but when she sat down at her desk she found that she had a hard time focusing her eyes on the screen.

Ellie finally gave up and went down the hall to drop in on Dave. She stuck her head around the door and caught him with his head drooping onto his chest, his breathing deep and noisy. She was tempted to drop a book or slam the door and then tease Dave about his lapse, but he looked so peaceful, his face relaxed, his mouth hanging slightly open, that she didn't have the heart. She closed the door softly and went back to her office.

She sat for a moment in front of her computer, resting her fingers on the keyboard as if about to start typing, but then she pushed the keyboard out of the way and lowered her head onto her arms. The next thing she knew there was a hand on her shoulder gently shaking her awake.

"Lieutenant Commander. Hey, Somers."

She wiped her mouth on her sleeve and raised a bleary face from the desk, a Post-it note sticking to her cheek. Teddy was bent over her, and Mike and Dave stood in the doorway behind him.

"What?" she said. "What is it?" She pushed herself upright in her chair.

Teddy grimaced. "The skipper wants to see us."

■

Dave tapped on the half open door, and they heard Traub call for them to enter. They filed in and took seats.

The commanding officer had a large room to himself, but otherwise his office had the same cheap wood-paneled wainscoting and stained, blue industrial carpeting that decorated the rest of the building.

"I heard about the SAR last night," Traub said, then paused, and Ellie tensed, waiting for what he would say next. She thought that she sensed the others bracing themselves as well.

"I wanted to say congratulations on a successful rescue and a safe return."

Ellie glanced over at Dave and Teddy. Dave had closed his eyes briefly, and Teddy couldn't repress the quirk of a smile, though he quickly pulled his face into a serious expression.

"It sounds like it was a messy night, and I heard you had some complications. You had to shear the hoist, is that correct?" He addressed the question to Teddy.

"Yes, sir," Teddy acknowledged.

"Then you decided to employ the ERD."

This time Ellie answered. "Yes, sir. Petty Officer Hoffman and the survivor were in the water, and though we were getting low on fuel, we thought we had a shot at getting them back in."

"You knew you'd have to get low to have a chance?"

"Yes, we talked about that," Ellie said.

"You all agreed to try it?" he asked, with a slight emphasis on the word "all."

Ellie hesitated only a moment before replying, "Yes, sir. We all agreed."

Traub turned back to Teddy. "We haven't had occasion to use the ERD here in a SAR since it was developed. How was it to set up?"

"Took no time at all, sir."

"Good. I understand I can't ask you how it was in practice, since you didn't end up using it."

"Not as it was intended, sir."

For the first time Traub looked at Mike. "You distinguished yourself last night. Am I right in thinking it's your first SAR?"

"Yes, sir," Mike said, the fair skin of his neck turning red.

"That's quite a first mission. You've shown you've got the mettle for the job, though you may very well go the rest of your career without another SAR like that one."

"Oh, I hope not, sir."

"Well," Traub said. "Good job. You all look tired. Why don't you take the day off and get some sleep."

They took that for their dismissal, and they started to get up, but he said, "Lieutenant Commander Somers, would you stay a minute?"

Ellie sat back down in her chair. She felt rather than saw the quick glances the others shot at her before they left the room.

"Close the door behind you, McDonald," Traub called out.

As Ellie sat there, she felt exactly as she had as a child, standing at attention in front of her father's desk.

"Lieutenant Commander Somers," Traub began.

Ellie waited, her hands in fists in her lap.

"This is not an easy job we have here," he continued. "We're sending crews out in the kind of conditions that no one else is willing to fly in. It's always risky. That's part of the job, so I don't want to sit here and criticize the choices you made during a mission. It's too easy to second-guess, but I do want to ask you a question, and I want you to answer me truthfully."

Traub paused and he seemed to expect something, so Ellie said, "Yes, sir."

"Do you think that you might have pressured your crew into agreeing to go along with your suggestion?"

Ellie forced herself to look the CO right in the eye. "Maybe."

"So you knew that they weren't completely comfortable with the plan?"

"I knew I could do it," she said.

"You're a good pilot, Somers, but have you ever heard the saying, 'A superior pilot is one who stays out of trouble by using his superior judgment to avoid situations which might require the use of his superior skill'? That's something you might want to think about."

Ellie nodded, but silently disagreed.

Traub appeared to sense something of her thoughts because he regarded her steadily, and this time, after a few seconds, Ellie looked away.

■

She found Dave, Teddy, and Mike all waiting for her a short way down the hall.

"You all right?" Dave said.

"Fine," she answered briefly.

"Was it bad?" Mike asked.

Ellie just shook her head.

There was a little silence.

"Hey," Teddy said brightly. "I've got an idea."

"What is it?" she asked, trying to summon up interest.

"How does Marcy's sound?"

Dave groaned. "Oh no. Last time we went, I spent most of the next day in the head."

"It's the best Mexican food in town," Teddy said.

"It's practically the *only* Mexican food in town," Dave countered.

Teddy turned to Mike. "You like Mexican?"

"Sure."

"Three to one," Teddy said. "You lose this argument every week, you know. I don't know why you bother."

"I don't know either," Dave replied. "I've got to get my wallet. I left it in my desk."

"I need to take a piss," Mike added.

"We'll meet you guys outside," Teddy said.

Ellie and Teddy continued along the corridor and out the door. Teddy saw Sam before Ellie did.

"Commander Pantano, hey, just the person we wanted to see right now," Teddy exclaimed with false enthusiasm.

"I'd like to talk to Ellie for a minute," Sam said. "Do you mind?"

"I don't mind, but Lieutenant Commander Somers might. Let me give you a piece of advice—now's not the best time."

Sam didn't move from where he leaned comfortably against the wall of the building. "How did your talk with Commander Traub go?"

"It went just fine, thank you," Teddy replied.

"I wasn't asking you. I was asking Ellie. How did *your* talk go?"

Ellie turned sharply. "How did you know the skipper talked to me separately?" she demanded. Then, in sudden understanding, "You had something to do with that, didn't you?"

"Oh, I hope so," he responded, unperturbed.

"I can't believe you would do something like that," Ellie said, initially too surprised to be angry.

"I just want you to be a little more careful. You won't listen to me, I thought you might listen to the skipper."

The shock passed and the anger set in. She took a step forward and pointed a finger at him. "Now you listen to me. I care about my job, and what's more, I'm damn good at it."

"That's a matter of opinion," Sam answered quietly. "I tell you one thing, if I was in trouble, I don't know that I'd want you to be the one in charge of the rescue."

"That would be smart, 'cause I'd be tempted to leave you there," Ellie said, using sarcasm to cover the fact that she was stung.

He shook his head. "It's just a matter of time. You're not indestructible, Ellie, no matter what you think. One of these days, I can promise you, your luck is going to run out."

"Boy, this hits the spot," Teddy said around a huge mouthful of beef enchilada. "I love this place. I think I should just move in here."

"You think the person who decorated is color-blind?" Dave asked.

The restaurant had red fake-leather chairs and gray industrial carpeting. The windows were bordered by frilly green and white curtains, the tables were covered with pink vinyl tablecloths. The walls were decorated with plastic vines and paintings of Mexican villages.

"You're so picky," Teddy said. "I think Mikey likes it." Teddy eyed Mike's empty plate. "But you're not holding your own there, Somers."

Ellie had only managed a few cautious bites. "I don't want it to come back up," she said.

"Don't worry about that. It's the great thing about Marcy's—it tastes nearly as good coming up as going down."

"Gross," Mike said.

"Do you mind, Teddy? Some of us are trying to eat here," Dave added.

Teddy ignored him. "Hey, Ellie, I know something that'll cheer you up. You don't know about what happened last night after we dropped you off at home."

"I don't remember you guys taking me home."

"That's not surprising," Dave said, "seeing as 'carried you home' would be a more accurate description."

Teddy was not going to be deflected. "Anyway, as I was saying. After we dropped you off, we went back out—"

That got Ellie's attention. "Back out?"

"It was still early," Teddy said. "Well, early enough. We went into town, to the P Bar, and Lazure went right to work. You should have seen the girl he started hitting on—she was ugly as a monkey's butt. Lazure was buying her drinks, trying to get her to go home with him, and she was taking the drinks but she was also lecturing him about how he's just like all the other guys. She claimed that she'd had more one-night stands than a hooker, and she'd made up her mind she wasn't going to sleep with another man until she had a wedding ring on her finger. So what do you think Lazure did?"

Ellie took the bait. "What?"

"He proposed to her," Teddy announced.

"No way."

"Yes way. Not only that, they started making wedding plans. Pretty soon they were talking about how many people they'd invite, how many bridesmaids and groomsmen to ask, whether to have it in Alaska or back where she's from, in California. Then she said that she wanted to be married outdoors, in a field somewhere, or on the beach. Lazure said what do you mean, they have to get married in a church so it's recognized by God. They started arguing about it, then the woman said, 'That's it, the wedding's off. I'm outta here.' And Lazure said, 'What? You can't do that,' like he was really upset. She got up off the stool and said, 'Watch me,' and walked right outta there. We practically had to hold him back. I told Lazure that I'm a believer now. If he'd been an atheist he might have been married now. Makes you think, eh? Somebody up there likes Lazure, of all people."

"All right," Dave said. "Enough."

"So you admit it's true?" Ellie said.

"Of course it's not true," Dave denied it, but he spoke without his customary overbearing tone.

"Mike?" Ellie said. "Is it true?"

Both Teddy and Dave laughed, and Mike looked sheepish.

"Wasting your time asking Mike," Dave said.

"He was passed out alongside the bar," Teddy explained. "Spilled his drink, threw up, and passed out right in the middle of the mess."

"And you left him there?"

"We made sure he wasn't gonna choke," Dave said.

"What about you?" Ellie asked Teddy.

"What about me?" Teddy acted affronted. "I was the model of decorum. I had to keep these two in line."

"Teddy acts the same whether he's sober or swimming in booze," Dave said.

Teddy smirked.

"That wasn't a compliment," Dave informed him.

"A hit," Ellie declared, laughing, as Teddy's smirk disappeared. "Now pay the check. I need to catch up on some work this afternoon."

"But we have the afternoon off," Teddy reminded her.

She made a face. "I'm far enough behind already. But it is hard to go back to the grind after a night like last night."

"There'll be another," Teddy said.

"Sure, but when?"

At that moment, the Russian freighter was entering U.S. waters, following the shipping route to Vancouver. However, the boat wouldn't stay on course.

CHAPTER 10

"Watch out, Lazure. She's coming on," Teddy cried. "I think she's got you."

"I see her," Dave growled. His car spun to the right, and Ellie's rocketed past, bouncing off the wall to the sound of screeching brakes and crumpling steel.

"Crap." Ellie tossed the joystick in the air and then caught it again.

The doorbell rang.

She glanced up, momentarily confused. Then she remembered. "I forgot I told that reporter guy he could stop by. Will you let him in, Teddy? I've got one more chance to turn Dave into a candidate for the junk heap."

Teddy got up off the couch and returned with Whalen in tow, just in time to hear the spectacular sound effects of another crash.

"Dammit," Ellie said.

"Finally, it's my turn." Teddy reached for the joystick.

"Actually, it's Mike's," Dave corrected him.

"You have a PlayStation?" Whalen remarked.

Ellie handed the controller over to Mike. "Kick his ass for me, okay?"

"Yes, ma'am," Mike said as Ellie stood up to greet her guest.

"Of course I have a PlayStation," Ellie answered Whalen's question. "If you don't fish or hunt, there's not much else to do around here."

"It's good for your hand-eye coordination," Dave added.

"Sure it is," Teddy said, winking at Whalen.

"What are you playing?" Whalen asked.

"Twisted Metal," Ellie replied. "It's a demolition derby thing."

"It's Somers's favorite. I think it gets that urge to crash out of her system," Teddy put in.

"Not funny, Teddy," Ellie said. "Why don't we go into the kitchen to talk." She led the way, and as they were crossing into the other room, they heard the sound of another crash, and Mike's voice cursing. Ellie grinned and shut the door.

"You want something to drink? A soda or something?" Ellie offered.

"No, I'm fine."

Ellie pulled open the fridge and grabbed a can of A&W for herself.

"I haven't had a root beer in years," Whalen said.

"Want to change your mind?"

"Sure, I'll take one."

Ellie retrieved another. "Glass?"

"No, can's fine."

She handed over the soda and sat down at the table. Whalen took the chair across from her.

"Do you mind if I use a tape recorder? My shorthand's not so good."

"I've been hanging around Teddy for too long," she said. "I tend to spout nonsense."

"I promise I won't use it against you."

"Oh, that's all right, if you *promise*." Ellie rolled her eyes.

"So you've learned not to trust reporters, huh?"

"Let's just say I've gotten in trouble before, talking to reporters."

"I'll make you look good."

"But will you make me look sober and responsible?"

He hesitated, wondering if he should lie, but she saved him from having to make that decision by saying, "What the hell. I suppose I've done enough damage already. Tape away."

"Great. Thanks." He dug the tape recorder out, pressed RECORD, and set it on the table. "I have a few general, background questions. I'll start off easy. What made you want to join the Coast Guard?"

"I always wanted to fly."

"When I think flying, I don't usually think Coast Guard," Whalen said.

"You're right. I didn't either. I figured one of the branches of the military was the way to get there. For a while I thought I might want to fly jets. They have all that power—like steering a rocket."

"What changed your mind?" Whalen asked.

"For one thing, how many women do you see flying jets?"

"The Coast Guard isn't bursting with women pilots either."

"True, but the Coast Guard doesn't have any gender restrictions. Their policy is that women can do anything that men can. There might be the occasional guy who has a problem with women flying, but in the armed forces it's practically institutionalized. If I'd really wanted jets, I'd have gone for it, no matter what, but I started thinking, what's the point? You have to get through the training, and then when you get there—*if* you get there—what are you doing? You're probably flying training missions the rest of your career. I mean, how many dogfights do you hear about these days? I wanted to do something. In this job, on a good day, you get to save someone. I don't know how these older guys can bear to retire. They'll have to drag me out by the heels. I can't imagine giving it up."

On impulse, Whalen asked, "What did your mother do?"

"She was a housewife. I don't know that she ever had a job in her entire life, even for a summer."

"There's nothing wrong with that, is there?"

"No, not if it's by choice."

"What about your father?"

"He was in the Navy. A pilot. A Korean War hero."

"He must be very proud of you," Whalen said.

"Must he?" Ellie looked amused. "Why do you think my mother never worked? It was because my father wouldn't allow it. He doesn't believe women should work."

"So he doesn't approve?"

Ellie thought about her last conversation with her father—it had been at least a year ago now, but the memory still gave her a sick feeling. "No, he doesn't approve." She tried to soften it with a smile, but it looked more like a grimace.

"Um . . ." the reporter searched for a new topic—one that would be less painful. "How do you like Sitka?"

"I love it," she said without hesitation. "The flying is the most challenging you'll find anywhere except maybe Kodiak. Nothing in the Lower Forty-eight can compare. It's the kind of flying pilots talk about the rest of their careers."

"I meant how do you like the town. Do you ever think of anything but flying?"

"Yes, sure . . . well, maybe not a lot," she admitted, laughing.

Now Whalen knew how to get her back in a good mood. All he had to do was switch back to her favorite topic. "You know, I could see you flying jets. I could see you—what do they call it—pushing the envelope, and those jets, they're impressive machines. You sure you never have a twinge of regret?"

"Not a flicker," she vowed. "You might not have the speed, but you get more than you give up. In a jet you just barrel along, and at high speeds, human reaction time isn't fast enough, so the computer is doing a lot of the flying. In a helo you can go forward, backward, stop and hang out. Whatever you want, you can do. As a pilot, I don't think it gets any better."

Whalen must have looked unconvinced because Ellie said, half to herself, "How do I explain it? You know that dream, when all of a sudden you can fly? You ever have that dream?"

"Yes, I've had that dream."

"That's what it feels like for me, flying helicopters. The helo responds like your very own set of wings. You can't imagine the sense of freedom you get from that. As for the machine, have you ever seen one of our Jayhawks up close?"

Whalen shook his head.

"That's your first mistake. You can't write this article without seeing one."

"Can we go now?" he asked.

She stood up. "Absolutely. Let's go."

Whalen followed her out through the living room to the front door. Dave, Mike, and Teddy were still huddled around the TV, focused intently on the screen.

"We're headed over to the hangar," Ellie said, opening the door. "We'll be back in a bit."

"Ellie, hold on," Dave called. "It's almost seven, and Alex's barbecue started at six. You want us to wait for you and all go over together?"

Ellie stopped in the doorway. There was a long pause before she replied, "You guys go on over. I think I'll skip it. I've got this interview thing . . ."

"Oh, come on," Teddy said, and at the same time, Whalen said, "We can always do this tomorrow."

"See," Dave put in. "You can come."

"Don't be such a party pooper," Teddy coaxed.

"No, really—" Ellie said.

"We're not gonna go if you don't," Teddy threatened. "Isn't that right, Mikey?"

"That's right."

"Doesn't look like they're going to take no for an answer," Whalen observed.

"They're going to have to," Ellie said. "I wasn't invited."

There was a short silence.

"It must have been a mistake," Dave said. "They're having everyone. Officers, enlisted . . ."

"No," Ellie assured him. "It's not a mistake."

"How do you know?" Teddy broke in. "It might have been."

"No. I heard him telling people about it, but when I walked up, he didn't say anything to me."

"But that's not right," Teddy said.

"We're certainly not going," Dave declared.

"No way," Teddy backed him up.

"Don't do that. Just go, okay? For Alex's sake. I know he feels bad as it is."

"But—" Teddy began, but Ellie cut him off.

"Just go. I'll see you guys later." Not waiting for an answer, she stepped outside and waited for Whalen to join her, then closed the door behind him.

"Should we take my car?" Whalen asked.

"I usually walk. It's only a few minutes."

The Coast Guard housing consisted of long, brown-shingled units with several apartments in each. They were plain, rectangular boxes, but they were set against tall pines, and there were flower pots on the steps and children's bicycles propped against the siding. The best part, Whalen thought, was that the road was called Lifesaver Drive.

They had reached the exit and made the right onto Airport Road before Whalen got up the courage to ask, "So why weren't you invited? Don't you get along with this guy? Or is it what we were talking about before? Is he one of the rare ones that have a problem with a woman pilot?"

"Alex? No, Alex is great. We get along fine. It's his wife that doesn't like me much."

"Oh," Whalen said. Then with greater understanding, "Oooh."

"It's nothing like *that,*" Ellie said, correctly interpreting the second "oh." "There's nothing between me and Alex. It's too small a base to mess with stuff like that. No, his wife just doesn't like me, and she isn't the only one. Let's just say I don't get invited to a lot of dinner parties."

"But it seems like you don't really mind."

She glanced at him. "Why do you say that?"

"Because of what you said to your friends back there."

"No. I mind. But I don't want Teddy and Dave to go on a crusade for me. It wouldn't help, and it would probably just make things worse. I figure it comes with the job, and I love the job, so . . ."

And in that simple sentence, in that summing up, Whalen caught a glimpse of Ellie's life. The Coast Guard might be a great place for women in comparison with the armed forces, but it still didn't change the fact that she was a woman in a profession dominated by men. They might accept her, they might even be pals with her, like Dave and Teddy, but she would never completely belong. Many of the other pilots were married, and they couldn't invite Ellie back to their homes. The gulf between her and their wives was too great. They could invite someone like Dave home—a bachelor the wives were able to flirt with delicately and tease about when he was going to settle down. Where could Ellie fit into that scenario? On what ground could she and the wife of her colleague meet? And if that was the case, how well could she really fit in with the other pilots?

He was about to ask her another question, something about how she could be happy under the circumstances, but he found they had reached the door of the hangar.

Ellie punched in a code, opened the door, and led him down a short hallway. She halted before another door on her left. "You ready?"

"Sure."

She ushered him through into the huge expanse of the hangar. The H-60 Jayhawk crouched on the concrete, gleaming under the lights, the paint waxed to a high sheen.

"Take a look at that and try to tell me that's not an amazing machine." Ellie glanced over at him, to gauge his reaction, but found

Whalen was staring at her instead of the helo. "Don't look at me, look at the helo," she ordered.

He obediently switched his gaze to the aircraft, but he was still thinking about what he'd observed on Ellie's face. Seeing her expression, he had the answer to the question he hadn't had the chance to ask. He knew how she was happy in a job where she was not invited back to her colleagues' homes, where she had to prove that she belonged, not once, but every day. He'd seen it in her face when she looked at the helo.

Whalen studied the machine, and he thought he might even be able to understand her feeling. He had imagined an ordinary helicopter, about the size of a car, maybe a station wagon, and delicate, like a machine version of a dragonfly. This helo was sixty-five-feet long, about the size of an eighteen-wheeler. The blades of the main rotor were thick and heavy and impossibly long; the diameter of the rotor was almost as long as the helo itself. He imagined the power generated by those enormous metal blades beating the air.

It was also the most immaculate, well-cared-for aircraft he had ever seen. It was painted with Coast Guard colors of white and orange on the body, and it had a black nose, giving it the look of one of the old-time WWII bombers. Whalen couldn't see the slightest sign of flaking paint, smears of grease, or any wear at all. It looked like it had never been rolled out of the hangar.

"Go on, climb in," she said.

Whalen stepped forward and climbed in the right-hand seat— traditionally the pilot's seat. Settling back into the fuzzy seat cover, he curled his right hand loosely around the cyclic and his left around the collective, resting his feet on the pedals. Then he tried to imagine what it would be like to feel the helo rise beneath him.

Ellie had circled round the front and climbed into the left-hand seat.

"This is making me want to learn how to fly helicopters," Whalen said.

"I recommend it, but I hate to break it to you, you wouldn't be flying a bird like this. This is a fifteen-million-dollar machine. It's a fully equipped, instrument rated helicopter, which isn't too common. What that means is it's got all the bells and whistles and some serious power. Without that power I wouldn't have been able to climb up the face of that wave the other night."

"Is this the helo you flew?" he asked.

"This is it," she tapped the helicopter's tail number located on the instrument panel.

"They sure got it cleaned up."

"They take real good care of these babies. They do constant maintenance, and they basically take them apart and put them back together every six hundred hours of flying time. It also doesn't hurt that the guys who maintain them are also the guys who fly out as the flight mechs."

"If there was an emergency right now, would they take this helo?"

"No. This isn't the ready helo. Looks like they haven't brought in the ready helo yet for the night. I guess it's out on the tarmac." Ellie leaned out and called over to one of the men on top of another identical helo, working on the main rotor. "Hey, Manny, is the ready helo still out?"

Ellie ducked back inside and told Whalen, "Seems like the duty crew got called out."

"A SAR?" Whalen asked.

"No, Manny said it was a medevac. We get more of those than SARs."

"But I imagine the SARs are more exciting."

"Sometimes, but the medevacs, depending on the weather and the route, can get pretty hairy too. The truth is that they're all great. It can be the middle of the day, middle of the night, you might be brushing your teeth when you get that call or hear the whoopee, and who knows, you may be going out to save someone's life. I'd do it every day if I could."

"How often do you get calls?"

At that moment the whooping siren sounded. They both jumped.

"That's the second time," she said, throwing him a look. "Boy, you're spooky."

"I think that somebody up there doesn't want me to finish an interview," he replied.

"We'll finish it first thing tomorrow. I promise." Ellie held up two fingers. But it was a promise she wouldn't be able to keep.

CHAPTER 11

"Can you fly?" That was the first thing the duty officer said when he saw Ellie. "You haven't been drinking, have you?"

"Not a drop. I'm ready to go."

"God, I'm glad to hear that," he said. "I've been doing the random recall, and no one's answering."

"Everyone's over at Alex's—he's having a barbecue. Have you tried my place yet?"

"Got the answering machine, like everyone else."

"Try again, and yell into it for Teddy or Dave to pick up. I left them there playing video games, and I think they might still be at it. Talk loud enough, and they'll pick up. If they're still there, it will give us a full crew."

The duty officer was already dialing.

"What is it? Medevac? SAR?" she asked.

He covered the mouthpiece. "Law enforcement," he said.

■

The Coast Guard cutter *Anacapa* was in the Dixon Entrance at the southern tip of Prince of Wales Island when the watch on the bridge saw a boat on the radar.

The *Anacapa* was patrolling the A-B line or "approximate boundary" line—a disputed area of water that marked the fuzzy boundary between Alaskan and Canadian waters. Both countries kept a close watch on fishing vessels in the area during the summer months to make sure that the Canadian fishing vessels didn't stray over into U.S. waters, and vice versa.

The issue was more complicated than a border patrol; the two countries had been sparring for more than a decade over the depletion of the salmon stock, and relations remained strained. A few years back, tensions had risen so high that for three days Canadian fishermen blockaded an Alaskan State Ferry, preventing it from leaving the terminal at Prince Rupert. There had also been several incidents of both sides confiscating vessels that weren't in violation, which complicated the issue even more. So the appearance of a blip on the radar drew the attention of the *Anacapa*. However, this vessel was at the western edge of the Dixon Entrance, too far out to be a good spot for salmon fishing, as the salmon tended to stick to the coast. It might have been a ship on its way down to Vancouver, except that it wasn't moving.

After a few minutes' consideration, the captain of the *Anacapa* decided to head out into the gulf to check it out. The water was a glassy calm, but the clouds hung low over the ocean like a gauzy veil, bringing the visibility down to a quarter of a mile. As a result, they had to get close to make out the outline of the ship through binoculars, and to discover that it wasn't a fishing vessel. A closer look revealed the Cyrillic lettering on the rusty hull.

"What's a Russian freighter doing sitting there off the coast?" the quartermaster said.

"Why don't we find out," the captain suggested. "Let's raise them on the radio."

It took several minutes to contact them, then several more to get an English-speaker, who turned out to be the skipper of the freighter. He reported that they were having a small engine problem, but they should have it fixed soon, and then they were going to continue on to their destination, Vancouver.

"Let us know if you run into any problems with your repairs," the captain said and signed off.

The captain turned the *Anacapa* back into the Dixon Entrance, and they checked out a couple of fishing trawlers before encountering the second incongruous vessel. This blip was moving toward them, on a steady westward course, and it appeared to be moving at a high speed. The *Anacapa* turned south to intercept it, but barely got there in time to catch a glimpse of her through the fog.

It was a pleasure craft, but with a very powerful engine.

"Good thing we don't have to worry about that one," the quartermaster said. "Because we sure couldn't keep up with it."

"What do you think that boat was doing headed west at this time in the evening?" the captain said.

"Out for an after-dinner spin?" the quartermaster guessed.

"In this weather?"

"It is a little strange," the quartermaster agreed.

"What if that boat was headed somewhere . . ."

"Where?"

"Out to that freighter," the captain said. "Bear with me for a minute. They say the Canadian border is the new point of entry for drugs, now that surveillance is stepped up along the Mexican border. Maybe the inspections at Vancouver's port are getting too intense? What if that's a go-fast?" the captain said, employing the term specific to the fast boats used for drug running. "Utilizing cigarette boats to rendezvous with a mothership works along the Florida coast, why not here?" The captain glanced at the quartermaster. "Sound crazy?"

"No, sir."

"Then what do you say we get someone down here that can keep up with that boat?"

That's when the quartermaster put in the call to the command center at Juneau, requesting assistance, and the call was relayed down to Sitka.

■

Twenty-seven minutes after the whoopee sounded, the helo lifted off the tarmac and headed south. Inside was the same crew from the SAR less than a week before, with Ellie in the right-hand seat, Dave flying copilot, and Teddy and Mike in the back. Ellie swung out over the ocean, roughly following the coastline, though they couldn't see it through the fog.

Ellie and crew had passed the tip of Baranof Island and the mouth of Chatham Strait when they got the report from the *Anacapa* that the two targets had converged. The captain's guess had been correct, and now the only question was whether the helo could reach the scene before the Russian ship offloaded all the cargo and the go-fast put enough distance between them to outstrip the radar.

The Jayhawk passed the entrance to Sumner Straight, then they were flying along the shores of Prince of Wales Island. The A-B line slanted across the southern tip of the island, but they still had at least fifty miles to go, as Prince of Wales was twice as large as the state of Rhode Island.

Then the *Anacapa* passed along the news that the go-fast had pulled away from the freighter and was on the move. The Jayhawk was still too far away to pick up the target, so Ellie brought the helo up in the hopes that the elevation would increase the radar's range, and she put on a burst of speed as well. It seemed to do the trick. In minutes, Dave was able to radio the cutter that they had the go-fast on their radar and were in pursuit.

The boat, unaware it was being tracked, was not running at anywhere near top speed, and the Jayhawk closed the distance quickly. When the radar signaled that they had caught up with the target, Ellie said, "I'm going down for a visual."

"Do it," Dave agreed.

"Passing eight hundred. Seven hundred. Six hundred," she read off as she brought the helo down. "Passing five hundred. Four." She kept a careful eye on the altimeter in case the fog extended right down to the ocean's surface, but at fifty feet they punched down through the cloud, and they could see the flat calm of the ocean, placid and eerie in the hazy air.

They were so low the helo seemed to skim over the surface of the water, and Ellie flew with a closer concentration. As a pilot, you didn't often fly low and fast, not unless there was a good reason. A small mistake, easily correctable at a higher altitude, might be unrecoverable.

The fog foreshortened the horizon and closed in above them, and everyone inside the helo strained their eyes to peer ahead, searching for the telltale sign of a wake.

"Where is it?" Ellie muttered.

And then, as if summoned by her question, there it was. There was a disturbance in the water, and then the boat itself, its speed throwing up a rooster tail of water behind.

"Gotcha," Ellie said.

"Yes, but how do we stop them?" Teddy asked from the back. "I wish we had a couple of those guns they've approved for the helos in Florida to stop the drug runners down there. One shot from a sniper rifle, I could take out their engine."

"I'll try to raise them on the radio," Dave said.

"I don't think they're going to say, oh, sure, we'll stop and wait for a cutter to arrive and board us, do you?" Ellie said.

"I have to try," Dave pointed out.

The boat had certainly spotted the helo, but it kept on running even as Dave tried to contact them. Dall Island loomed up out of the mist, to port, and the boat swung in a wide arc, heading for the waterway between Dall and a smaller island wedged between Dall and Prince of Wales.

Ellie followed, and the steep banks—thick with the deep green of hemlock and cedar—heightened her sense of speed. Soon she was within twenty yards, then ten, keeping just above the arc of water spewing from the vessel.

"What are you doing?" Dave demanded.

"Getting closer," Ellie said.

"I can see that, but why?"

"I'm trying to stop them. I think they need a little persuasion."

"Oh no. No, Ellie."

"Come on," she said. "Let's have some fun with this."

"Ellie—" Dave started to say, but before he could finish, she had nudged them forward until they were right above the go-fast, and she was taking them lower, until they felt a wheel bounce off the top of the boat's cabin.

This brought a startled cry from Dave. Then Ellie brought them down again, the wheel hitting hard enough to dent metal and sending a shudder through the helo.

"Bring us up, Lieutenant Commander," Dave said. "Now." He spoke in a tone that Ellie couldn't ignore, and she reluctantly complied. She eased back on the cyclic and pulled up on the collective, dropping back behind the boat. Then the helo began to yaw, the nose swinging slightly to the right. At first Ellie thought that she simply hadn't used enough left pedal to counteract the torque caused by pulling up on the collective, so she applied more pressure, but if anything, it seemed to make it worse. She slowed the Jayhawk, reducing the torque, but the aircraft continued to yaw, the body swinging so far around that they were looking out at the steep bank of trees to their right, even as the craft continued forward flight. She jammed down on the left pedal and nothing happened. "I'm losing the tail rotor," she yelled. "Pedals not responding."

She dimly perceived Dave chanting into the radio, "Mayday, Mayday," but her concentration was focused on trying to keep from impacting the water as the helo spun like a slow top. The body of the helo continued to twist, and they were now facing backward. There was only one way she knew to stop the spinning and get her men out. She made the decision almost instantaneously, and it was that quickness that saved them.

"I'm going to try to land on the water," she said. "Teddy, Mike, pre-pare to ditch. Prepare to ditch."

Everyone was watching the water as she brought them down, and they all three yelled "Okay," just as she felt the friction of the water slow, then stop the fuselage from spinning.

"Bail now. NOW!" Ellie yelled, engines running, maintaining a kind of hover with the lower part of the helo submerged.

Over the headset she heard scuffling from the back.

"They're out," Dave reported.

"I'm going to try to give them some space, then we'll go for a con-trolled shutdown," Ellie said as she carefully water-taxied forward. When they shut down, the helo would roll, and then the rotors would hit the water. Even with the engines turned off, the blades would shatter like glass, and she didn't want to be anywhere near Mike and Teddy when that happened.

"Almost time to shut it down," she told Dave. "Get that door open."

Next to her, Dave jettisoned his door, but Ellie didn't want to take her hand off the controls, so her door remained on.

"Ready to shut it down?" she said.

"Ready."

Ellie continued to man the cyclic and collective while Dave chopped the engines and immediately applied the rotor brake. Ellie tried to keep the helo upright as the rotors slowed, but she felt the craft rolling to the left.

Then everything seemed to happen at once. The helo lurched and the retreating blade impacted the water. It struck with enough force that it nearly ripped the transmission off the top of the aircraft, and inside the cockpit the impact felt like hitting a brick wall while going forty. Ellie's head was snapped sideways and slammed against the doorframe. She felt a jagged pain shoot through her skull, and her vision started to darken. She might have passed out, but the shock of the freezing water filling the cabin revived her.

In this scenario, Ellie had been taught to stay strapped in until the water covered her face, but it felt like extraneous advice—the water poured in so fast it seemed as if, all of a sudden, she was submerged. She opened her eyes to the murky, stinging salt water, so dark she couldn't see. She fumbled with her harness. How deep had the helo sunk already? Her lungs were burning, and she was still going down.

She tried to find the door release, but she soon realized that she couldn't waste any more time. The helo was sinking like a stone, with her in it. Dave's door was open, so she half swam, half pulled herself through to the left-hand side. Dave was no longer in his seat, and she felt relief knowing that at least she had gotten her crew out.

She managed to exit the helo, but she knew she was losing the battle. She could feel the darkness of unconsciousness descending. She triggered the CO^2 cartridge on her life vest, but she must have been too deep, and the water pressure was too much for the small canister. She started swimming for what she thought was the surface, but then she wasn't sure the helo hadn't rolled again as it was sinking. She might very well be swimming for the bottom of the ocean. It was her last thought before she blacked out.

CHAPTER 13

The first thing Ellie was aware of was the pain—a throbbing ache in her head. She opened her eyes. Above her she saw a plain white ceiling. When she looked to her right, she saw the top of an IV stand and the plastic bag of clear liquid that hung from it. She followed the tube into the back of her hand, where they had taped the drip into a vein. That was all she could see without lifting her head, and the ache made her want to keep her head as still as possible, though a groggy, disoriented feeling signaled that she must have painkillers in her system.

Then she heard what sounded like the door to her room opening, and the top of a woman's head appeared. A nurse rounded the side of the bed, and Ellie could see she was reading from a clipboard. She set it down and, with a ripping of Velcro, unstuck a blood pressure strap and reached for Ellie's arm. It was only then that the nurse looked at her, and when she saw Ellie's eyes were open, she gave a yelp and jumped back.

"Hello," Ellie said, her voice coming out in a croak.

The nurse pressed a hand dramatically to her chest. "I wasn't expecting you to be awake. Why didn't you call me when you woke up?"

"Didn't know your number," Ellie replied, her voice loosening to a weak but normal tone.

The woman smiled at her. "Not very original, but it seems that you're feeling better."

"I'm feeling, but I don't know about the better part. It's like a jackhammer's going in my head."

"What do you expect when you get in an argument with a large piece of metal?"

"What happened?" Ellie asked her. "I remember getting called out, but after that it's just flashes."

"That's not unusual with a head injury. In most cases the memory returns. I wasn't on duty when you came in, but your friend may be able to help . . . and you might be able to help us by getting him out of the way for a while."

"Teddy," Ellie said.

"How did you guess?"

"What has he been up to?" She felt as if the hammering in her head was already lightening.

"He keeps stealing puddings from the kitchen. He thinks we haven't noticed."

"I'll straighten him out," Ellie offered. "Just send him in here."

"I think I'll take you up on that."

The nurse went to find Teddy, and Ellie was left still flat on her back. She explored with her right hand, found the control for the bed, and located the button to raise herself to a sitting position. It didn't make her feel any better, but it didn't make her feel worse either.

A moment later Teddy pushed the door open. She had been expecting a big greeting, but he barely smiled, and instead of coming over to the bed, he pulled up a chair and sat a few feet away. She noticed that he looked tired.

"How are you feeling?" Teddy asked, but when he spoke, he didn't quite meet her eye.

"Like hell," she said, expecting him to make some joke about how she looked it too. He just nodded.

"You all right?" she asked him.

"Me? I'm fine."

"How about the other guys?"

"Fine."

"Thank God." She hadn't realized how tense she'd been until she heard his answer. She relaxed back against the bed. "Teddy, tell me what happened."

When he spoke, he seemed wary. "What do you mean, what happened?"

"I don't remember too much."

"You don't remember?"

"The nurse said it might have something to do with the head injury. I remember the call. I remember the fog. I remember finding the boat, following it, and a flash of something, like the world spinning, and then I think I remember water. Breathing water. That's all."

"You went down in the helo," Teddy told her, staring down at his hands. "Mike's the reason you're still around. He gave you mouth-to-mouth, got you breathing again."

"I wasn't breathing? Well . . ." Ellie was speechless for a second. When she regained her voice, she said, "How about that. The kid's a hero."

"That's what they're saying."

"And the go-fast? Did they get the go-fast?"

Teddy shook his head. "The duty helo diverted on its way back from the medevac, but they didn't follow the boat. They helped us instead. They got to us just before the *Anacapa* did."

"The cutter too? You mean they left the freighter?"

"Yeah."

"They all got away?"

"It's probably only heroin headed straight for the elementary schools."

"Don't try to cheer me up, Teddy," she said, though she wasn't even sure he was trying to. It had sounded like one of his jokes, but he had said it almost bitterly.

"How did we go down?" Ellie asked.

Teddy didn't look at her.

"Teddy."

He looked up, and then back down again. "I was in the cabin. I'm not the best person to say."

"Was there a malfunction with the helo?"

"You mean you couldn't possibly have fucked up. It must have been one of the mechanics, right?" His response was so sudden and so biting, it was as if he had been waiting to erupt.

The shock of his attack threw Ellie for a moment, then she tried to backpedal. "No, I didn't mean—"

"There was nothing wrong with that aircraft. I'm just as good at what I do as you are. Better. I might joke around, but I take my work seriously. I would never do anything to jeopardize the crew."

"And I would?"

There was an awful silence. Then Teddy said, "You did."

Ellie wanted to contradict him. She searched her memory, but came up with a blank. "How?" she asked.

His voice was tight as he spoke. "We were following the go-fast when it turned into a channel. You came down low and bounced a wheel off the roof. When you pulled back, the tail rotor must have dipped into the water thrown up behind the boat and damaged a blade. We started losing torque control."

"Oh." Ellie closed her eyes. She strained her brain, trying to cut through the fog of painkillers. She remembered the low fog, the channel, the speed of the go-fast, just those few brief images. She didn't remember bumping the boat, but Teddy would have Mike and Dave to back him up on that. Had the tail rotor impacted the rooster tail when she tried to back off? Had she simply not used enough power, causing the tail to drop? Would she have made that kind of mistake? It felt like she was living a nightmare, not being able to remember.

"That's all you have to say? 'Oh.' That's it?"

"What do you want me to say, Teddy?" she asked, helpless in the face of his anger.

"You're something else, you know that? You're one of a kind. How about an apology? I guess that never crossed your mind. We were all telling you to pull up. You just didn't listen."

"I'm sorry, okay? I'll listen next time. I promise. But could you ease up a little? I'm sure I'll hear about this from the CO . . . not to mention Dave. I bet he's waiting outside for his turn, right?"

Teddy looked at her. Then he said, "No," but he said it in a strange, strangled voice.

Ellie hadn't thought she could feel worse. "What is it? What's wrong with Dave? You said everyone was okay."

Teddy was silent.

"If you don't tell me right now, I'm going to rip out this IV and go find someone who will," she threatened, and she meant it. She felt she couldn't stand another second with this awful feeling like she couldn't breathe.

"You weren't supposed to know till you got out of here. That's what the doctor said."

"Screw that. Don't you dare pull that shit on me. How bad is he hurt?"

"He wasn't breathing when he came up either. Mike got you breathing again, and I couldn't . . ."

It took Ellie a moment to finish the sentence for herself and then to grasp the implication. That meant that Dave . . . she felt a wave of nausea. Dave couldn't be gone—not Dave, with his self-righteous rants, his ridiculous handlebar moustache, and those occasional smiles that he couldn't quite control.

She could tell from the expression on Teddy's face that he was replaying the event in his head. In her imagination, Ellie saw Teddy swimming up to Dave's body as it floated on the swells.

"Jesus, Teddy. I'm sorry."

"Yeah? Well, you've got a hell of a lot to be sorry for."

"What do you want me to do, Teddy? Say it again? I'd say it a million times if I thought it would do any good, but it won't. I wish it could."

"You don't get it. I think you *should* try saying it a million times. Maybe then you'd learn something—you tried to be a hotshot pilot, and now Dave's dead. I was there, and I couldn't help him. You have no idea how that feels."

Teddy didn't stop there. "Now to top it all off, you claim not to remember—so you don't have to admit you fucked up. Trying to save your own ass, and screw the rest of us, right? Not this time. This time I say screw you. Screw you." He stood up abruptly, almost knocking the chair over. Then, without another word, he turned and left the room.

Ellie sat up for a long time, watching the doorway, hoping that he might come back.

He didn't.

CHAPTER 14

"After reviewing all the information and hearing the testimony of the witnesses, we have concluded our investigation into the crash of CG 6047."

While the president of the Mishap Analysis Board spoke, Ellie sat as straight and still as she could manage. It was almost over, she told herself. After more than a month of waiting, the ordeal was finally coming to an end. In the first few days after the crash, she had dreaded the decision of the MAB because she knew that the three-man panel would decide her future, but after a week of sitting in her apartment, she had realized that the final determination couldn't come soon enough. Living only a few hundred yards from the base in the midst of all her colleagues meant she had to watch them passing by on their way to work and then again on their way home. It was a blessing that Teddy lived in the barracks closer to the base, so she didn't have to see him, but she saw Mike and Sam, and she even found herself forgetting sometimes and watching for Dave. That was the worst—that and not flying.

She could hear the helos when they took off. Even with the TV on and all the windows closed, she could hear the beat of the heavy rotor blades, and when they banked away heading out over the water she could feel the turn in her hands and feet. Closing her eyes, she tried to pretend she was flying again, but then there would come a sickening moment of doubt. Imagining a turn, she found herself thinking—had she done it right? She didn't trust herself anymore, and if she had to think about it now, when she was only mimicking the movements in a chair in her living room, how would it be back in the air? And back in the air not only on a clear day, but during a storm, with gale force winds and no visibility. How could she trust herself to fly the way you needed to under pressure—instinctually, without hesitation? If she started flying from her head, she was in trouble. You had to fly with your hands and your feet. They said you really became a pilot when you learned feel. Some people never did, just as certain people who learned to play the piano went on to solo careers and others ended up teaching children their scales. But there were times when the concert pianist started hitting wrong notes during an important recital, and there were pilots who, under pressure, momentarily forgot how to fly. It didn't only happen to rookies. It happened to people who had been performing in difficult situations for years. Suddenly, inexplicably, they lost it. Is that what had happened to her?

So she sat, watching her old life outside her window and wondering if she could ever return to it, even if the results of the inquiry were favorable. And if they weren't . . . she could still be a commercial pilot, she supposed, but she would have to get licensed, and that cost money. She didn't know where the money went, but she'd never been able to save anything from her salary. She'd have to get a job, save up for the fees, and then maybe, if she was lucky, she'd get a job ferrying passengers somewhere. However, there were days—the bad days—when she thought that not being a pilot might be the best solution after all, and that's when she started to think that the hearing couldn't come soon enough.

The president of the MAB continued. "On the evening of the thirteenth of July, at nineteen hundred hours, Lieutenant Commander Somers responded to a call from the cutter *Anacapa*. While in pursuit of a boat suspected of illegal trafficking in drugs, the helo experienced a loss of tail rotor and the crew had to ditch the craft in the water. The Mishap Board has determined that the accident was pilot error, brought about when Lieutenant Commander Somers, despite protest from her crew, descended to intimidate the boat, and the tail rotor impacted the wake."

She was able to listen to that without emotion. That finding she had known about ever since they'd told her that the MAB had decided not to raise the helo. The area of the channel where she'd gone down was over 700 feet deep. Divers couldn't go down below 230 feet, so it required an automated retrieval. For an automated retrieval, contracting a Navy ship would have been the best solution. However, there were only two ships on the West Coast that the Navy used for salvage, and neither was available. They considered hiring a civilian contractor, but for an automated retrieval, it would be considerably more expensive than using Navy salvage and, with budget constraints, cost was a significant factor. The fact that there were no bodies to recover, and that they had a good idea what caused the crash, left the board with little justification for the expenditure.

Ellie knew that the real question being decided here today was their recommendation concerning her future. If she could eventually return to flying, then she didn't care what they threw at her. Generally, they didn't ground a pilot for pushing the envelope—it was part of the job—but usually pilots were flying on a SAR where there was an overriding reason. The standards on a law enforcement call were less clear, especially when one of the crew died in the resulting crash.

Would they let her fly again or not. That was the question.

"With respect to Lieutenant Commander Somers, the board recommends—"

Ellie could feel the weakness in her legs and arms. She was so nervous she felt dizzy.

"—that she be permanently removed from flight status."

Ellie had her answer.

On the way out, Commander Traub stopped her with a hand on her arm. Anyone else she would have shaken off, but she stopped for her CO.

"I'm sorry, Ellie," he said, and he looked as if he meant it.

She wanted to say thank you, but she wasn't sure if she could get the words out.

"I hope you'll stay with us," he continued, but he must have seen something in her face because he added quickly, "At least take some time to consider it."

She shook her head—all along, she had known what she would do if they jerked her wings. She said, her voice not quite steady, "I'm sorry, sir. I'll have my resignation on your desk by tomorrow."

C H A P T E R   1 5

Someone was ringing her doorbell. Ellie opened her eyes, then sat up, rubbing at her cheek where the fabric of the couch had left a waffle pattern on her skin.

Ellie had the feeling that the doorbell had been ringing for some time already, but she'd been reluctant to return from the comforting void of sleep. Since the trial, she'd spent as much time as possible sleeping. She had moved her things off the base to an apartment in town, and since then had left that apartment as infrequently as possible, going out mainly to stock up on food. After buying groceries, she always paused in front of the liquor store, and it was only through sheer stubbornness that she was able to resist smoothing things over with a shot or two. Instead she escaped through sleep, and even when she was awake she felt sluggish and listless, as if life itself were a dream.

Ellie lay back down and tried to bury her head under the cushion of the couch, but the doorbell rang again. She threw the pillow across the room and pushed herself up. While she sat there, trying to shake off the numb stupor of sleep and hoping that whoever was at the door would go away, it rang yet again. With a groan, she heaved herself up off the couch and crossed to the window, bending one of the blinds to see who was standing at the door, but when she looked, she almost didn't believe it.

Sam stood waiting patiently, his hands in his pockets.

Ellie considered cleaning up a little before letting him in, but just the thought of it made her tired. Why bother, she asked herself. She crossed to the door and opened it as he was raising his hand to ring the bell yet again.

They stood there for a moment, regarding each other. Then Sam said, "Can I come in?"

She stood back, opening the door wider to allow him to enter. He stepped inside, and she pointed him through to the living room.

All the blinds were drawn. The room was lit by the flickering blue light of the television, illuminating the plates and glasses strewn on the floor around the couch and littering the coffee table. It looked bad, but not, she thought, worse than it had been these last weeks.

"Sit down," she offered, gesturing at the couch.

He kicked over a glass on his way and bent to pick it up.

"Leave it," she said. "Don't bother."

He hesitated, then took the extra step to the couch and sat down. He looked so clean, his pants pressed, his hair neatly brushed, and he looked so serious—even more than usual.

She took the chair opposite.

He massaged his hands nervously. "So, how are you?"

"Fine."

He darted a look around, as if to say, This is fine? She pretended not to notice.

"I know I'm not exactly the person you wanted showing up at your front door . . ."

He trailed off, but she didn't contradict him. The truth was that she was having a hard time caring. She tried to revive the old animosity, but she couldn't seem to summon the energy.

"I wanted to talk to you," Sam said.

She picked at the fabric on the arm of her chair. "Yeah?"

"I have some information, and it could be good news for you . . . potentially . . . I mean it might be."

"Yeah?" she said again.

Sam frowned at her. "You sure you're all right?"

"I'm fine. I'm just tired." She tried to work up some interest, for appearances' sake. "What's this news, then?"

He seemed reassured by her question. "I think there might be a chance—a good chance—you can get them to raise the helo."

Her heart thudded hard once, then subsided. "Why would I want them to do that?"

"Why? So we could know for certain what happened."

"There's no point. I already know what happened."

"Did you remember something?" he asked eagerly.

"No, but the Mishap Board ruled on it. That's the end of it." She shrugged.

"It shouldn't be. They should have raised the helo."

"Why? They knew the cause of the accident, and they didn't have the budget."

"But it was all circumstantial evidence. Strong circumstantial, true, but circumstantial. Teddy and Mike were in the back, you can't remember, and Dave . . ."

More than anything, Ellie wanted to close her eyes and go back to sleep. "It's over, Sam," she said wearily. "I resigned. I'm out."

"You can appeal." Sam leaned forward over his knees in his eagerness to convince her. "If you get a lawyer, you can appeal on the basis of flight safety. Use the fact that they don't know for certain why the helo went down, that the only reason they didn't raise it was due to cost, and that they might be endangering their people. Do that, and there's a good chance you can force them to bring the helo up. You might not even have to get a lawyer. You might only have to threaten to raise a stink because of this news I got today. A friend of mine over in Navy salvage called me. There's been a change in the scheduling, and one of the salvage ships is going to be up here in a couple of weeks doing pier repair over in Adak, and they might have a few extra days to come over and help us. That news, along with the threat of an appeal, might be enough to persuade them to bring up the helo now—to avoid having to spend twice as much to hire civilian contractors to do it later."

Ellie was shaking her head before Sam even finished. Even if they raised the helo, the evidence would probably support the finding of the board, and then it would feel as if she were being convicted all over again. It wouldn't change anything that had happened. It wouldn't bring Dave back.

"I appreciate what you're trying to do, but I think I'll pass," she said.

"I don't understand. I thought you'd grab at any chance to come back."

At one point, she would have thought so too. She started to say, "I don't have the money for a lawyer—" but Sam interrupted.

"I told you that I don't even think you would need to hire one.

Threatening to hire one might be enough. I'll tell you what. You don't have to do anything. If you want, I'll talk to the skipper for you."

"No. Thanks, but no."

"Why not?"

How could she explain the lethargy she couldn't seem to shake? And she didn't even want to acknowledge to *herself* the fear that lurked beneath it, so instead of trying to answer, she turned a question on him.

"Why would you want me back? I thought that you would have liked nothing more than for me to get my wings jerked."

"I never said that."

"You said you didn't approve of the way I flew, and I have to give you this—you warned me. You knew something like this was going to happen."

"No," Sam denied it.

"You said so. You said eventually my luck would run out. Well, it did. I didn't think what I was depending on was luck. I thought I was relying on skill. Turns out I was wrong, and you were right. I wasn't a good enough pilot."

"There was nothing wrong with your skill, but there's more to being a good pilot than skill. It's true, I didn't think you were a good pilot, but you could have been."

"Could have," Ellie repeated.

"Still can be," Sam amended quickly.

His pity, she discovered, was much worse than his hostility had ever been.

"Thanks for coming." She stood up as a signal to him that their talk was over.

He looked up at her, then slowly rose as well. "It seems like I've made a mistake," he said.

When she didn't contradict him, he nodded sadly. "I'll let myself out."

He left the room, and she heard the front door close behind him. Then, she wasn't sure why, but she crossed to the window, and peering out through the blinds, she watched him walk away.

CHAPTER 16

"Hey," the bartender rested his elbows on the counter near Ellie. "The guy down the other end of the bar wants to buy you a beer. That okay?"

Ellie looked down the bar and caught the eye of a decent-looking guy with the deep, leathery tan of a fisherman. She tilted the inch of warm beer in the bottom of her glass. She was used to getting hit on in bars, and consequently was very good at fending off unwanted advances. Her first rule was never to accept a drink, but this time she hesitated. She hadn't talked to anyone in what felt like a long time—and she wouldn't mind another beer. She told herself that just talking to the guy wouldn't hurt.

She said, "I guess he can do what he wants."

The bartender went down to the taps to pour another, and the man picked up his beer, said a word to his friends, and walked down to where she sat.

Ellie had come to the Columbia Bar because she was sure that she wouldn't meet anyone she knew there. It was the kind of place where fights broke out, where "Rock You Like a Hurricane" by Scorpion was always playing on the jukebox, and where the bartender told the same dirty jokes over and over. It was not the kind of place where her friends went to hang out, and most of the locals avoided it as well. It was a Friday, and while every other bar in town was packed, Columbia Bar was nearly deserted.

It had been almost a month since she had moved off the base; the summer was chilling into fall, and the crowds of tourists were thinner every day, along with her chances for finding employment. After Sam had come to visit, she had suddenly found the apartment unbearable, so, recently, she had spent her days on the trails around the town. In the morning she would walk up Lake Street, past the high school, and into the woods. The cross-Sitka trail ran just beyond the parking lot, and ten yards in, she would be surrounded by a forest of paper birches so tall that the first branches sprouted from the trunks almost fifty feet above her head. She loved the way it made her feel like she was in the middle of the wilderness, away from the town, and the air station, and all the reminders of her rootless existence.

Ellie didn't know why she stayed. There was nothing in Sitka for her. It was a beautiful place, surrounded by peaks that rose up in a majestic, green-sided, snow-tipped backdrop, but it was small—population under nine thousand—and it was made even smaller by the fact that there was no neighboring town down the road. Plus, the isolation seemed to have protected it from the march of time. It was a town of shingled houses and sidewalks, where kids set out folding tables to sell lemonade and cookies. It was the kind of place that, when the basketball team qualified to go to the finals in Juneau, the town raised the money to send the band along to cheer them on. Everyone appeared to know one another, and she was sure they knew her as well. The local paper, the *Daily Sitka Sentinel*, had covered the story on Ellie—with pictures. There was no anonymity. There was no forgetting. But she couldn't seem to bring herself to leave.

Instead she escaped as best she could in her walks along the trails. The problem was that she still had to return in the evening to her empty apartment. She had borne it for a while, but the silence had finally driven her out, and her solution had been the Columbia Bar. She had been coming here for a week, and this was the first time anyone had spoken to her other than the bartender, who had favored her several times with his comedy routine.

The man reached her at the same time as the bartender with the fresh beer. She raised the glass and said, "Cheers."

He raised his bottle of Miller Light and took a long swallow. Then he put his glass down and leaned against the bar. "So . . ." he said.

"So . . ." she echoed, smiling.

"So," he said again. "We were wondering if you're the gal that crashed that helicopter."

She stopped smiling. "What's it to you?"

"Just wondering, is all."

"That's me," she said, taking another sip.

"I thought so." Then he turned and walked back along the bar to where he'd been sitting before.

Ellie realized she was still holding the beer. She put it down so fast the liquid sloshed over the sides and onto the bar. Before she could reconsider, she got up and walked down to where the man stood with his back to her.

"Do you have something you want to say to me?" she asked him.

He looked over his shoulder. "Nope."

"I didn't think so. Nothing I hate more than a coward," and she turned and headed for the door.

There was a short silence behind her, but then she heard his voice. "Must be hard to live with yourself then," he called.

She stopped and spun on her heel. "Excuse me?"

"I guess it's not so hard to live with yourself if you get a little help from a faulty memory," he amended.

"Yeah? Who are you to talk to me? I've saved fourteen lives. How many have you saved?"

"None, but I never killed anybody either."

Ellie had nothing to say to that. She turned again for the door and walked out into a rain as fine as mist. It didn't seem to fall but to hover in the air around her. As invisible as it was, she was wet by the time she reached home.

 Sam sat at his desk, hunched over his knees. He stood abruptly and walked toward the door of his office. He got halfway before he stopped, turned, and sat back down.

The next time he got all the way to the door before he halted, his hand on the knob.

He muttered, "Damn," then he opened the door and started down the hall.

The CO had an assistant whose desk was just outside his office. Sam greeted him, "Hey, is the skipper in?"

"He's in his office. You want to talk to him?"

"Only if he's not busy," Sam said.

"I think he's on the phone with his wife."

Sam started backing up. "It can wait."

"No, hold on. He should be just about done. Let me check." Petty Officer Jackson got up and stuck his head in Traub's office before Sam could retreat.

"He says go right in." Jackson opened the door wider for Sam to go through.

Sam entered and stood in front of the CO's desk.

"Sit down," Traub said, waving at a chair. "You had something you wanted to talk to me about?"

Sam lowered himself into a chair, crossed his legs, and cleared his throat. "Yes, sir. It's about Lieutenant Commander Somers. There's a situation I think you should be aware of." He took a deep breath and launched into the lie. "Officially, I have reason to believe she is going to retain a lawyer to appeal the decision of the MAB on the grounds of flight safety. And personally, I think we *should* raise the helo to determine the true cause of the accident. Also, I happen to know that the Navy salvage ship *Salvor* is in the area and could perform the recovery."

Traub appeared to mull over Sam's information. "Is this lawyer going to be submitting a motion to raise the helo?"

"Officially? He's working on it."

Traub nodded thoughtfully, and from his next words, Sam knew that he had understood not only what Sam had said, but also what he had not said. "Let me guess. This lawyer works rather slowly?"

"Yes, sir. And this window of opportunity with the *Salvor* is very short," Sam added.

Traub nodded. "Officially, I will forward this information up the chain of command, and I'll add my recommendation. I should probably disapprove, but personally, I think you're doing the right thing."

The rain continued into the next day, and the next, and on through the week. On the first day of it, Ellie got up, showered, dressed, made coffee, then sat by the window and watched it drill the pavement in hard waves and shiver the boughs on the Western hemlocks.

The next day she heard the steady, relentless patter of it before she even opened her eyes. She lay there in bed, the covers half kicked off and twisted, wondering how, in the year and a half she'd been in Alaska, she had never noticed how depressing the rainy season was, the low but constant murmur of drops striking the roof, the dim, predawn light that lasted throughout the day, the bleak, dismal sameness of it. She kept sliding in and out of sleep, and she didn't manage to get out of bed until the afternoon.

By the third day she couldn't take it anymore. With no particular destination in mind, she put on her boots and jeans, dug her umbrella out of one of the boxes she hadn't bothered to unpack, and headed out into the rain.

There was a cruise ship docked in the harbor—she had assumed they were done for the year, but it must have been one of the last of the season. It seemed as if most of the vacationers had elected to stay on board, but there were small clusters of people wandering through the streets, in and out of the shops.

Ellie followed one of the groups into a store. The front was filled with Alaska-themed knickknacks for the tourists: shirts, mugs, hats, pins, key chains, post cards, Christmas ornaments, even oven mitts. As she wandered back among the aisles, she found a section of camping supplies with tents and stoves and bear mace in a container that looked like a small fire extinguisher. There was a wall of shoes—hiking boots, rubber galoshes, running shoes. There were windbreakers in rainbow colors, Polartec vests, and heavy winter jackets. She reached the furs: fur hats, fur stoles, fur-lined gloves and baby booties, jackets made of wolf and reindeer skin. And then she came upon the leather jackets. They weren't Alaska-themed. In fact, the tag said that they were Italian leather. She ran her fingers along the sleeve of one and discovered that the leather was almost indecently soft beneath her fingertips. She slipped the jacket off the hanger, and found that it was a bomber, like the kind she used to picture herself wearing when she was a pilot. Suddenly she wanted that jacket. The fact that she wasn't a pilot anymore didn't lessen the desire. She hadn't wanted anything like this in years. She searched for the price and found it hanging from the sleeve.

She took one look at the tag and started to put it back on the hanger, then she hesitated. Draping the coat over the rack, she shrugged out of her windbreaker, dropped it on the floor, and took up the leather bomber, sliding her arms in the sleeves. She turned and found herself looking into a full-length mirror hanging at the end of the aisle. It looked just as she had imagined it would.

Why had she tried on the jacket, when she knew she couldn't afford to buy it? she asked herself. She was about to return it to the hanger when an idea occurred to her. Instead of putting it back, she held it out, as if admiring it, but she was really looking for the white plastic tag that set off the store alarm when you tried to exit. She checked the collar and the cuffs and didn't find anything. Her head seemed to be very clear, and she did a quick check for mirrors or cameras. There were still a good number of tourists in the aisles and even a short line at the counter wait-ing to pay. Both employees were at the cash registers. In season they had more staff, but most would have gone back to school or on to other jobs. If she was going to do it, now was the best time. She quickly rolled up the leather jacket and hid it inside her windbreaker.

Then, with her windbreaker tucked under her arm, Ellie wandered through the aisles, pausing nonchalantly by a rack of hand-painted bar-rettes. She caught a glimpse of her face in the mirror at the top of the revolving stand. She looked distracted, almost absent-minded, but she felt like she had grabbed an electric wire. She felt like the whoopee had gone off in her head.

The store started to empty out, and the line at the register dwindled till there was only one person, who was buying what looked to be a small army of dolls. Ellie lingered so long near the counter that the other salesman, who was now free, asked her, "Can I help you with anything?"

When he spoke, it sent a little thrill of fear through her. She wondered if his question was too sharp. Did he suspect something?

"No, I'm just looking. Thanks, though."

"Let me know if you need anything."

She nodded, shifted the jacket on her arm, and made her way down the aisle toward the entrance, her shoes squeaking on the linoleum. The place seemed suddenly deserted. The crowd she had come in with had filtered out and left a heavy, hanging silence.

Ellie stopped, picked up a pencil box, turned it over in her hands, and set it down again. There was only about five yards of space between her and the exit. Fewer than ten steps and she would be outside and headed home.

She took them slowly, casually, but counting them in her head. One, two. She was away from the protection of the aisle and in the open. Three, four, five. She was approaching the white plastic towers bracketing the doors, ready to sound the alarm. What would she do if it went off? Would she run? The salesman would surely recognize her, and then it would be in the papers. She could see the headlines, "Disgraced Coast Guard Pilot Caught Shoplifting." Everyone would see it. Teddy. Sam. The CO. The only person who wouldn't see it was Dave.

All this flashed through her head in the time it took for her to lift her right foot and swing it forward for step six. One more would take her through the barrier.

Ellie lifted the foot that would carry her through the gate with a gut-twisting feeling of exhilaration.

He swooped down from behind, laid his arm around her shoulders in a vicelike squeeze, and used his hip to pivot her back into the store. The force of his momentum carried her along with him. It was as smooth as a dance step, and like the best of leads, he made it feel inevitable.

"Hey, Ellie," he said, carrying her along through T-shirts and baseball caps and back into the porcelain with ornate Russian designs in honor of Sitka's Russian roots.

He kept up the chatter while he steered her deeper into the store. "Nasty weather out, isn't it? The weather doesn't bother some people, but it always gets me down. I'm not used to it. I was just thinking about you. Wondering what you were doing." Once they were far enough away from the register, he stopped and turned to her. "So, how are you?"

"I've got a better question," she said. "Who are you?"

Ellie had a good memory for people, but even if she hadn't, this man was not someone that she would have forgotten easily; she thought he might be about the best-looking man she'd ever met. He was tall, with a slender athletic build, and his face—well, she might even have said he was too pretty if his features hadn't been textured with age. He was somewhere in his late thirties, she guessed. But the one thing she was absolutely sure of was that she had never seen him before in her life.

"Who are you?" she repeated the question in a hissing whisper. Fear still beat through her.

"How about this question," he said, with a smile that showed he was enjoying himself. "How about, 'What do I want?'"

"How about it?" she said, not sure if she should be relieved or worried about that smile. His grip was tight enough that she didn't think she could easily jerk free, and she didn't want to make a scene. At least not yet.

"I want to help you," he explained. "I want to help you avoid an embarrassing situation."

"What . . ." she started to say, intending to feign ignorance, but without removing his hand from her arm, he pulled her windbreaker from where she had tucked it in the crook of her elbow, and shook the leather jacket free.

She fell silent, sensing that was the best tactic for now.

With his one free hand, he separated the two jackets and tossed hers back. Then he juggled the leather jacket in his hand until he had it by the seam. He turned the pocket inside out and showed her the bulky white plastic tag attached to the lining.

Ellie felt her breath catch, then it came out in a laugh. "That was a close one. You can let go of me now. I'm not going to run off."

Slowly, almost suspiciously, he eased his grip. There was a second when his fingers remained curled around her arm. Then his hand dropped away.

"I guess I should say thanks, but I'm wondering why you left it so late. One more step and I would have been through."

"I wanted to see if you were really going to do it. I thought you might . . ."

"Chicken out?" she suggested.

"I was going to say, 'Think better of it.'"

"Are you the police?" she asked, suddenly suspicious.

It was his turn to laugh. "Do I look like the police?" He held his arms out as if for inspection.

"No," she admitted. "Then, I guess I should thank you."

"No, you shouldn't." He grinned, his cheeks creasing, his eyes narrowing to slits, giving him a sly look.

"What?" she said, confused.

"You shouldn't thank me," and as he said it, she felt certain that he was laughing at her.

"Why not?"

"Because I'm just returning the favor."

She was more bewildered than ever. "What favor?"

"You saved me once. Now I get a chance to save you in return—"

She was beginning to think she had a nut case on her hands until she heard his next words.

"—though saving you from the jaws of the store alarm hardly compares to snatching me from the churning waters of a Pacific storm."

"What?" she said again. It was all she could manage. Her brain was having a hard time processing this turn in the conversation.

"I believe I have the honor of being the last person you rescued. Rather dramatically."

"That was you? When the hoist went and we used the ERD . . ."

"That was me."

"The one who wanted to do it again the next day," she said.

"You remember." He seemed pleased.

"It's not exactly the normal response when we rescue someone."

"No?" He was still smiling.

"No," she said, smiling back. They stood there a moment.

"Well, I guess I'm glad we brought you in," she said. "We're even now."

"Hardly even. Actually, I was hoping that you'd let me thank you by taking you out to dinner."

"Oh? Um . . ." she intended to say no thank you, but she ended up saying, "Where?"

"A new place."

"There aren't any new places. Certainly none that are opening just in time for winter."

"It's been in the area for a few months, but you probably haven't heard of it because it's relatively exclusive."

He looked earnest, but Ellie sensed a hidden joke, and she wondered if it was at her expense.

"When do you want to go?" she asked.

"So you'll come?"

She hitched her shoulders in a shrug.

"Are you busy tonight?"

She thought about pretending to be busy for appearances' sake, but boredom won out over pride.

"Are you sure you can get a reservation at this *exclusive* new place?" she asked.

"It'll take some doing, but think I might be able to swing it."

"All right. What time?"

"I'll come pick you up at seven?"

"I live right off Lake Street. Turn on Hirst and look for the beige apartments on your left. I'm on the ground floor, door's to the right as you're walking up the path."

"I'll be there."

"There's just one thing," she said.

"What's that?"

"I still don't know your name."

"That's right, you don't." He shifted the leather jacket to his other arm and held out his hand. "Nicolas Andreakis."

She took his hand. "Ellie Somers."

"I know," he said.

"Oh . . . right."

He held her hand a moment longer, then let go.

"I guess I'll see you tonight, then," she said, taking a step back.

"Don't you want this?" he hefted the jacket on his arm.

"I'm not going to let you buy it for me," she told him.

"I wasn't thinking of that." With a quick yank, he ripped the lining of the pocket at the seams. Another yank, and he pulled the plastic signal from the fabric. Then, lifting the lid off a teapot on the shelf, he dropped the plastic piece in.

"That's why they should put it through the leather. It serves them right for trying to be clever." He held out the jacket as if for her to put on, his eyes dark and steady on hers.

She saw it for what it was. It was a dare.

Ellie slipped her arms into the sleeves, and without another word, walked steadily toward the entrance. This time she didn't linger, didn't look at the register. She walked right through the store alarm and out the door.

She stopped outside, under the awning, and glanced back inside the store.

Nicolas raised a hand.

She snapped open her umbrella at him, then swung it up over her shoulder to protect the leather and stepped out into the rain.

CHAPTER   2 0

The Navy salvage ship USS *Salvor* rounded Cape Muzon at daybreak and headed north up the Kaigani Strait between Dall Island and Long Island. Her radar tower, booms, and sharp, low profile made the ship look huge, modern, and oddly out of place sailing through the deserted stretch of land. Seven nautical miles up the strait, and the same distance from the U.S.–Canada border, she deployed her sidescan sonar and began "mowing the lawn," sweeping up and down over a search area half a mile square. The ship had a good posit on the location of the crash from the EPIRB signal, which went off when the helo hit the water. Five hours into the search, the *Salvor* had a good contact for a possible location of the wreck, and she anchored over the site.

The land sloped steeply down on both sides of the strait, which was over seven hundred feet deep at its center. To investigate the contact, the *Salvor* deployed the remotely operated vehicle Deep Drone. The ROV made the dive to the site and spent three hours photographing the Jayhawk where it lay upside down, its rotor head partially buried in a bed of silt. For the crew of the *Salvor*, the ROV was like putting a hand on the bottom of the ocean—and an eye. The minisub had a video link to the ship, and the crew made tapes and took pictures for evidentiary purposes. Finally, satisfied with the pictures, the captain had the ROV place a pinger on the helo so it could be found in the morning. The *Salvor* then pulled the drone out of the water to wait for daylight.

The next day, the slight chop kicked up by the wind in the channel barely caused a roll on the 250-foot ship. The crew attached a Kevlar line and a wire strap to the mechanical arms of the ROV and sent it down

again to the wreck. The sub shackled the wire strap and line to hard-
points on the underside of the helo, after which the ship's winch slowly
hauled the aircraft to the surface. The crew attached a boom to the helo
and lifted it aboard. The helicopter rocked briefly at the end of the line
when it came free of the water and settled on the fantail, where it sat,
dripping.

CHAPTER 21

Ellie had to laugh when she saw Nicolas pull up in front of her apartment that evening. She laughed because of what he was driving. The majority of the vehicles in town were trucks made by Ford, Chevy, or GMC, but he came in a BMW . . . a BMW convertible. It was a ridiculous car to be driving. Every year Sitka got more than twice as much precipitation as was needed to sustain a rainforest. That led her to question where he had gotten it . . . and why. Did he imagine that it would impress her? Then she realized that she had to cede him that point—it *had* made an impression.

Nicolas climbed out of the car and started up the walk, and Ellie saw that he was wearing faded jeans and an old sweater. Even though she had only half believed him about the restaurant, she had doubted enough to struggle over what she should wear. During her years in the Coast Guard, she had spent her days in a one-piece flight suit and her evenings in jeans. Now that she didn't have to wear the flight suit any longer, she lived in jeans. When she looked in her closet for something to wear to dinner, she found that she didn't have much else. Her dates in the Coast Guard hadn't been the kind that she would even think about dressing up for, and Sitka was definitely an informal town. She owned a single dress—black wool—that she had worn to her uncle's funeral a year ago, and she'd had to decide between the dress and the jeans.

Ellie's mother, in her valiant but vain efforts to interest Ellie in clothes and fashion, had repeated the rules of etiquette often. One of them, Ellie remembered, was that if you didn't know what to wear, it was better to be too dressy. Ellie figured that her mother must know about these things because she had spent her life agonizing over just these kinds of decisions: what to wear to an afternoon wedding, finding the perfect housewarming gift, whether to use place cards when giving a dinner party. They were the only decisions that Ellie's father would allow her mother to make: the trivial ones.

Ellie had always thought of her mother's emphasis on these details as both irritating and sad, but when Ellie saw Nicolas on the walkway, she knew a little of the dismay her mother felt when she miscalculated. She had chosen to follow her mother's advice and wear the dress, and it had turned out to be the wrong choice. This, Ellie thought with despair, was what her life had come to. This sort of thing never would have bothered her in the past—nothing but flying had ever been that important. Without flying, she felt exposed, laid open to ridicule in the smallest things.

There was no time for her to change. At the last minute, before Nicolas rang the doorbell, she ran back into the living room, grabbed the leather jacket, and put it on over the dress. The diversionary tactic seemed to work because he didn't appear to notice the dress at all. When she opened the door for him, he said, "I like your jacket."

"I'm taking a gamble that the clerks at the Trading Post don't hang out at this new place you're taking me," she replied.

She noticed that the corners of his eyes crinkled when he smiled. "It's a safe bet. You ready?"

Ellie followed him down the path, and when they reached the car, Nicolas went to the passenger side and opened the door for her. That made her pause. She knew in most places it was considered a courtesy, but it had always made her feel awkward. On a whim, she walked past him and around to the driver's side. She tried the door, discovered that it was unlocked, and slipped into his seat.

Nicolas was left holding the open passenger door. Ellie leaned across the seat. "Are you getting in or what?"

He climbed in and handed her the keys. "I just want to warn you, this car isn't mine."

"I think I can make it from here to wherever you're taking me," she said. "In this town, I know it can't be far. Now, where are we going?"

He directed her back to Lake Street. They took the right onto Halibut Point Road, then the left onto Katlian. At first, headed down Lake Street she worried that he might be taking her to Marcy's, and she heaved a sigh of relief when they turned. Then she was certain that it was the fancy steak house down Halibut, but the turn on Katlian convinced her that it must be the Pilot House. Of course none of these places were new, but there was no way she wouldn't have heard about a new place—especially an exclusive one.

She didn't put it together until he directed her to take the turn into the parking lot for Thomsen Harbor.

"You're not taking me out on a boat, are you?" she said, half laughing.

"You scared to go out with me?"

"It's kind of a point of pride when you're in the Coast Guard, not to put yourself in a situation where you need to be rescued. I hate to remind you, but your track record isn't so hot."

After she said it, she realized her slip and was relieved when he didn't point out that she wasn't in the Coast Guard anymore.

"Don't worry. We'll be nice and safe and boring," he promised, leading her down the gangway to the docks.

Thomsen was the largest of Sitka's four harbors, and it was an impressive structure. All of the harbors were solidly built, but Thomsen was like a small town. It stretched a quarter mile along the shore, and if you tallied the maze of walkways, the total length would add up to several miles' worth of wooden docks. These docks were twice as wide as those at Crescent, and they were equipped with streetlights.

In the summertime, it was almost like a neighborhood, if a transient one. Many people sailed up the Inside Passage, living on their boats, and they would come to Sitka, dock at Thomsen, and stay a few days, or weeks, or even months.

As they walked along, Ellie wondered which, in the tangle of masts and rigging, was his. They walked the length of the dock and had taken a left along the outer edge before she thought to ask him if he'd gotten a new boat.

"No. I'm renting this one," he said.

"Is this boat the new place you were talking about?"

"It is."

"I'm guessing that the great chef you were talking about is you?"

"You'll see."

When he stopped, she discovered the reason they had walked so far. The boat he stood in front of was so large it had to be docked on the outer edge of the harbor—it wouldn't have fit into any of the regular slips. It was over a hundred feet long and had four stories of smoky, tinted windows.

This couldn't be the boat, she thought. Last summer she'd met the crew of one of these fancy yachts drinking at the P Bar, and she'd heard how much one of these cost to rent: at least a hundred grand for a week, and that wasn't including expenses. Nicolas didn't look like he had that kind of money.

She was about to call him out on the joke when a man came striding down the gangplank, arm outstretched eagerly before he even reached them. He captured Nicolas's hand and shook it vigorously. "Welcome aboard, Mr. Andreakis."

"Captain, this is Ellie Somers," Nicolas performed the introductions.

Then Ellie had her hand pumped. "A pleasure. Please, come on board. Everything's ready."

"I appreciate your being able to accommodate us on such short notice," Nicolas said as he started up the gangway. Ellie followed silently.

"We offloaded our last customers a couple days ago, and we're about to head back down to warmer waters for the winter, so it's no problem," the skipper replied over his shoulder. "The table is set up in the forward cabin—or you can have drinks out on the upper deck."

"The upper deck, I think." Nicolas looked to Ellie for confirmation.

She nodded as if she were regularly asked to choose between the deck and the forward cabin of a luxury yacht.

"I'll let them know. Can you find your way up?"

Two minutes later they were on the upper deck, and the ship was pulling away from the dock. It was the perfect evening to be standing at the bow of a yacht with the wind in her face, blowing the tingle of cold into her cheeks. The dreary gray drizzle of the morning had disappeared; the evening sky was a deep blue, and the air was crisp and dry and so clear that it felt like you could see to the end of the earth if only it didn't curve away. The change would have been almost miraculous if it hadn't been Sitka, where the weather seemed to change from one minute to the next. In Sitka—in most of Southeast Alaska—Ellie had discovered that you appreciated days like these.

The sun was setting earlier every day now, and the last rays of the day lit up the snowy tip of Mount Edgecumbe, the massive, hulking volcano that dominated the horizon to the northwest of the town. A covey of bald eagles wheeled and dove at a school of fish off the starboard bow.

Ellie was watching the eagles strike the water with feet outstretched, so she wasn't prepared when she glanced over to port just as the yacht was passing the air station on the narrow tip of Japonski Island. She hadn't seen the base since the trial, and at the sight, she was caught in a sudden piercing wave of loss. She had been enjoying the novelty of sailing out of Sitka Channel in a yacht, but with one glimpse of the old buildings, she knew that she would trade a hundred yacht trips to be back there—back home.

She looked away quickly and found that Nicolas was watching her, and his seemingly permanent expression of submerged amusement was gone, replaced by a serious, searching look.

"Can I have that drink?" she said with a self-conscious smile.

"Sure. Of course. I'll go see what's keeping them." He seemed flustered, but the situation was saved from awkwardness by the appearance of one of the crew, carrying the drinks.

They stayed out, enjoying the view until the sun dove into the water and the sky turned purple, then black with a carpet of stars. Without the sun, the air cooled quickly, and they turned their backs on the stars and went inside, rubbing their hands together and blowing on their fingers. It was warm in the cabin, the room lit by the flickering candles on the table set for two. A crew member standing near the door sprang to life when they entered, leaping to pull out a chair, ostensibly for Ellie, but she slipped into the one opposite, leaving Nicolas to take the proffered seat. However, when the young man, who introduced himself as Andrew, offered to refresh their drinks, Ellie agreed to that quickly enough.

He left with their empty glasses, and Ellie and Nicolas were alone again. They had been standing out on the deck for some time, but the wind and the water and the sunset had called for silent appreciation— and now this quiet room called for conversation.

Ellie glanced around. One wall was all windows, the others were a warm cherry wood. Above the table, a crystal chandelier threw out a soft glow.

"Do you like it?" Nicolas asked her.

"Very much. I have to hand it to you—you were telling the truth. This place is new to the area and pretty exclusive, but how do you go about renting a yacht for the evening at the last minute?"

Nicolas shrugged it off. "You make a call, give them a credit card. It's not a big deal. You heard the skipper. They dropped off their last passenger a few days ago."

Of course, Ellie thought, he still needed a credit card that would cover a charge that size. She wondered where he'd gotten his money, but she thought it might be rude to ask.

Andrew returned with their drinks. They both took a sip, and there was a little silence between them.

"So," Nicolas said. "Did you do any more shopping after I saw you this morning?"

Ellie couldn't help laughing.

■

Nothing was ordinary that evening—not the setting, not the wine, not the food. Ellie knew instinctively that the conversation had to match. She couldn't ask the usual mundane questions: Where are you from? What do you do? Are you single? Married? Divorced? It didn't matter how curious she was about the answers, this night was a night apart.

So they talked about extraordinary things—they talked about the SAR. She told him how close he had come to not being found and what had been going on in the helo, and she was able to hear from him what it was like from a rescuee's point of view. That SAR led Ellie into stories of other rescues, many that she had no involvement in, but which had become legend in the Coast Guard. She realized at the end of the evening that she had done most of the talking, and the only thing she had really discovered about her dinner companion was that he was a very good listener.

Dinner seemed to whirl by in a blur of alcohol and food, and those two things, combined with the gentle movement of the boat, seemed to bend time so it felt like a mere hour or two before they were thanking the skipper and walking back down the gangway to the dock.

Ellie hadn't looked at her watch all night, and when she glanced at it in the pool of light from the street lamp, she couldn't believe the time.

"It's late," she exclaimed.

"Yes, I guess it is," Nicolas said. "I'll take you home."

It hadn't been what she meant at all. She would have been more than ready to suggest a drink at a bar, but she couldn't very well contradict him now. They made their way back along the dock to the parking lot.

The BMW was the only car left. Nicolas started around to the passenger door, but he checked himself.

"Sorry," he said. "I've noticed you don't much like having doors opened for you."

"Very perceptive. How did you pick that up, I wonder?" She smiled.

"I wonder," he echoed dryly. He crossed in front of the car and opened the driver's door with the key. He climbed in and pulled the door shut behind him.

Ellie bent and pulled the handle on the passenger door. It didn't give. It was still locked. She bent down to look through the window and found him grinning at her from the driver's seat. She tapped on the glass with a knuckle, and he fit the key in the ignition so he could roll down one of the power windows an inch.

"Yes? Need anything?"

"You made your point," Ellie said, tilting her head to speak into the narrow opening. "Would you open the door now, please?"

"Certainly. My pleasure." He clicked the UNLOCK button.

She opened the door and slid into the seat as he started the engine.

"You're all right to drive, aren't you?" she asked.

"I'm fine," he assured her, pulling out of the parking lot and turning toward her apartment.

She tried to think back and remember how much he'd had. After finishing their drinks, they'd gone through a bottle of wine with dinner. She tried to recall how many glasses she'd drunk, and couldn't count them in her mind, which was a bad sign. He had always been filling her glass, but she couldn't remember if he ever filled his own.

"Not a big drinker?" she said.

"Not really."

"You on the wagon?" she asked, though she was sure he had sipped at his wine, and people she had known with a history of drinking problems usually tended to stay away from it completely.

"No. It's just that I like being in control."

She couldn't resist this opening, especially after their discussion about the SAR during dinner. "And that's why you sailed right into the middle of a nasty storm alone?"

"Yes."

"Explain that one to me."

"I shouldn't think I'd need to." He glanced over at her. "You of all people should know that sensation—when you feel as if the whole world has shrunk to the dimensions of the cabin of a boat . . . or the cockpit of a helo. All the other bullshit in your life drops away, and all that matters is what you do in the next moment because that's going to decide whether you live. Or don't. It's all up to you. Not many people understand the allure of that kind of simplicity. That kind of control. I think you do."

"Huh," she grunted, looking away, out her own window.

He let the silence ride with them as he drove the short distance to her apartment. He pulled over in front of her walkway, put the car into park, and shut off the ignition.

"Well," she said. "Thanks for dinner."

"Dinner was my thank you, remember? And you can't thank someone for thanking you—where would it end?"

"I don't know, but I think we're more than even now. That dinner plus the last-minute save at the Trading Post—I think that adds up to one life."

She had spoken flippantly, but he rebuked her with his answer. "No, it doesn't. At least not if the life is your own. Then you feel as if you can never say thank you enough."

Ellie realized that no one had ever thanked her before because she had never actually spoken to any of the people she had saved. "You're very welcome," she told him.

There was a pause.

"I had a good time tonight," he said.

"Me too."

"You know, I'm in town for a few days."

"Oh?" she said, trying to sound nonchalant.

"Any chance you're free Friday?"

Ellie cracked a knuckle, thinking about the empty days stretching out in front of her. "Sure. I'm free."

"You pick the place this time?"

"Okay." She opened her door. "Friday, then."

As she got out, he leaned toward her, out over the passenger seat. "Need any help with your front door?" he asked.

"No, that I think I can manage." And she swung the car door shut on his grin.

C H A P T E R　　2 2

 She ended up taking him to Marcy's. She debated it in her head for a full day before she decided to go—more out of impatience with her indecision than out of reasoned thought. She dreaded running into one of her old friends. She tried to reassure herself with the thought that the chances of seeing anyone were slim, but during the meal she wasn't able to stay focused on what Nicolas was saying. Her eyes kept straying back to the doorway, and the longer they stayed, the more nervous she got.

When they were done with the meal—which at Marcy's didn't take long—she told herself there was no reason to stick around. Half her attention was on the door and the other half was scouting for their waitress, when Nicolas said, "I have a proposal to make." His words barely registered. "Oh yeah?" She glanced briefly at him then back at the entrance.

He got her attention with the next two sentences. He said, "I'm flying out tonight. I was wondering if you'd come with me."

Her gaze snapped back to his face. "Come with you? You're kidding, right?"

"No."

"You barely know me. Why would you want me to come with you?"

"Maybe so I could have your full attention without having to share it with a doorway. Are you expecting someone?"

He hadn't said anything during the meal, so she had supposed that her watch over the entrance had gone undetected.

"No, I'm not expecting anyone."

"Then am I boring you?"

"No," she smiled. "You're not boring me."

"You'll come with me, then?"

Now she laughed. "Just because I'm not expecting anyone, and you're not boring me, it doesn't follow that I'll come with you. I don't even know where you're going."

"Does it matter?"

"That depends," she replied.

"On what?"

"On where you're going."

"You can choose. Wherever you want to go."

"Oh right."

"The jet is waiting at the airport."

"The jet?" In Alaska it wasn't unusual to own a plane, but they were usually single- or twin-engine prop planes, not jets.

"It's a very small jet," he said.

Ellie just shook her head.

"So where do you want to go?"

"Why do you think I'd go anywhere at all with you?" she asked.

"Because you haven't said no."

"I'll say it now. No."

"You don't mean it, though. I don't see how you can turn me down."

"I'll show you how." She held her hand up for the bill, but it was a futile gesture, as their waitress was in the back.

"I thought the adventure would appeal to you," Nicolas said.

"Oh, you did? I may be adventurous, but that doesn't mean I go off with strange men in their jets, even if they are only very small ones."

"Why not? What do you have keeping you here?"

She couldn't answer that because, in truth, she had nothing keeping her here—nothing but the illusion that if she stayed close to the air station, her old life was somehow not out of reach, not irretrievably gone.

"I don't know anything about you," she said, evading his point.

"That's easy enough to fix. What do you want to know?"

She hesitated, torn between shooting him down cold and this opportunity to satisfy her curiosity. Curiosity won.

"What have you been doing in Sitka for almost two months?" she asked.

"I haven't been here for two months. I left right after you saved me."

"So what were you doing here two months ago, and why are you back now? Are you here for the fishing?"

"I'm here on business."

She waited for him to elaborate, and after a moment, he did.

"My father is interested in buying a cruise line, or possibly starting one of his own, and he's heard the way to make the best use of the ships is to run them in the Caribbean in the winter, and up to Alaska in the summer. I was researching what the other Alaskan cruises offered and the possible ports of call."

"That was the first visit. What about this second one?"

"I booked myself onto a cruise to see what the competition had to offer. We stopped here . . ."

Ellie remembered the ship that had been in port.

". . . I was wandering around the town, and I happened to recognize you. I followed you into the store, intending to introduce myself and thank you for saving my life, and I happened to see you trying on the leather jacket . . . you know the rest."

"No, I don't. What happened to your cruise?"

"We had a dinner date," he reminded her.

"You had a boat to catch."

"I have my priorities."

"What about your father? He can't have been too happy about that."

"I'm used to him not being happy with me in general," Nicolas said with a bitterness that Ellie recognized from personal experience. She almost said something but caught herself just in time and, as a result, swung from near sympathy to sarcasm.

"It's Daddy's money, then," she said.

"You don't approve?"

"You're just a playboy." When he didn't deny it, she felt a distinct sense of disappointment. She caught the eye of the waitress and signaled for the bill.

"But I play hard," Nicolas countered. "Come with me and try for yourself. There doesn't always have to be a purpose for everything. You'll find out there's a certain wicked satisfaction in doing something for absolutely no reason at all. You don't need a reason to come with me. Do it for the hell of it."

"There's always a reason," Ellie said.

"Just because you always have a reason, doesn't mean everyone else does."

"Why did you rent that boat and go out alone?"

"You have me there. That time I did have a reason. I wanted to see the sun set."

"That amounts to no reason at all. You could have seen that from the shore."

"Have you ever seen the sun set while you're sitting in a boat alone with water in every direction, as far as the eye can see? It's the most amazing experience. It feels like you're the only person on earth. It's so quiet, you might almost imagine you could hear the hiss when the sun touches the water."

"Yes, but you wouldn't have been able to see the sun, not with that storm. By the way, did you know there was a storm on the way?"

He looked at her. "What should I say?"

"The truth," she replied, though she already knew.

"I didn't intend to go so far."

"I think you did."

"All right," he agreed.

"All right?"

"I told you I played hard," he said. "Any more questions?"

She drummed her fingers on the table, thinking.

For the first time all night she wasn't watching the door, and that was the moment that Teddy stepped through with two other Coasties. One of Teddy's companions spotted her, and nudged Teddy. Teddy looked over and stopped short. After a moment's hesitation, he seemed to make a decision, and he crossed to where she sat.

"Ellie," Teddy said softly, almost hesitantly.

Ellie's head jerked up, and her first thought when she saw him was that, in all the time they had been friends, he had never called her Ellie. As informal as he was, as close as they had been, he had never crossed that line. Not until just now. Now that she had resigned from the Coast Guard. Now that she wasn't an officer anymore.

"Hey." Teddy stuffed his hands in his front pockets as if he didn't know what else to do with them. "I don't mean to interrupt . . ."

A minute ago her greatest fear had been that Teddy would come into the restaurant, see her, and turn around and walk back out . . . or that he would studiously ignore her. She hadn't thought that there was even a chance he would come up and speak to her. But now that he had, all she could think of was what had changed—how he had walked out of her hospital room the day after the crash, then the weeks of silence. She had been so sure he'd stop by after the hearing. He hadn't even called.

She said, "What do you want, Teddy?"

"I was wondering if you and your uh . . . friend might like to join us." From the questioning glance Teddy shot at Nicolas, Ellie knew he hadn't recognized Nicolas from the rescue.

"We already ate."

"Oh." Teddy looked down at the plates that were still sitting on the table. "Right. Well . . . I was wondering if I could talk to you—it won't take a minute."

Ellie was suddenly so angry she could feel the blood rushing to her cheeks. Now—when he just happened to run into her—now he wanted to talk.

"Sorry. I can't. I'm leaving," and she glanced over at Nicolas meaningfully.

Nicolas understood what she meant by that look. She was accepting his invitation—or rather his challenge.

Teddy didn't understand the hidden meaning in her words, but he did know that she was angry. "Listen, I wanted to say I'm sorry about what happened," he said. "I was messed up for a while about what happened with Dave, and I took it out on you. I've been meaning to get in touch, but . . . Could I call you tomorrow? Is that okay? There's something I need to talk to you about. It's important."

Ellie was about to explain to Teddy why calling the next day wouldn't do much good as she wouldn't be there, but she abruptly changed her mind. "Sure. You can call." He could try, she thought to herself. She just wouldn't be there to answer.

"I don't have your new number," he pointed out.

She took the pen the waitress had left to sign the credit card receipt and scribbled her number on the edge of a napkin.

"Here," she held it out to Teddy. Then she turned to Nicolas. "You know what? I think I'm ready to get out of here."

Nicolas grinned at her. "What are we waiting for?"

"I have no idea." Ellie got up and retrieved her leather jacket from the back of her chair. "Excuse me," Ellie said to Teddy, who was standing in her path as if he didn't quite believe she was really leaving.

"Sorry." Teddy stepped aside, and Ellie brushed past.

"I'll phone you tomorrow," Teddy called after her.

"You do that," she said over her shoulder.

Ellie walked from the restaurant with the sure knowledge that Teddy was still watching her through the large windows at the front of the restaurant. "Hey," she whispered to Nicolas once they were outside. "Hey, open the car door for me, will you?"

"*Now* you want me to open the door?" he whispered back, striding alongside her.

"I said so, didn't I?"

"This kind of stuff is what gives women a bad reputation," he said, rounding to the passenger door, and sweeping it open with as big a flourish as she could have wished for.

He rounded to the driver's side and got in. "You want me to gun the engine too?" he asked.

"I think it would be a nice touch. You've got a flair for this."

"Came in handy during high school."

"So I'm petty and childish," she said. "Do it anyway."

He pulled away from the curb with a satisfying roar.

"Now what?" he asked.

"My place. So I can pack a bag."

"You're going through with it?"

"I'll tell you one thing—I'm not planning on being around to get that phone call tomorrow," she said.

"Is that the only reason you're going? So you can make your old buddy feel stupid?"

"Does it matter to you?"

Nicolas thought a moment. "No," he admitted.

"That's good, but it's not the reason," she told him.

He made a left onto her street, pulled up in front of the curb, and turned to look at her. "So what's the reason?"

She leaned toward him, and she noticed that he pulled back a little. "You want to know?" she said, dropping her voice to a tone of husky intimacy.

"Yes."

"I'm really, really . . ."

He raised his eyebrows.

". . . bored."

He smiled, almost, she thought, in relief. "The sooner we get going, the sooner I can help with that."

"I'll be back in ten," she promised.

As she let herself back into her apartment, she made another split-second decision. She determined that when she left Sitka with Nicolas, she would be leaving it for good. He was right, there was nothing here for her. She'd spend some time with Nicolas, and then strike out on her own—she'd start a new life for herself away from all this.

When she entered, Ellie went straight to the kitchen and pulled out the box of garbage bags. Then she walked through the rooms, a trash bag in her right hand, her duffel in her left. Everything went into one or the other. Without thinking about it too much, she threw out her few dishes, her plants, most of her clothes, even the small stack of paperbacks that she had bought in an effort to fill the empty hours. She unplugged the phone. She left the big things—the TV, the PlayStation, the VCR. She figured whoever moved in next could use them.

When she was done, she had filled four Hefty double-plys, but there was still space in her bag. It had taken more than ten minutes, but not by much. She tried not to think about the fact that she had lived a life so easily left behind.

Ellie emerged onto the sidewalk, the duffel slung over one shoulder and two knotted trash bags in each fist.

"Is that your luggage?" Nicolas asked through the open window as she approached.

She heaved her load onto the curb by the trash cans and climbed back into the passenger seat, her duffel on her lap.

"You didn't say you were only coming for a long weekend," Nicolas remarked, looking at her half empty bag.

"I need to stop at my landlord's house. She lives one street over."

"What, so she can watch your cat?"

"So I can tell her that I'm moving out."

"When are you going to do that?"

"I just did."

"So," he started up the car. "After we drop off your key, where do you want to go?"

She shrugged. "Surprise me."

Teddy phoned Ellie the next day at eleven. Then again at twelve. He called every hour on the hour until he was sure that even Ellie, no matter how late her night had been, couldn't still be sleeping.

When he called, it just rang and rang and rang. The last time Teddy let it ring twenty-seven times before he gave up. Had she unplugged the phone? Given him the wrong number? Or maybe she was ignoring him. Well, let her, he thought. Ellie was only punishing herself because it would be just that much longer before she heard the news. Then he thought about the possibility that someone else might run into her and tell her, and he picked up the phone and tried again. He wanted to be the one to tell her . . . and he wanted to know who that guy was—he had looked strangely familiar.

Teddy let it go on for what felt like an eternity of rings before hanging up again. Then he sat for a moment, considering.

Less than five minutes later, he found Sam in the hangar, running a rag over the bumper of his truck. The crew often used the hoses meant for the helos to wash their cars. Sam had turned the surface of his into a mirror.

"Hey, Commander Pantano," Teddy said. "Can I have the keys to your truck, there?"

"What for?" Sam asked, raising the wiper and giving the glass a squirt of Windex.

"To drive it. Why else would I ask for the keys?"

Sam stooped for a clean cloth and leaned over the hood to get the center of the windshield. "Why don't you ask me if you can borrow my truck instead of asking me for my keys?"

"Okay, so can I borrow your truck?"

"I just washed it," Sam said, stepping back to admire his work. Then he bent and rubbed at a speck of dirt on the door.

"You washed it, so now you're never going to drive it again? Anyway, Tom's outside waiting to wash his car."

"What do you want it for?"

"I'm going over to see Somers, to tell her the news."

"I thought we decided not to tell her anything until we had something definite to tell."

"*We* didn't decide. You did," Teddy said.

"If I remember correctly, you didn't disagree."

"Well, I ran into her last night."

"Where?"

"She was at Marcy's. Eating dinner calm as you please with some guy."

"What guy?" Sam asked.

"I don't know what guy. Though I could swear that I've seen him before . . ." Teddy broke off to search his memory again, but dry and dressed, Nicolas had looked quite different from the figure in the survival suit, hair wet and dripping from the storm. "Anyway, when I saw her, it seemed crazy for us not to tell her. Plus, she might find out anyway, and if that's the case, I think she should hear about it from someone she knows."

"I see your point," Sam relented.

"Ah, the man can be made to see reason," Teddy said, holding up his hands in a hallelujah. "It's real nice of you to let me borrow it, sir."

"I'm going to do better than that," Sam told him. "I'm going to drive you."

Teddy couldn't suppress the momentary expression of horror. He tried to cover it up by saying, "That's okay, sir. You don't have to do that. I might not be able to pilot a helicopter, but I can manage a car all right. I wouldn't want to put you to any trouble."

"It's no trouble."

Teddy opened his mouth to reply, but found that he had been out-maneuvered.

A few minutes later, Sam pulled up in front of Ellie's apartment. They both got out and walked together up the path. Teddy pressed the bell, and they waited for her to answer.

"She's ignoring us." Teddy rang again, this time keeping his finger on the bell.

"It might take a while," Sam said. "Be patient."

Teddy rang a few more times before he gave up, saying, "I'm going to check the windows." The blinds were down on the window in front, so he disappeared around the side. He was only gone a minute when he called out, "Commander. Sir. Come here." His voice sounded urgent, and Sam hustled around the side to where Teddy stood by one of the low windows.

"Did you find her?" Sam asked. "Is she in there?"

"No."

"Then what is it?"

"Take a look in the window," Teddy said.

Sam looked. "So?"

"What do you see?"

"I don't see anything."

"Right. Don't you think that's strange? No glasses on the tables. No clothes on the floor. No newspapers. Nothing. Somers is a terrible slob, and here's her place, completely neat after living in it for a month? No way."

"We'd better go see her landlord," Sam said.

The landlord came to the door in answer to their ring. She wore jeans and a sweatshirt, her iron-gray hair pulled back in a ponytail.

"Ellie Somers?" she said. "Yes, she rented an apartment from me, but she came 'round last night and dropped off the keys. I told her that she had to give thirty days' notice. She said she was leaving that night, but she'd send me the check for the next month. I felt kinda bad, since I know she's been through a lot—"

"She said she was leaving?" Sam broke in.

"That's what she said."

"Did she say where she was going?" Teddy asked.

"No. I was curious myself, but I didn't want to pry. I didn't get the feeling like she was moving down the street. It seemed like she was leaving for real. More than that I can't tell you."

Sam said, "Thanks," and they retraced their steps down the path. They were quiet as they climbed in the truck and headed back to base.

They were crossing the bridge when Teddy burst out, "I should have known."

"Known what?" Sam said.

"I should have known she was leaving. She just about told me. I said that I had something to talk to her about. She said she was leaving, so I asked could I call tomorrow? She had this little smile on her face, and she said, 'Sure, you can call.' Then she turned to the guy she was with, and she said, 'I'm ready to get out of here.' God, I'm so thick."

"Hindsight," Sam said. "Even if you had realized it, what would you have done?"

"I'd have said, 'Somers, they brought up the helo.' If I'd told her that, you think that anything could have gotten her out of town before we knew what they found?"

"Maybe not. But it's out of our hands now. It might even be best this way. The expert they brought in is looking at the helo now, but chances are he'll find that you were right, and the tail rotor hit the water as she was pulling up."

"I guess, but what if I was wrong? What if it was something with the helo, a malfunction or something?" Teddy said. "If that's the case, how will we find her? She could be anywhere."

"We'll worry about that when we get there," Sam said. "If we have something to tell her, we'll find her. Wherever she is."

CHAPTER 24

"Hey, we're here," Nicolas woke Ellie with a hand on her shoulder.

"Mmm, yeah, I'm awake," Ellie said, sitting up and trying to pretend she hadn't been fast asleep. She hoped she didn't have a string of drool down her chin. She rubbed her face with both hands, then ran them back over her hair and tightened her ponytail.

"So where's 'here'?" she asked.

"Why don't you come outside and see?"

She followed him to the exit and, ducking out of the door, she felt a warm night breeze brush against her skin. In Sitka, the sun could be warm, but the air always carried the damp chill of the ocean. The nights in Sitka were never balmy, the air never like this hot dry wind.

When they had taken off, she'd looked out onto acres of trees, mountains rising on all sides. Now, in the bright lights that circled the tarmac, all she could make out was flat dun-colored sand and scrub brush. She had left thick green pines and a silver blue ocean and had arrived at what appeared to be an empty expanse of desert.

"We're in the middle of nowhere," she said, accusation in her tone.

"People do occasionally come to spend some time in the middle of nowhere," he replied.

When she'd said, "Surprise me," she'd thought San Francisco, Chicago, New York, Hawaii. She didn't bother to hide her disgust.

"Why would anyone come here?" she said.

"You don't like it." It was more statement than question.

"What's to like?"

"You haven't seen everything," he said.

"What's to see? More sand? A gas station along the road?"

"Come down," he motioned for her to descend the stairs, "and take a look."

"Fine," she thumped down the steps and stood beside him on the asphalt.

"Around this way." He took her by the arm and led her behind the tail of the plane.

She stopped when she saw what was on the other side.

It was a city of lights and color rising from the middle of the desert. There was a huge, hulking pyramid, the illuminated turrets of a castle, a skyscraper that glowed green, another that seemed to be made of gold.

"What the hell is it?" she said.

"Can't you guess?"

She shook her head, her mind blank.

"That," he gestured extravagantly with one arm, "is Las Vegas."

"Vegas," she murmured.

"Home sweet home."

She turned to look at him. "You *live* here?"

He was staring out toward the bright strip of light. "We moved here from Greece when I was eleven."

"I thought your father was in shipping."

"He is."

"And he lives in the middle of the desert?"

"That's my father. He gives new meaning to the word 'overachiever.'"

"I guess some things don't get passed down," Ellie kidded.

Instead of being angry, Nicolas surprised her with a laugh. "You're right there. I haven't done one useful thing in my entire life. It's harder than you think to manage that, but I figured that my father had done more than enough for two and the world needed a rest."

"I think I'd like to meet your father," Ellie said.

"God forbid," Nicolas shuddered dramatically. "But there's no danger of that. He's never in town this time of year. Still too hot."

"I think it feels great."

"Now it does, but try going out tomorrow at noon. Lucky for us, most of the amusement here is indoors and well air-conditioned. The car's over there if you're ready." He pointed to a limo that had pulled up across the landing strip.

When the bags were stored in the trunk, and they had climbed in the back, Nicolas asked Ellie if she wanted to drive down the Strip, or if she wanted to go straight to the hotel.

"The Strip, please," Ellie responded.

In less than five minutes they were there, and she was peering out the window as they rolled by the casinos, each one more fantastic than the last. There were so many lights it seemed bright enough to be day, and though Ellie knew it must be late, the sidewalks were jammed with people. There were packs of young men alongside gray-haired ladies and couples pushing baby strollers.

It was dazzling no matter where you were coming from, Ellie thought, but the contrast to Sitka was almost overwhelming. It felt as if she'd been dropped into the middle of a huge, crazy circus.

The car turned left, down a long driveway bordered by lush green lawn and dotted with fountains. Ellie looked up at the building and read the name in huge, red, Roman-style letters: CAESARS PALACE. The entrance had a tiered awning, glowing bright pink and flanked by marble statues.

"You live in a casino?" Ellie said, pulling back in from the window to look at him.

"My father has a house in the desert, but I thought you wouldn't want to be out in the middle of nowhere. When I'm in town, I usually stay here."

The door on Ellie's side of the limo was opened for her.

"You might have to get used to it," Nicolas said with a nod toward the door. "Even when you're not trying to impress your friends."

There was nothing for her to do but step out, though she felt shabby in her jeans. She could go almost anywhere in Sitka in jeans—and she had forgotten what it felt like to be so out of place. It was too soon for homesickness, she told herself.

The man who had opened the door for her obviously wasn't a bellboy. He was dressed in a suit, his hair was slicked back, and he had a huge smile on his face. Ellie couldn't help but stare at his teeth. They were so white they almost glowed, and every tooth was perfectly even. She was so mesmerized by them she almost didn't see his outstretched hand.

"I'm Greg Daniels," he said, capturing her hand and shaking it enthusiastically. "It's great to meet any friend of Nick's."

At the sound of his name, Nicolas appeared around the car.

"Nick," he nearly bellowed. Nicolas got a heartier shake than Ellie, and a slap on the shoulder as well. "Where have you been? I was starting to think that the Andreakis family had forsaken us here at Caesars and gone next door."

"It's Greg's job to make sure we lose all our money here and not someplace else," Nicolas explained to Ellie.

"I'm here to keep you happy," Greg agreed, completely unfazed. "Is there anything I can do for you? We've got some drinks chilling in your room, can I order some food? Do you need anything while you're in town? A car? Appointments at the spa?"

Behind them, a bellboy was lifting Ellie's duffel out of the trunk. Greg instructed him to "Put the bags in the Bacchus Room." He turned back to them. "Will that room suit you all right?"

"That's fine," Nicolas said.

"I wish I could've had something better for you, but at the last minute, and on a Friday . . ."

". . . there wasn't anyone less important than me to bump," Nicolas finished for him. "The others all lose more than I do?"

"You generally lose a respectable sum," Greg assured him.

"That," Nicolas said to Ellie, "is why Greg is so good at his job. I'm as sarcastic as I know how to be, and he comes out with a response like that, and he says it with a straight face. Now, you have to wonder, is he feeding me some of my own medicine or is he genuinely trying to reassure me? Sarcasm or flattery? Or both?"

Greg smiled serenely.

"The genius is that he's whatever I want him to be. It's up to me to interpret it any way I like," Nicolas said.

"Whatever you want," Greg agreed. "Can I show you to your room, so you can freshen up?"

"No thanks, Greg. I think we can find it ourselves."

Nicolas held his hand out, and Greg reluctantly handed over two plastic card keys, saying, "Can I do anything, get anything—"

"If we need you, we'll call you." Nicolas dismissed Greg with a nod.

"It was so nice to meet you," Greg said to Ellie. "Be sure to call if there's absolutely anything—"

"Enough," Nicolas said. "Buzz off."

At this snub, Greg's smile seemed, if anything, to widen. Without another word, he disappeared into the casino.

"That was incredibly rude," Ellie said.

"I've learned it's the only sure way to get rid of him—not necessarily an easy task, I assure you. You've got to make it clear he's not wanted. Otherwise he tends to follow you around, trying to do things for you, and failing that, just trying to flatter your ego."

"I would've thought that'd be something you'd love."

"See, I can tell you're being sarcastic. You'll need some practice if you want Greg's job. Come on, let's go to the room."

She followed him through the door and across an expanse of marble and gilt, past a replica of the statue of David, and to a bank of elevators. When they reached their floor, Nicolas walked up to a set of double doors flanked by brass columns and illuminated with recessed lighting. Above the door a plaque read BACCHUS.

The door led into a vestibule with corridors leading off to the right and to the left, and straight ahead it opened onto a huge area that encompassed both living room and dining room. To one side was a cluster of brocade couches and armchairs piled high with cushions, and on the other side, a dining table that seated eight. One wall was taken up by three huge windows, looking out over the carnival lights of the Strip.

"Greg was apologizing for this? I'd like to know what the nice rooms are like," Ellie said as she crossed to the windows and stood looking out.

"I can tell you. The 'nice' rooms, as you term them, are the villas. My father stays there when he comes to town. About eleven thousand square feet—"

"Eleven thousand square feet?" Ellie interrupted. "That's . . ." she paused as she calculated, "that's bigger than the hangar back at the Coast Guard station."

"Might be."

"That must be the biggest hotel room in Vegas."

"No, there are bigger."

"But that's the size of a mansion. What do they do with all that space?"

"They have what you'd expect in your normal mansion," Nicolas said. "Swimming pool, billiard room, library, gym. It varies from place to place, but they're all designed to overwhelm. And you can't forget the little things that make it all worthwhile, like a Matisse hanging in your bathroom, or a butler on call twenty-four hours a day."

"You're kidding, right? Tell me that you're kidding."

"That's Vegas. Believe the unbelievable."

"So how much does it cost to stay in one of these villas?" she asked.

"It depends. Are you talking about the ones at the Bellagio? Or the MGM Grand? Or the Hilton? Or the ones here at Caesars?"

"The ones here."

"Nothing."

"Nothing?"

"You can't rent them. You have to be invited, and when you're invited, it's free."

"Another one of these exclusive things?" she said, retreating to the chair and collapsing as if the thought of it exhausted her.

Nicolas followed, perching on the arm of the couch opposite. "Exclusivity works. It's human nature. We want things we think we can't have. If it becomes a mark of status, then an invitation to the villas becomes a draw for the whales—the really big gamblers. In some of the other casinos, where the villas are older and can't attract the high-stakes players, you can rent them out for fifteen to twenty thousand."

"A week?"

"No. A night."

"This place is insane."

"That's why I wanted to bring you here. I thought you'd fit right in."

"I don't fit in with all this money," she protested.

"I didn't mean with the money. For the gamblers, it's not about the money. You'll see. When we go down to the casino you'll understand what it's really about." And Nicolas stood.

"What, you mean now?"

"You're not tired, are you?" Nicolas's voice had the flavor of a challenge.

Ellie recovered quickly. "Not at all."

"Then it's time to have some fun. You ready for some fun?"

"Always," she said.

CHAPTER 25

Ellie followed Nicolas through a series of dark rooms where the ceilings were painted black, the floors were covered with deep red and gold carpet, and the walls were hung with portraits of emperors.

The first few rooms they passed through were filled with slot machines—lights flashing and bells ringing. Then they moved on to the tables—craps, blackjack, and a section set off for baccarat. In the gloom, the green felt of the tables seemed to glow.

As Ellie looked around her, she was surprised by the number of people still in the casino. She knew it was late—she felt it in the grittiness behind her eyelids—but from the crowds she would have guessed it was only eight or nine o'clock. She started looking for a clock to check the time. She asked Nicolas, but he showed her his bare wrist. "No watch," he said.

"You seem to know your way around. Is there a clock anywhere here?"

"You don't know much about casinos, do you?" he said.

"No, I don't," she admitted.

"They don't ever put clocks up in casinos, and you'll notice, they also don't have windows."

Automatically she glanced around. He was right. There were no windows.

"There's a reason for that," he told her. "They want you to lose track of time. They want to keep you here and keep you playing because the longer you play, the more chance there is you'll lose. That means no reminders that would call attention to the fact that you've been at it for two, or ten, or twenty hours."

"No one goes for twenty hours."

He just looked at her.

"Okay, maybe sometimes, but it can't happen often."

He smiled, his eyes crinkling at the corners. Already she knew that smile was dangerous.

"Let's go play," he said.

Nicolas threaded his way through the tables. Then he stopped. "I forgot. The cash machines were back by the elevators. I usually sign for the money, so if you want, I'll get some chips for you and you can pay me back. Just tell me how much you want."

"How much *I* want?" she repeated. Then she recovered herself and said, "I can't afford to gamble. I thought I'd just watch you."

Nicolas shrugged and said, "All right," but Ellie had the distinct feeling that he was disappointed in her—that she had fallen short of expectation.

He led the way to a room that was larger than the others. This one was circular, with a high domed ceiling. Nicolas headed for the center—for the high-rollers' tables.

There were only two other people playing—a Japanese businessman in a suit and an American in jeans and a button-down shirt with a bolo tie. As Ellie and Nicolas approached, the latter whooped, jabbing his fists up in victory. The businessman watched, expressionless, as the dealer swept away his chips.

It was time for a new shuffle, so Nicolas stepped forward and took a seat. The dealer looked up from cutting the cards and said, "Hello, Mr. Andreakis."

"Hello, Brian," Nicolas replied. "How have you been?"

"Not bad, not bad. Would you like to play?"

"Yes, and I'll need some chips."

Ellie saw Brian signal, and almost immediately, there was a man at Nicolas's elbow. "How much would you like, Mr. Andreakis?"

"I'll start with fifty," Nicolas said.

The man filled out a paper and held it out on the tray for Nicolas to sign.

Ellie knew he couldn't mean fifty dollars, but she didn't quite believe it until she looked and saw the zeros in the amount column—four of them.

They gave him chips of three colors: black, purple, and orange. There were eleven stacks on the felt in front of Nicolas, ten to a stack. Ellie counted three orange piles, three purple, and five black. From that, she was able to determine that the black were worth a hundred, the purple five hundred, and the orange a thousand.

The players all placed their bets. Nicolas carefully compiled a stack of chips and pushed them forward. There was almost as much money in that one bet as she had to her name.

Ellie twined her hands together behind her back and watched as the cards were dealt. The man in the bolo had a sixteen; he slapped the table, saying, "There goes my luck." Nicolas's two cards added up to eleven, the Japanese businessman had a total of nineteen, and the dealer had a queen showing.

Before drawing another card, Nicolas said, "I'll double down," and pushed forward another stack equal to the first. Nicolas and the bolo tie scratched the table with their forefinger and were each dealt a third card. The bolo tie busted with a face card, but Nicolas got a ten, for a total of twenty-one. The dealer flipped his card over. It was an ace. Both Nicolas and the dealer had hands totaling twenty-one, but only the dealer's was a true blackjack.

"Blackjack wins," Brian said and swept away all the chips on the table.

Nicolas grinned at Ellie and put his next bet in the box.

Over the next few hands, Ellie watched Nicolas lose more than half his stack of chips. He won an improbable hand when, hitting on eighteen, he got a three and beat the dealer's twenty, but then he lost again. Before she would have thought possible, Nicolas was placing the last of his chips in the box. He plucked a couple of orange chips off the pile and rolled them over to Brian. Brian nodded and said, "Dropping two thousand for the dealer."

The cards were dealt, and Nicolas had a thirteen. He hit and got a six for nineteen. The dealer flipped his card and showed sixteen. The rules dictated that the dealer had to hit on sixteen, and the next card he turned over was a four. Almost apologetically, Brian swept away the last of Nicolas's chips.

Nicolas turned to her. "You want to get a drink?"

Ellie nodded silently, and he led the way. She thought that they were headed back in the direction of the elevators, but with all the rooms linked together like a honeycomb, she couldn't be sure. They ended up at the entrance to something called the Shadow Bar. A few steps led up to a room lined with three deep, red velvet walls, and one notable exception. The fourth wall—behind the bar—was taken up by two huge screens that showed the gyrating silhouettes of two women dressed only in top hats. Ellie and Nicolas took two stools by the bar, and Nicolas ordered the drinks—beer for her, seltzer for him.

"You having fun?" Nicolas said, spinning his stool toward her.

"Sure."

"I want the truth," he chided.

"It was . . ." she hesitated, glancing uneasily at the screens and then away again.

"Yes?"

"I guess . . . it wasn't as exciting as I thought it would be."

"Of course it wasn't." He turned to accept the drinks and paid the bartender. He handed her the beer and took a sip of his seltzer.

She took her beer, but set it down, saying, "What's this 'Of course it wasn't?' You lost fifty thousand dollars."

"So?"

"So?" Then she said sarcastically, "You know, you're right. You didn't work for it. You're just throwing away Daddy's money. I don't know why you even bother."

"It's less boring than a lot of other things I could be doing," he said. "But if you were to try it . . . now *that* would be exciting."

"Me? You know how much I have in my bank account?"

"No. How much?"

"Six thousand, two hundred and forty-two dollars. Give or take a few cents. How could that be more interesting than your losing fifty thousand? It doesn't compare."

"It's a lot to you."

"Comparatively," she said dismissively.

"Yes, comparatively. What else is there but comparatively?"

"Don't get all intellectual on me."

Nicolas took a sip of his seltzer, and Ellie curled her hands around her beer.

"And what would I do if I lost?" she said. "I'd be completely dependent on *you.* "

He grinned. "It's a terrifying possibility, isn't it?"

"You have a talent for understatement. So, on the one hand, there's horrifying consequences if I lose, and what would I get if I won?"

"Money. But what you'd get isn't the point, is it? It's what you stand to lose. That's what makes it exciting."

"So why don't you put all yours on the line, however much it is?"

"I get an allowance," he said. "I can't lose it all. Even if I lose all I have at the moment, he just gives me more."

"You don't have to take it."

"You mean turn him down and deprive him of the pleasure of lording it over me? I wouldn't be so hard-hearted. And you're changing the subject."

"What do you do for amusement when I'm not here?" Ellie asked.

"If you stick around, I'll show you."

Ellie took a sip. When she put her beer glass down, she carefully centered it on the napkin. Then she said, "Okay."

"Okay what?"

"Okay, get me the goddamned money."

"How much?"

"How much do you think?"

"Six thousand, two hundred and forty-two, give or take a few cents?"

"And get it for me in hundreds."

"You want it that small?" he said, deadpan.

"Get out of here." She picked up her beer and pretended that she was going to empty it on him. When he left, she didn't put it down. She lifted it to her mouth and drank the whole thing in a few long, convulsive swallows.

As Nicolas led the way back to the tables, Ellie could feel the tingle clutch at her stomach, then spread like heat up into her chest and arms. This tingle was different from the feeling she got when she headed out on a SAR. Even with the wind blowing gale force, and the rain falling so hard you'd think you were hovering under a waterfall, the kick in her gut hadn't been like this. That had a beat as steady as a pulse. That was a surge that she could focus. As much as she had been accused of being wild and irresponsible, she had never felt wild or irresponsible. In fact, she had never felt so strong, so even, so responsible as the times when she had been doing her most dangerous flying. This was different. This felt crazy and stupid and illicit. This felt dangerous in a way that flying never had.

"You can sit at any of these tables," Nicolas said to her, with a gesture that took in the circular room, and the room beyond, and the one beyond that.

"Why don't we go back to the table where you lost?" she said.

"That's for high-rollers."

"So?"

"The minimum bet is five hundred."

"So?" she repeated.

"I thought you might want to start out slow."

"Why would I want to do that?"

He paused, as if trying to think of a reason. "You know what? I have no idea. By all means, let's go back to Brian."

But Brian was no longer there. He had been replaced by a tower of a woman with hair so blond it looked white and deep crow's-feet at the edges of her mascara-crusted eyes. Her hair was piled up on her head, giving the impression of even more height, and she stood ramrod straight, with the posture of a queen.

Nicolas touched Ellie's arm and said, "I wouldn't advise that table now. That's Vicki. She's a real gorgon, and she's got a reputation for being unbeatable."

Sure enough, Ellie noticed that all the other tables were full, while Vicki had seven empty seats ranged in front of her. Vicki stood motionless, her hands resting on the felt, one laid over the other, her eyes fixed on an indistinct middle distance.

Nicolas continued, "As a dealer, you don't want to win. If you win, you don't get as many tips, and you can make a lot on your tips—especially at the high-rollers' tables. But Vicki doesn't seem to care about that. It's almost as if she takes pride in it."

Ellie studied her, and suddenly Vicki looked back, her pale blue eyes unblinking. "I'm sure she does," Ellie murmured.

"We'll have to wait until another spot opens up," Nicolas said.

"The hell we will." Ellie walked toward Vicki's table and took the seat in the middle, directly in front of the dealer.

Vicki followed her progress, until Ellie was seated and had set down her chips. Then she shifted her eyes beyond Ellie's shoulder and said, "Good morning, Mr. Andreakis."

"Good morning, Vicki. This is my friend, Ellie Somers."

Vicki looked at Ellie. "Good luck, Ms. Somers," she said, patting the table in front of Ellie, but somehow she made the gesture of goodwill seem sinister.

"Thank you." Ellie, with a feeling of bravado, put ten black chips—double the minimum bet—in the box.

Vicki dealt the cards. Ellie found herself with a three and a seven, and Vicki had a six showing. "I'll double," Ellie said, placing another thousand behind the first and scratching the table for another card. It's a third of my savings, she thought. A third of everything she had in the world. She felt excitement burn up into her neck and cheeks. This was certainly the stupidest thing she'd ever done, and there was no taking it back now.

Vicki slipped a card from the plastic sleeve and turned it over. It was a queen, and Ellie had a twenty.

Vicki turned her down card over. It was also a queen. With a sixteen, Vicki had to hit. She dealt herself another card. It was a king. She had busted.

In two minutes, Ellie had added two thousand dollars to her small fund. She had done something stupid and had gotten away with it—more than gotten away with it. She experienced a rush of intense relief that felt almost like joy.

On the next hand, Ellie was dealt two aces. She split the hands, as she had seen the Asian man who had been sitting next to Nicolas do, and with a thousand riding on each, she drew a blackjack on one and a nineteen on the other. The dealer had a ten showing, and turned over an eight. Ellie had won again, her blackjack paying 3–2 odds instead of just even.

Nicolas leaned over and said, "You lied to me. You have played before."

She shook her head. "I'm a fast study."

"You didn't learn that from me."

Those two hands gave her courage. Ellie bumped up her initial bet to fifteen hundred and won. She increased it to two thousand, then to three. Her first loss came when she bet five thousand. Seeing that pile of chips disappear took her breath away for a second. Then she realized that she still had over twenty thousand in chips in front of her.

She decreased her bet, deciding to play it more cautiously, and she lost again. And again. At this point some people might have thought about quitting, getting out while they were ahead, but that didn't occur to Ellie. She was caught up in the excitement of losing. It was stronger than the excitement of winning because it was sharpened against an edge of fear.

She kept telling herself that her luck had to turn . . . and then it did. She had a run of hands where the cards all went her way. Vicki was busting often, and Ellie had a series of good draws where she was able to double down on her bet, and suddenly she had as many stacks of orange chips as she'd had of black when she sat down. That was enough money to make her pause, even in the midst of the excitement. With this much money, she could take some time and travel. Or go back to school. Or both. She had thought that she didn't care about winning money, but the truth was that she never imagined she might win this much. The pile of chips on the table in front of her wasn't just money; it was opportunity.

"Will you reserve this spot for me?" she said to Vicki.

"Certainly." Vicki took out the clear plastic circle to reserve her place, though all the other seats at the table were still vacant.

Ellie motioned to one of the waitresses, a brunette at least fifty years old, her calves still firm and high, but her legs loose above the knee and the skin of her chest puckered like wrinkled paper above the squeezed cleavage.

"Could I get a whiskey and some cigarettes?" Ellie said. "Single malt, and Marlboro Reds if you have them."

"Seltzer for me," Nicolas added.

Ellie wandered over to watch another table, and Nicolas followed her without a word.

The waitress came back with their drinks and Ellie's cigarettes. Ellie took a swallow of her whiskey, and it burned a trail of heat down her throat to her stomach.

She offered a cigarette to Nicolas.

He shook his head.

"Let me guess," she said. "You don't smoke."

"No, I don't."

"You don't drink. You don't smoke. What do you do?"

He smiled and took a sip of his seltzer.

"Damn it," she said.

She went back to the table and sat down, and Vicki removed the plastic RESERVED sign. Ellie slid the minimum forward and Vicki dealt.

But it was different this time. Ellie had lost the recklessness of her earlier play, and her sudden restraint appeared to bring bad luck with it. In what seemed like no time, she had lost ten grand. In an attempt to turn the tide, Ellie tried going back to her old style of play and started increasing her bets. She told herself that with a couple of big hands she could get it back, but the run of the cards was against her, and the pile of chips disappeared so quickly it seemed to be melting.

She started making crazy, desperate bets in an effort to win back what she had lost. On one bet she doubled down, and when the hand was over, she found she'd lost ten thousand over one card—an ace for the house.

When those chips were cleared away, the pile in front of her was pitifully small. In reality, it was only five hundred or so less than what she had started with, but she didn't stop to think of that. She pushed half of what was left into the box and waited for the cards.

The first was a five. Ellie groaned inwardly. It was all over.

Vicki dealt the second card, and Ellie couldn't believe her luck. It was a six. A face card would make it twenty-one. It wasn't blackjack, but she'd take it.

Now she just needed to see what Vicki would have showing. To Ellie, it seemed the nearest thing to a miracle. Vicki dealt herself a six as well. It couldn't have been better for Ellie. A six meant that if Vicki turned over a face card she'd have to hit.

Ellie took the rest of her pile of chips and placed it behind her first bet, but she took a five-hundred-dollar chip off the top and pushed it across to Vicki.

"Dropping five hundred for the dealer," Vicki called out. Then she patted the table in front of Ellie again. "Good luck," she said, and this time Ellie thought she didn't look cold so much as she looked sad.

Vicki dealt Ellie the next card. A nine. Ellie allowed herself a smile. That would be enough. Surely it would be enough.

Vicki flipped her down card. It wasn't a face card as Ellie had hoped. It was a two. She hit another, and that was a three. Ellie couldn't believe it. Vicki had eleven.

Slowly Vicki drew the next card.

And, just like that, it was over. Vicki had drawn a queen.

She didn't meet Ellie's eyes as she swept away the last of the chips.

"Do you know what they say about you?" Ellie asked Vicki.

Vicki was already busy tidying her table, ready for another customer. "Yes."

"You don't win any more than any of the other dealers, do you?"

Vicki stopped what she was doing and looked at Ellie. "The house always wins," she said.

"Not always," Ellie contradicted her.

"Always . . . ," Vicki said, ". . . when you play until you lose."

CHAPTER 27

When Sam landed the helo, the ambulance was waiting nearby, lights flashing through the sheeting rain. He waved to the medics that it was okay to approach, and the victim was unloaded as quickly as care would allow. The ambulance pulled away, and Sam powered down, unbuckled his seat belt, and climbed stiffly out of the helo.

Teddy climbed out the side door and bounced up next to him. "That was awesome," he said. "Totally awesome."

They had picked up a teenage boy who, while climbing with his father, had fallen two hundred feet down a cliff face. The rescue team had reached the boy, but he had been unconscious, and they hadn't wanted to move him far for fear of a spinal injury. They had called for a hoist extraction, but it had been a tricky thing. Sam had been forced to hover the helo with the rotor blades only fifty feet away from the sheer rock cliff, with a cross wind trying to drive them into the wall.

"I don't know how you held that hover for so long, sir," Teddy said. "I swear, even Somers couldn't have done it better."

Sam didn't have to answer that because Teddy didn't give him a chance.

"You're the man. Gimme five." Teddy did a dance spin and held his palm out behind his back.

"Cut it out, Teddy," Sam said.

"What do you mean 'cut it out'? You flew that helo like it was a butterfly. That kid's gonna live to see fifteen because of us. I think that's cause for celebration, don't you?"

"That's the job, Teddy," Sam said. "It's just the job."

"Well, we did a damn good job."

Sam smiled a little then. "We did all right today."

"All right," Teddy muttered. "He says we did 'all right.' Hey, Lieutenant Ruzick," Teddy called out to the copilot who was coming around the other side of the helo. "Commander Pantano here says we did 'all right.' What do you think of that?"

"That's more than he usually says," Ruzick replied.

"For Pete's sake—" but Teddy didn't get to finish what he was about to say because Petty Officer Sachs came running up to them.

"McDonald, Commander Pantano, the skipper wants to see you both in the conference room as fast as you can get there."

"What did we do this time?" Teddy said. "I swear, every time I come off a damn good rescue—"

"I think it's about the investigation," Sachs panted.

"They find something?" Sam asked.

"I don't know, but it sure seems like something's up."

Without another word, Sam and Teddy headed for the hangar.

 It was very late when Ellie and Nicolas returned to the suite. Nicolas searched his pockets for the card key while Ellie leaned wearily against the wall. He finally found it, opened the door, and Ellie followed him inside. They hadn't left any lights on, and after the bright corridor, the hallway seemed dark in the faint pre-dawn light.

"You want a drink or anything?" Nicolas gestured toward the kitchen.

"No thanks, I think I've had enough for tonight."

There was a pause.

"Quite a night, wasn't it?" he said.

"Mmm, yes." She was acutely aware of how close they were standing.

He smiled at her—she could see the gleam of his teeth. "I'm glad you came," he said softly.

"Me too," she replied, her voice nearly a whisper.

He seemed to lean toward her. She was sure that he was going to kiss her, but then, abruptly, he took a step back instead.

"You can have the master bedroom," he pointed down the short corridor on the left of the vestibule. "That's where I told Greg to put your bag. I'll take the spare," he indicated the corridor opposite, to the right.

"Oh . . . all right." Ellie struggled to hide her surprise.

"I don't know about you, but I'm beat."

Was she imagining things, or did she hear a note of apology in his voice?

"I'm pretty tired," she said.

"So, I'll see you in the morning."

"The morning," she agreed.

Ellie went down the left-hand corridor, and Nicolas the right. Just before entering her bedroom, Ellie glanced over her shoulder, but Nicolas had disappeared inside his room. All she could see was the door closing behind him.

■

Ellie slept, shades drawn, well into the bright desert afternoon. She emerged from her room, groggy and hung-over, to find Nicolas stretched out on the sofa in jeans and a T-shirt, his face hidden behind a newspaper, his bare feet propped on the arm nearest her. Even though they hadn't slept together, just waking up and finding him sprawled on the couch reading the paper seemed somehow intimate.

On the coffee table to his right there was a dish with scattered crusts and the dried, bright yellow slick of egg yolk. There was also a large silver dome over another plate.

He lowered his paper. "Sleep well?" he asked.

"Nothing like losing your life's savings to help you sleep like a baby," she said, dropping into the armchair.

"I ordered you breakfast," he gestured to the silver dome. "But I think it's cold by now."

She peeked underneath and rescued a cold triangle of toast. She spoke around a mouthful. "So what now?"

"What now?" he echoed.

"Where do we go from here?"

"I thought maybe dinner? Since you slept through breakfast and lunch already."

She laughed. "That's not what I mean, but okay. Dinner sounds good. And then?"

"Drinks?"

"You don't drink," she said.

"But you do."

There was no arguing with that.

"And then?"

"And then we'll see," Nicolas replied.

Ellie wondered if that was suggestive. She rather hoped it was. Maybe last night he truly had been tired. He wouldn't have invited her to Vegas if he hadn't been interested—at least that's what she told herself.

Nicolas had claimed one couch, so Ellie took the other, and they spent the hours before dinner in front of the TV. Nicolas found a classic cartoon channel, and they ended up watching *Tom and Jerry* and *Woody Woodpecker* episodes. Nicolas made her laugh with his running commentary on the psychological impact these cartoons would have on children, though every time she laughed, the dull hangover ache in her head flared up.

At one point Nicolas got up to go to the kitchen and tickled her feet as he passed by. She let out an involuntary shriek and pulled her knees to her chin.

"Aha, a weakness," he said. "I'll have to remember that."

He disappeared into the kitchen, returning with a glass of water and something cupped in one palm.

She drew her legs up again, but though he stopped by her couch, he didn't try for her feet. Instead he offered her the water.

"What's that for?" she asked him.

"To wash these down." He held out his cupped palm, and she saw that he was holding two aspirin. "You look like you might need them."

"Thanks," she said, reaching out to retrieve the two pills and thinking that she couldn't even remember the last time someone had taken note of what she might need.

It was only when she turned from the TV and saw that it was almost dark outside the windows—the lights of Vegas starting to shimmer in the dusk—that she realized the afternoon had worn into evening. She had to think about taking a shower and getting dressed, but first she asked Nicolas where they were going.

"I'm taking you to my favorite place," he said. "A little restaurant called Michael's."

"Dress code?" she asked.

"Anything. It doesn't matter. I'm going like this." He wore a pair of jeans so old they had ladders of wear up the thighs.

Taking her cue from Nicolas, Ellie put on her old flight pants and a T-shirt. She imagined he was taking her to a publike restaurant with wooden booths, graffiti scratched into the tables, colored glass shades over the lights, and a menu dominated by pizza, burgers, and beer.

She saw nothing in the entrance to make her think differently. They crossed the street to the Barbary Coast casino, which was supposed to be a neon version of a pirate's hangout. When they entered, Ellie noticed the owners had tried to make the interior look like the inside of a ship by decorating with brass and oak and dressing the dealers in yellow silk shirts with billowing sleeves, but this effect was overwhelmed by the row upon row of ringing, flashing slot machines Ellie and Nicolas had to thread through to reach the back corner.

Nicolas led the way up a couple of steps to a wooden door inlaid with an intricate stained-glass window. He pushed it open and ushered her into another world. Ellie found herself standing in a small room, almost a boudoir, done in plush velvet and deep mahogany. The diners were seated in high-backed wing chairs, as if in their own living rooms. Instead of a ceiling, a stained-glass dome arched overhead.

Ellie spent the first few seconds adjusting to the surprise, and in those seconds she lost her chance to grab Nicolas and retreat. She was stranded in a five-star restaurant dressed in a T-shirt and pants stained with engine oil.

The maître d' advanced on them, and she tensed preparing for a cold rebuff, but he greeted Nicolas with a smile. "Mr. Andreakis. It's been a while since we've had the pleasure of your company."

"I've been away," Nicolas said.

"And your father? I hope he's well."

Ellie noted that people always seemed to ask about his father.

"He goes to Greece for the summer. I wouldn't expect him back for another month at least, but I'm sure the very day he's in town he'll be here."

The maître d' beamed.

"I'm sorry I didn't call for a reservation," Nicolas said, looking around the restaurant. "You seem to be full tonight, as usual. I don't suppose there's any chance you can squeeze us in?"

"We always have a table for you, Mr. Andreakis. For two?" the maître d' said, glancing at Ellie, who was trying to hide behind Nicolas.

"Yes, two. You can come out now," Nicolas said to Ellie over his shoulder.

She gave him a narrow-eyed stare and stepped forward to stand next to him.

"Would you like your usual table, or something more private?" the maître d' asked.

"The usual will be fine."

"Then if you'll follow me." He picked up two menus and led them through the closely packed tables. Ellie could feel the eyes of the other

diners following them as they walked to a table in the center of the
room. Ellie noticed that the women were wearing dresses that flashed
with sequins, and the men were dressed in suits.

Once Ellie and Nicolas were settled at their table, the maître d'
handed them menus, saying, "If there's anything else I can get you,
please let me know." He left them, and Ellie opened her menu pretending to study it, but when he had gotten far enough away, she lowered it
and hissed, "Very funny, Nicki. I hope you're enjoying this."

"Enjoying what?"

"Next time I ask you something, remind me that you're a lying son of
a bitch."

"I didn't lie to you," he said.

"I asked you what I should wear and you said I could wear anything,
and that it didn't matter. How is that not lying?"

"But it didn't matter, did it?"

She paused, searching for a response. "You can't go around doing
whatever you want," she said finally.

"Why not?"

"Because . . ." Then she realized that she didn't have an answer.

"Rules are made to be broken," Nicolas said. "At least they are for
people like us."

"You mean people like you. People with money."

"No. I mean people with guts. People who are willing to go and do
what they want."

She instinctively felt that it was wrong, but again didn't quite know
how to rebut it. She was silent for a moment.

"So," he said. "Do you know what you want?"

"What I want?" she said, stalling. "You know, it hasn't been so long
since I resigned . . ."

He showed his teeth in a grin. "I meant what you want for dinner."

CHAPTER 29

Sam and Teddy arrived at the closed door to the conference room, both a little out of breath after their hurried
change out of their ADCs. They paused there, as if by
silent agreement. Teddy slicked down his hair with his
palms and blew a whoosh of air from a pursed mouth.
"Do I look okay?" he asked Sam.

Sam motioned for him to zip up the flight suit where the collar of his
T-shirt was showing through.

"Thanks," Teddy said.

Sam took hold of the doorknob. "Ready?"

"Ready."

When Sam opened the door, they were both startled by the number
of people sitting around the table in the conference room. There was the
CO and the members of the original Mishap Analysis Board, plus several
men they had never seen before, sitting at the end of the table.

"Petty Officer McDonald, Commander Pantano, please come in,"
Traub gestured for them to take seats.

They entered cautiously and took the two chairs at the head of the
table that were offered to them.

"How was the SAR?" he asked them in an undertone.

"Good," Teddy said.

"It went well," Sam agreed.

"Kid's okay?"

"He'll be laid up a while, but he should be fine," Sam answered.

"Glad to hear it. All right then." Traub looked to the assembled group.
The board's president leaned forward, resting his forearms on the

table. "If it's all right with you, we'd like to go over once more Petty Officer McDonald's version of the events the night of the crash."

"I'll do my best," Teddy said.

"Good. That's all we ask. Now if you would tell us again about the evening of the accident."

Teddy cleared his throat nervously, but when he spoke his voice carried its trademark calmness.

"We were called out at approximately nineteen hundred hours to assist the cutter *Anacapa*. They had come across a Russian freighter just outside the Dixon Entrance. They contacted the ship, which reported engine trouble, but the ship's captain said that they'd almost got it fixed and didn't require assistance. The *Anacapa* continued with their patrol along the A-B line, but a little while later they caught sight of a cigarette boat headed in the direction of the freighter. The captain had worked patrol down in the Gulf, and he thought it looked like a pickup, so they called us in for backup. They witnessed the rendezvous, and then they went in for the freighter, and we went for the go-fast."

"We reached the *Anacapa*'s position and headed due east in pursuit of the other craft. Conditions were difficult—the fog took the visibility down to a quarter mile, and Somers—excuse me, Lieutenant Commander Somers—was flying low, so as to keep under the cloud cover. We located the go-fast, which instead of continuing toward the coast, turned north into a channel near Dall Island. We followed." At this point in his story, Teddy hesitated.

"You followed," the president of the board prompted. "Remember, we're just going over what you've already testified to."

Teddy nodded and continued. "We were low to begin with, flying under the worst of the fog. That's when Lieutenant Commander Somers closed in, and brought us down on top of the go-fast. She was trying to intimidate them—"

"Don't editorialize," the president told him. "Just tell us what happened. I believe you said that Lieutenant Commander Somers didn't consult you before performing this maneuver, and that both you and Lieutenant Lazure protested."

"That's correct, but then she brought us up. That's when it happened. The helo started to yaw right. I heard Lieutenant Lazure shouting—"

"Did you hear anything else?" one of the other men sitting at the end of the table broke in to ask.

"Hear anything? You mean something over the headphones?"

"No, not over the headphones."

"I had the rotor right overhead, and my headphones on, and Lieutenant Lazure yelling—it was difficult to hear anything else."

There was a pause. Then the president said, "You were telling us that Lieutenant Lazure started to say something."

"Right," Teddy was still staring at the stranger at the end of the table. Then he looked back at the president. "That's right. Lieutenant Lazure started yelling, 'Left pedal, left pedal,' and Lieutenant Commander Somers yelled back something like, 'I'm losing the tail rotor.' It was amazing the helo was still in the air at all."

Teddy spoke calmly enough, but it was as if his eyes turned inward, and he was back in the helo, seeing it all again.

"Do you know if there were any warning lights beforehand?" the president asked him.

"I'm sure there were warning lights if the rotor struck the wash, but they didn't talk about them up front. They were probably too busy dealing with the situation."

"All right. Go on. The helo started to yaw . . ."

Teddy picked up the lead. "Then Lieutenant Commander Somers told us she was going to try to land in the water. I don't know how, but she did it. The water stopped the helo from spinning, and she ordered us to bail out. Petty Officer Hoffman and I exited the craft, and Lieutenant Commander Somers water-taxied away, for our safety. I'm not certain what happened next. I was swimming in the opposite direction, but it sounded like they executed a controlled shutdown."

Teddy paused there, obviously remembering what had happened next.

The president gave Teddy a moment to recover, then he asked, "I understand that you were all particularly close friends. How was it you were on the duty crew together that night?"

It wasn't a question that Teddy had been expecting. "We weren't. We had all been on a mission a few days before, but we weren't the duty crew that night. They had to do a random recall, and most of the pilots were at a barbecue and had cracked a couple of beers. We all happened to be at Lieutenant Commander Somers's house when we got the call."

"That's right," the president said. "I remember now. But where was the duty helo? Do you remember?"

"The duty helo was out on a medevac. I remember it because it turned out to be a prank call. We get one of those every so often. They went out to the village, discovered that there was no one suffering symptoms of a heart attack as had been reported, and headed down to back us up. Turned out they got there just in time to rescue us."

"Did anyone find out who was behind the hoax?"

"I don't recall."

"Could you have someone check that?" the president said to Traub.

Traub got up and left. Everyone else in the room waited in silence. Finally Teddy said, "Have you found anything?"

The president held up a hand. "In due time we'll answer all your questions. I have to ask that you bear with us a little while longer."

"Was there . . . I mean is there evidence of mechanical failure?" Teddy persisted.

"That's all I can tell you at this time. I'm sorry."

Teddy's jaw muscle clenched, but he nodded.

Traub ducked back into the room. "I have someone checking into that other issue."

"Thank you." The president turned back to Teddy. "And thank you for answering our questions after what I'm certain was a long day for you." Then he glanced over at one of the men at the end of the table, who dipped his chin in an assent.

"Petty Officer McDonald, I hope you don't mind if we come back with other questions as they arise."

"Not at all," Teddy said. "Anything I can do to help, and if you find anything . . ."

"We'll let you know as soon as we can."

Teddy stood, and Sam started to get up as well.

"Commander Pantano, if you don't mind, we'd like you to stay."

Sam sank back down into his chair.

Teddy stopped, and it looked as if he might say something, but when he looked over at the skipper, Traub jerked his head toward the door. Teddy hesitated, then obeyed.

There was a pause after Teddy had left, as if the president wanted to make sure he couldn't hear from the hallway.

The silence went on long enough that Sam was the first to speak. "I can't add anything to what Petty Officer McDonald told you. I wasn't involved in the incident."

"We know, but there was something we were curious about. When was it you decided that Lieutenant Commander Somers wasn't responsible for the accident?"

"How do you know I decided that?" Sam glanced over at the skipper.

"They asked me how I came to request that the helo be retrieved—since no appeal was ever filed. I had to tell them the truth," Traub explained.

"What we want to know," the president continued, "the question we want to ask you is, What made you so determined to raise that helo?"

"With all due respect to Petty Officer McDonald, he was in the cabin and not in the best position to determine the cause of the accident. The two people who could have told you—the pilots—were both unable to. It was all circumstantial evidence. I thought we should know for sure. I guess when it comes down to it, I took a chance on a hunch."

"It happens to have paid off."

"What do you mean?" Sam said. "What did you find out from that helo?"

"Come on, come on," Ellie said under her breath as she rattled the dice in the loose cage of her fingers.

"Seven or eleven," someone from around the table called out.

"A seven or eleven," she whispered. "Come on."

She wanted a quick hit. She needed a quick hit. All she had left of the thousand she had borrowed was resting in a pitifully small pile on the felt. After dinner they had returned to the hotel, and Nicolas mentioned that he wanted to play a few games before turning in.

"I'll teach you how to play craps," he'd said. "It's got the best odds of any game in the house."

She'd had a couple of drinks, found herself rolling for Nicolas, and winning. The people around the table cheered the new hot hand and a little crowd formed. Nicolas stood behind her, kneading her shoulders like a trainer with an athlete, caught up in the excitement of it. He was betting big—bigger than the night before—and backing up the bets, and it seemed like no time at all before she'd won him over seventy grand.

"It's not fair, I'm getting all your luck. You should use some for yourself," he'd said.

"You're forgetting one thing. I'm flat broke," she reminded him.

"I'll lend you some," but before he'd even finished the sentence, she was shaking her head no, though she was tempted. It had been fun rolling for that kind of money, but it wasn't the same as playing for yourself.

"I don't want to go into debt . . . I mean any more than I already am," she said.

"But this way you could win some cash," he argued. "Then you wouldn't have to be completely dependent on me."

"That's assuming I win."

"Look, you already won me thousands. Take this," he handed her an orange chip. "Consider it a commission."

She hesitated. "I'll only take it if we call it a loan."

"All right, a loan," he agreed.

But now there was only seventy-five dollars left of the thousand—three green chips. She bet twenty-five on the line, blew on her hand, and shot the dice. They rolled, bouncing up against the end of the table, and fell back. She'd rolled a three. Craps.

There was a groan around the table, which she echoed silently as the croupier swept away many of the chips on the table and paid out those who were betting with the house.

"Still your roll," the croupier said.

Only fifty left. She pushed forward another green chip, shook the dice, and sent them down the table.

They jostled each other, rolled, and came to rest up against the far wall. A four.

It was a long shot, but by backing up her bet, she'd get paid two-to-one odds. If she rolled another four before she rolled a seven, she'd have seventy-five to go with her fifty. Ellie placed her last chip behind the first.

She shot again.

A twelve.

She juggled them and side-armed the dice.

A three.

There was action on the table at every throw, but Ellie was focused on that four. She could even see it in her head. A pair of twos. That's how she'd get it.

She pitched the dice once more, and they went bouncing down the table. The first came to rest on a two, and she held her breath as the other did a slow roll. She saw the two disappear and the five come up.

"Seven," the croupier called. "Next roller."

Ellie turned away, and Nicolas took her elbow as they made their way out from the crowd around the craps table.

"I thought you said the odds were better with craps," Ellie said.

"You were up for a while there," he replied. "How much did you have?"

"The most? About five thousand."

At the time it hadn't seemed like enough—not compared to how much she'd been up the night before on the blackjack table, when she'd gone from six thousand to almost fifty. Only now, when it was all gone, did she think that five thousand was almost as much as she'd had when she came down here.

"Want to try again?" Nicolas offered. "You can make it back in no time."

"It's getting late . . ." Ellie said.

"Maybe, but I'm not tired. Are you?"

"You know, come to think of it, I'm not," she said. "Not even close."

It was light outside when they finally stumbled back to the room. Nicolas collapsed on his couch. Behind his head, outside the wall of windows, the sky was a pale pink, and the mountains in the distance were dark blue silhouettes.

"To look at you, you'd think that you've been hard at work all day," Ellie said, taking the armchair across from him.

"All night," he corrected. "Haven't we both?"

She snorted. "Do you call losing hard work?"

"Hell yes. You think it's easy, bearing up under this pile of money? I have to get rid of some of that dead weight—and all you'll take off me is a few thousand. I call that cruel."

"If it's such a burden, why don't you do something useful with it?" she said, kicking off her shoes and propping her feet on the coffee table.

"There's that do-gooder in you popping up. I leave all that charitable stuff to my father. He gives it away by the fistful. You should see all the plaques and certificates he's got up on his walls to reassure him that he's a great man. I take on myself the infinitely more challenging work of squandering the rest."

"That charitable stuff helps people," she pointed out.

"Yes, but that's not why he does it."

"How do you know?"

That seemed to annoy him. She didn't consider until later that she might have touched a nerve, and that was why he turned on her with his next remark. "Can you really say that the only reason you risked your life flying SARs was because you wanted to save people?" he demanded.

"I don't need to defend my actions to you," she said. He was just a playboy who did nothing but spend his father's money. What right did he have to question her motives? She got up from her chair. "I'm going to bed," she announced. And she did start toward her room, but she stopped before she reached the corridor. "It might not have been the only reason," she said, turning to face him. "But it was the most important one."

"That's the really sad part. You're lying to yourself and everyone else. Let me ask you this. You can't be a pilot anymore—that's over. So now what? What are you going to do? Go join the Peace Corps? Become a social worker? Please."

It wasn't really a question, so she didn't bother to answer. Instead she said, "You're a real asshole."

"Absolutely," he agreed. "But at least I don't pretend to be anything else."

She retreated down the hall to her room, slamming the door closed behind her, but that gesture took the last of her energy, and she leaned against the door, her forehead resting on the wood, too tired to move.

If she hadn't been standing there, she wouldn't have caught it—in the quiet that followed, she heard the muffled pad of bare feet.

Ellie straightened and brought her ear closer to the crack between the frame and the door, listening. Not a sound. Nevertheless, the hair on her arms prickled. She had the eerie feeling that he was there, right on the other side of the door.

She stood so long, listening to the silence, she was almost convinced she had imagined it. It was silly, she told herself, to think that she could sense his presence.

She was about to turn away when she heard his voice, very low.

He murmured, "I'm sorry."

This time he was so quiet she didn't hear his retreat. She only knew he was gone when she caught the soft click of his door closing.

Teddy was sitting at a table in the back corner of the Eagle's Nest with an empty beer glass in front of him when Sam walked in the door nearly an hour later. Teddy was sitting alone, even though nearby a group of his friends were playing a rowdy game of fooseball. He was staring morosely at a newspaper spread out on the table in front of him, though it was obvious he wasn't reading.

Sam crossed to the bar and ordered two beers.

"Two?" the bartender said. "What's the hurry?"

"One's for Teddy."

"One of the boys tried to buy him a beer earlier, but he wasn't interested. Something's got to be pretty wrong for Teddy to turn down a free beer."

"I guess I'll give it a try anyway," Sam said.

The bartender shrugged and drew two from the tap. Sam carried them over to the table and set one down right in the middle of Teddy's paper. The beer slopped over the side, and the newsprint soaked it up. Then Sam took the seat opposite.

Teddy stared at the beer for a moment, then he picked it up and moved it off his paper. "I don't remember asking you to sit down," he remarked.

"Usually when someone buys you a drink, you say thank you," Sam said mildly.

"It's a poor consolation prize. I'd rather have some information."

"How about both?"

Teddy looked up. "You mean it?"

"I stayed behind to persuade the skipper we should tell you. That's what took me so long."

"So long? What took so long about it? I knew it. He doesn't trust me."

"He trusts you—he doesn't trust your mouth," Sam said. "I convinced him you would be able to help, but I had to promise you wouldn't say a word about it to anyone—and I mean anyone."

"No problem."

"This is serious, Teddy."

Teddy shot him a pained look. "I know it's serious. Give me a little credit."

"All right, I'm sorry. It's just when you hear what it is . . ." Sam halted and the silence stretched out.

"For God's sake," Teddy said. "Tell me already."

"It's about the accident."

Teddy rolled his eyes. "I *know* it's about the accident."

"Right. Well . . . that's the thing," Sam said. "It wasn't an accident."

"Say that again," Teddy demanded.

"It wasn't an accident," Sam repeated.

"What's that supposed to mean?"

"It means that the helo was tampered with. It means that it wasn't Ellie's fault, and it wasn't your fault either."

"Christ. But how?"

"Someone planted a sort of homemade zip gun—pretty much just a pipe with a bullet—inside the cabin beneath the tail rotor gear box," Sam said. "Apparently it was very small and well camouflaged, but it still couldn't have been there long or someone would have spotted it."

"Smart. Anything on the outside we would've caught immediately."

"Or they might have chosen it because it was so easy to rig. It'd only take a second to reach up and attach it. In fact, the whole device was incredibly simple. Anyone could have made the gun itself, and the remote trigger wasn't that high-tech either. Someone on the go-fast probably had a remote that could set off the charge. It wouldn't have taken much to touch off the bullet, and it probably wasn't even loud enough to hear over the noise of the helo. Then, once the bullet punched through the gearbox, the fluid would have leaked out."

"But that should have touched off a chip tail transmission light, and probably a tail box temp light as well," Teddy said. "And the fluid wouldn't have blown out immediately. There should have been time to land safely."

"You're right. There should have been a warning light. But, as you said, maybe they didn't mention anything about it over the ICS because they were busy dealing with the situation. And they might not have had time to land if the bullet itself took out a tooth in the gear. There's also the possibility that they didn't see the warning light immediately. Think about what was going on at the time. There's any number of possible explanations, but it's something we can't know for certain."

Teddy nodded. "You're right. I can't blame it on them. It's my fault. I was in the cabin. I should have noticed the device."

"You can't excuse Ellie and Dave and then hold yourself to a higher standard," Sam said.

"The hell I can't."

"You weren't the only one who missed it. There were other people in and around that helo. They didn't see it either."

"Those guys we just talked to, they hold me responsible," Teddy said. "They think I should have seen it."

"No. That's not true."

"Then why did they tell you all this and not me?"

"Because . . . well, because they were relatively sure I didn't do it."

"And they think I did? I was in the helo, for God's sake. Somers and Lazure were my best friends. You," he said accusingly, "everyone knew you didn't like Somers. You were always on her case. In fact, I heard you say just a few days before the accident that it was only a matter of time, and pretty soon her luck was gonna run out. That could be interpreted as a threat."

"I was the one who got them to raise the helo," Sam pointed out, "and they couldn't think of a reason why I'd sabotage the helo, then when I'd gotten away with it, convince the skipper that we should bring it up."

"Ah," Teddy said. "Right."

"They decided to tell me what they'd found because they were hoping I knew something about it. They thought I'd been suspicious for a reason, and that was why I went to the skipper."

"Were you?"

"I had no idea," Sam admitted.

"Who would have?" Teddy said. "It's not something that comes to mind. I mean, why would someone want to do something like that?"

"I have to admit, they've got that figured out, and it makes me feel like an idiot for not thinking of it earlier."

"Well? What is it?"

"Think about it for a second. What were you doing when you went down?"

"Oh," Teddy said. "The drug smugglers."

"Right, and what happened when you went down?"

"Everyone left off the pursuit to come help us . . ."

"The boat got through, and even the freighter got away," Sam finished for him. "How much heroin or coke do you think that boat was carrying? It was probably enough that they could make it worth someone's while to ensure that the helo went down."

"Yeah, but who?"

"Anyone who had access," Sam said.

"Me? Mikey? *Dave?*"

"They haven't discounted anyone. As you said, a warning light probably went off, and whoever planted it must've thought that would give the pilot enough time to land safely. This device wasn't designed to cause injury; the main objective seems to have been to divert the pursuit."

"Anyone who worked on this base would know there's a good chance someone's going to get hurt," Teddy said.

"They say that a million or two can help anyone's conscience."

"You know what I say? I say that's a load of crap."

"Someone's responsible," Sam said.

"So what did you tell the skipper?"

Sam answered reluctantly, "Well . . . Frank's wife has a fourth on the way, and he doesn't make much in the way of salary. He could use the money. He might have put it away for the kids' college or something."

"You said that?"

"No. Not yet. I wanted to ask you what you thought."

"I think it stinks."

"Me too," Sam sighed. "They showed me a list of people who had access to the helo, and they wanted to know if I had any ideas. I told them I'd think about it and get back to them."

"And you want me to help you set them on someone?"

"I want you to try to think of anyone you think could have done this."

"No one I know," Teddy declared.

"Who else had access to the helos?"

"We have people come through."

"The helo had a six-hundred-hour inspection less than three weeks before the crash, and they told me that there's no way the device could have been installed before that. And they checked—no one got a tour of the hangar in that time. Do you have any other ideas?"

Teddy thought for a moment, but he obviously didn't come up with anything because he burst out, "You know as well as I do that it couldn't have been any of the boys. No way. There's got to be some other explanation."

"Can you think of one?"

"You're the one playing detective, why don't you think of something?"

"That's really helpfu . . ." Sam broke off. "Oh."

"Oh what?"

"You're right. You're absolutely right," Sam said.

"Of course I'm right," Teddy said. Then a moment later, "What am I right about?"

"I can't believe no one else thought of this."

"What?"

"There is another explanation—I mean people who aren't Coasties who have access to the helos."

"We don't let anyone near the helos if we're not watching them every second."

"Yes, we do," Sam said. "Think about it."

"Come on, I don't . . ." Teddy's eyes narrowed, then widened. "I can't believe I didn't think of that."

"It's so obvious that nobody did."

"The SARs," Teddy said.

"The SARs," Sam agreed. "It had to have been someone you picked up between the helo's last overhaul and the accident. How many people did you have in that helo the three weeks before the crash?"

"One," Teddy said. "There's only one it could be."

CHAPTER 33

"It was a memorable one," Teddy said. "The craziest SAR I've been on."

Sam caught the thread. "You're talking about when your hoist broke and Ellie pulled that stupid stunt with the ERD . . ."

". . . and we got Mike and the guy back in the helo, but barely. In fact, we almost missed the survivor out there. It was dumb luck we found him at all."

"But if you almost didn't find him—that doesn't fit. If he was the guy, he must have planned it. What you're describing doesn't sound very well planned."

"Something must have gone wrong," Teddy acknowledged. "But that's nothing new. The weather and the ocean wreak havoc with a lot of plans, but he's the one, all right. You know what he said when we finally got him inside the helo?"

"You told me, but I forgot."

"He said, 'Can we do it again tomorrow?' This from a guy who almost died."

"Misdirection," Sam said. "He was trying to throw you off guard."

"Wouldn't he have done better to act like most survivors?"

"So he's crazy. I guess you'd have to be crazy to think up a stunt like that in the first place."

"Sounds plausible," Teddy said.

"Then let's go talk to the skipper. He can pass it along to the authorities, they can track the guy down, and we can find Ellie and get her back here. Case closed."

Sam started to get up.

"Ellie," Teddy said. "Oh my God, Ellie."

"Yes, Ellie. Did you forget about her in all this?"

"No, but—"

"What? You don't want her back? Come on already," Sam took a couple of steps away from the table and stopped, waiting for Teddy to follow.

"Hold on, I gotta tell you something. I just realized . . ."

"Can't you tell me in the car?"

"No. Sit down a second, okay?"

Sam returned to the table and sat back down on the edge of his chair. "I'm sitting. What is it?"

"The last time I saw her—remember I told you about it? She was having dinner at Marcy's, and she was with a guy."

"And?"

"The guy . . ." Teddy leaned forward across the table, "Sam, he was the guy from the SAR."

At Teddy's words, Sam felt suddenly chilled, as if someone had opened the door to a cold wind.

"I thought he looked familiar," Teddy went on, "but I couldn't place him. When we hauled him in from the helo he was soaked, and you know people look different in those situations."

"But you're sure now?" Sam said.

"I'm positive."

"When was that?"

"The night she left," Teddy left the words hanging in the air. Then he tried to retreat from the implication of it, by adding, "But she wouldn't just take off with some guy she barely knows . . . would she?"

Sam just looked at him.

"Oh shit," Teddy said.

They sat in silence for a minute.

"You don't think there's any chance she was involved with the whole thing, do you?"

Sam looked at him sharply. "No." Then less certainly, "No. Do you?"

"No. Somers is crazy, but she loved her job. The problem is, if *we're* wondering about it, think about how the suits are going to react if, when they track this guy down, they find her with him."

"It wouldn't look good, but they're professionals. They'll figure it out in the end."

"You want to put her through that after what's happened already?"

Sam looked grim, then shook his head.

"What, then?"

"We've got to find her first," Sam said.

"Right." Teddy paused, then asked, "Do you think it's a coincidence—them meeting up and going off together?"

"Not a chance."

"Then what do you think he's doing with her?"

"I would guess that he wants something from her."

"Yeah, but what?"

"I don't know," Sam said. "But I hope we get to her before she finds out."

Ellie and Nicolas fell into a sort of routine. They stayed up late gambling and then slept late into the afternoon. They ordered room service, watched TV, and occasionally ventured out. The days were generally uneventful, but there was a peaceful, companionable feeling to them, and there were moments that stood out vividly in Ellie's memory.

The first occurred one afternoon, when they were both stretched out on their couches watching an old movie. As the sun set, it came in through the windows, and the glare off the television made it hard to see. Nicolas got up to close the curtains, but he didn't go straight to the window—he made it halfway before he stopped just behind her.

"What are you doing?" she said, tilting her head back and squinting up at him.

"I'm looking at your hair," he replied. To get it off her neck, she had fanned it over the arm of the couch.

"What, do I have dandruff or something?" she said.

"No. I just noticed how beautiful it is. It's nearly black." And then she felt his fingers, light and almost hesitant, playing with the strands. A second later he had turned to close the curtains, but she hadn't forgotten that brief touch.

Then there had been the lazy afternoon when they had wandered down to the shops inside the casino. Nicolas stopped in front of one that sold jewelry made from antique coins and announced that he was going to buy something for his aunt for her birthday. Ellie helped him pick out a beautiful pendant, a Greek coin from 334 B.C. that hung from a thin silver chain. That night, before going down to dinner, he had turned her around and fastened the pendant around her neck. She protested that it was for his aunt, but he silenced her, saying, "I don't have an aunt."

"That's downright sneaky," she told him, but she didn't take it off.

And there was the afternoon she woke up to find he'd bought a PlayStation and the newest version of her favorite game, Twisted Metal, as a surprise. She taught him how to play—and in a few hours he was beating her two times out of three. "I can't believe this is your favorite. You're terrible at this game," he said, laughing.

Then, of course, there were the nights spent down in the casino. After that second night at the craps table, she had given up the pretense of resisting. Now that she'd experienced the rush of the cards, it wasn't any fun to watch. Every night, depending on their mood, Ellie and Nicolas either took seats side by side at the blackjack tables, or stood together at the craps table. They consulted on strategy, commiserated over losses, and generally egged each other on to greater excess. She and Nicolas were partners in folly, though compared to Nicolas's losses, Ellie felt positively frugal.

She had borrowed and lost three thousand the first night. The next it had been four. It had gone like that, increasing by a thousand or two every night, and it went on—her debt quickly mounting though never seeming insurmountable—until the final night—her last night of gambling.

Ellie never remembered how it had started. Had she taken ten thousand to begin with or only five? Had she gone back and asked for more, or had he offered? How many drinks had she had? The waitress kept bringing new glasses as soon as the old were empty. All she knew was that in a blaze of reckless abandon, with a satisfying feeling of tragedy, she lost. And she kept losing.

She felt instinctively that it was right. She had lost her job, her friends, her honor (though she never would have spoken that word aloud) and it was only right, only fitting, that she should in some way commemorate all.

It went quickly, a mere two hours at the high-rollers' table—though the helo had gone down in seconds. When she needed more money, Nicolas, gambling right beside her, slid more chips over from his stacks. It could have been worse, though how much worse, she would never know. She hadn't stopped of her own accord, and as far as she knew, Nicolas hadn't reached anywhere near the limit of what he was prepared to give, but he had reached the limit of his credit. When he tried to sign for more, the floor manager explained quietly that before Nicolas could do that, he would need to settle his present debt.

After the floor manager left them, Ellie stepped away from the table, tripped, and almost fell, but Nicolas was beside her and caught her arm. She found she needed the support to make it to the elevator. When they reached the suite, Ellie dropped into the armchair, closed her eyes, and found that the room was spinning slowly around her. "Oh God," she said.

"What? Are you going to throw up?" Nicolas said, ready to jump up from the couch.

"I might. If you don't stop the room from whirling around like this."

"Open your eyes."

She did. "That's better," she sighed.

"You need a trash can, just in case?"

"No," she flapped a hand. "I always make it to the bathroom in time."

"Why don't I find that reassuring? You want some coffee?" When she didn't answer immediately, he said, "I'm going to order you some coffee."

She was still drunk, but at the same time she could feel tomorrow's hangover pressing her temples in a vise. She had no idea how much money she had gone through. At that moment she felt like she would have given almost anything to be back at the air station, bored out of her mind, griping about the rain and the paperwork.

"What are you thinking about now?" he said. "You've got the most terrifying expression on your face."

"Nothing."

"Come on, 'fess up."

If she hadn't been drunk, she probably would have put him off with a joke, but she was at that point of inebriation when the urge for confession struck, so she told him. "I was thinking about how, just when you realize you've lost something, you start thinking about how much it meant to you."

Nicolas smiled, but it was a sad kind of smile. "You should console yourself with the thought that once you get it, you can't remember why you wanted it so much in the first place."

"That's not always true," Ellie said, even while she struggled to think of a situation in which that wasn't the case. It was like running in water, trying to get her brain to work.

"Yes and no," Nicolas said. "It's the difference between desire and contentment—but some people aren't built to appreciate contentment."

"I can't guess who you're talking about. Come on, I'm drunk, but I'm not that drunk."

"I'm including myself in the categorization."

"But it's so depressing."

"You can look at it this way. You might not have a very happy life, but it won't be boring."

"Right now a little boredom doesn't seem so bad." She pressed her hands to her head as if she were trying to hold it together.

"You must be really tired to say something like that."

"Wasted," she agreed. "But you said it before—squandering money is a tiring business."

"What you've been doing this past week hasn't been squandering," he assured her.

"What is it then?"

"The way you've been playing? That's called throwing it away."

She let her head flop back on the chair. "Now you tell me."

"I wouldn't have dreamed of saying anything before this. I was having too much fun. I finally found someone who seemed to lose as much as I do."

"I don't have any idea how much it was. Do I want to know?"

"Probably not."

"Oh God," she said again. "What the hell am I going to do?"

"It's easy enough to fix."

"And how do I do that? Should I rob a bank or something?"

"No, that's not necessary. It's very simple. All you have to do is agree to do a little something for me—"

Every night when they returned to the room, she had wondered, Would this be the night? Every night the answer was no. If she'd had the courage—if he hadn't been quite so good-looking—she might have made a move herself. Instead she had decided to wait and leave it up to him, and finally here it was, but not in any form she'd anticipated. He had to have known she was willing. She had to assume he'd chosen this route so she wouldn't get any ideas about what it might mean. Maybe he thought she was after his money. Or worse, that she was trying to land him as a husband. She felt cheap and ashamed and disappointed, but she didn't want him to see that. She tried to rise as if in indignation, but she had to steady herself against the chair. Then she said, "What the hell do you take me for?"

He looked bewildered.

"Let's get this straight right now—I don't sleep with anyone for money. I don't care how much I lost."

Nicolas started to laugh.

"What's so funny?"

"I'm sorry, but . . ." and he broke down laughing again, "but I wasn't proposing that you sleep with me to work off your debt."

"You weren't?"

"I mean I'd be willing to sleep with you, if you insist, but my services don't come cheap. Of course I could always put it on your tab . . ."

It was so silly she had to laugh along with him, though she could feel that she was blushing furiously. It would have been better to have made a pass at him and get turned down. That would have been less embarrassing. She tried to continue the joke, saying, "If you put it that way, it's tempting, but I don't think it's a good idea for me to get any deeper into debt."

He gave an exaggerated sigh. "All right. Good night, then."

"I've already blown my chances for a good night," Ellie said ruefully.

"Sleep well?" he suggested.

"I've drunk enough that I might still have a shot at that."

She turned and made her way back to her room, and sure enough, she didn't remember anything after she hit the bed.

CHAPTER 35

"So?" Sam quizzed him. "What did you find out?"

He and Teddy were back at the Eagle's Nest, huddled at the same table in the corner.

"Nothing at the hospital," Teddy reported. "Mike got checked out by a doctor, but the survivor took off. Didn't stick around to see anyone and certainly didn't fill out any of the paperwork. You get anything?"

"I tracked down the owner of the boat that went down, the *Black Rose*," Sam said. "It was registered to a local guy. Sold it the day before. Cash. A bunch of fishermen on the dock saw the survivor sail it away, and one talked to him, but nobody got a name."

"So we got nothing on him."

"At least we can be relatively sure that we guessed right before we go running after Ellie," Sam pointed out.

"Yeah, but that doesn't help if we can't find her. Did you try her folks?"

"Yes."

"And?"

"Why was it, Teddy, that you wanted *me* to call?"

Teddy pursed his lips, then admitted, "I had a bad feeling about it. She didn't talk about her parents much, but from what she did say, I gathered her father is a tough cookie. I guess she wasn't exaggerating?"

"No, she wasn't exaggerating. Her mother answered, but she wouldn't talk to me. She handed me over to Ellie's father, and I didn't get past square one with him. I could barely get a word in edgewise. You don't want to know what he said—about his own daughter."

"You could always call back later and try to get her mother to talk to you."

Sam shook his head. "I can't call back. Not after what I said to him."

"You didn't!"

"I did."

"What happened to Commander Pantano the politician?"

"Shut up, Teddy."

"To think that there was a real person underneath all this time."

"I lost my temper, but yelling at people doesn't get you anywhere," Sam said. "Now if Ellie calls her parents, they certainly won't tell us."

"That's true, but yelling makes you feel better."

"It was stupid of me to go off like that," Sam insisted.

"Of course it was. But don't you hate those people who are always smart? As a matter of fact, I think that's why I didn't like you much."

"You were way off. I'm dumber than most," Sam said. "Think about it. Why am I even doing this? Ellie has made it obvious that she hates me."

"She doesn't hate you," Teddy said. "Strong dislike maybe, but not hate."

"Great."

"If it makes you feel any better, I'm starting to like you all right. Do a couple more stupid things and, before you know it, we'll be best friends."

"Great," Sam said again, without enthusiasm.

"I thought that would cheer you up. So what now?"

"I'm thinking."

"Can we get the manifests for the evening flight? I bet the person sitting next to her is our guy," Teddy said.

"I thought about that. The problem is we'd have to pull some serious strings to get the manifest—I think it might even be against the law to give out that kind of information—and I don't see how we could keep something like that from the skipper."

They sat in glum silence.

"My brain hurts from thinking," Teddy said. "Maybe we should go to the skipper with this."

"You're giving up already?"

"I don't know what else we can do. It's better than leaving Somers out there with that guy."

"We don't know for sure that she's with him. We should at least find that out before we give up and tell the skipper."

"And how do we do that?"

"We can try her landlady again. Last time we were there, we didn't ask her much after we found out that Ellie had left. Maybe she saw something."

"Maybe," Teddy said, but his tone was dubious.

"You have any better ideas?"

Teddy rapped with his knuckles on his skull. "Empty. Hear the echo?"

"Let's go, then."

It took less than five minutes to reach the house. When the same woman answered their knock, Sam greeted her. "Hi, we came by to see you a few days ago . . ."

She stood in the wedge of the screen door, almost as if blocking their entrance. "I remember. You were asking about Ellie Somers."

"That's right," Sam said. "We were wondering if we could ask you a couple more questions."

"Tell me again why you wanted to know?"

"We're friends of hers, and we're trying to find her."

"If you're friends of hers, why didn't she tell you where she was going?"

Teddy stepped forward and spoke. "As you can probably tell, we're with the Coast Guard, and after she . . . um . . . left, she didn't feel comfortable around us, but I have a picture of me and her together, so you'll know we were friends." Teddy dug out his wallet and extracted a snapshot. In the picture Ellie had him in a headlock, and they were both grinning.

The landlady took the picture and squinted at it. "Some friend— looks like she's trying to strangle you," she observed as she handed the picture back, but she stepped out onto the stoop, letting the screen door shut behind her. She fished a pack of cigarettes from her pocket, shook one out, and lit it. "I'm sorry about being so suspicious, but since you came by, there have been some other people around asking about her."

"Did they say who they were?"

"They said they were something to do with the Coast Guard."

Teddy and Sam exchanged looks. It must have been someone investigating the sabotage.

"Did you remember anything when you were talking to them?"

"No. Nothing more than what I told you last time. I wish I could help. I've got some mail of hers, but she hasn't called for it, and like I told you, she didn't let on to me anything about where she might be going."

"We wanted to ask you if she was with anyone when she came by that night."

The woman took a drag on her cigarette. "She came up to the door by herself, but now that I think back, the car was still running as I was talking to her, so there must have been someone with her."

"Are you sure she didn't leave it running?"

"I stayed out on the stoop to smoke, and I saw her get in on the passenger side, so yes, I'm sure she was with someone. Besides, I don't think it was her car. Didn't she drive some kind of truck?"

"Yes," Teddy said.

"See, this wasn't a truck. I remember noticing it because this car was a convertible, and I thought that was strange—someone with a convertible around here."

"Thank you. What you've told us helps," Sam said. "It helps a lot."

"If you find her, tell her that I've been keeping her mail."

"We will."

As they returned down the walk, Sam said, "That answers it. She went with him. I guess you're right this time, Teddy. We should probably tell the skipper. I can't think what else we can do."

"There's one thing," Teddy said.

"What?"

"I just remembered, I saw the car too, and she's right, it was a convertible. We know he doesn't live here, so he must have rented it."

"Can you rent a convertible here?" Sam said.

"Worth a shot at the rental place anyway, wouldn't you say? In fact, my favorite bartender's brother works down at Allstar. He'll help me out if he can."

Half an hour later, Teddy returned to where Sam sat waiting in the truck.

"So?" Sam asked as he climbed in.

"The bartender's brother was there—Tony. Great guy. I told him that I beat a guy in a poker game, and he skipped town without paying me. I said I was trying to track him down, and I didn't know anything about him except that he'd been driving a convertible. Easiest thing in the world. Tony remembered him. Who's gonna forget a guy renting a convertible here? He went and got me a photocopy of his rental application, complete with driver's license. His name is Nicolas Andreakis."

"Where does he live?"

"Guess," Teddy said.

"I don't want to guess. I want you to tell me."

"You're no fun. He lives in Las Vegas. Okay?"

When Sam didn't reply, Teddy said, "Well, what do you think?"

"I think we could hop a flight to Seattle and get a connection to Vegas from there," Sam replied.

"What? Tonight?"

"Why not?"

"Because . . . because we need to put in for leave, and we need to let the skipper know where we're going."

"We'll put in for leave, but we're not going to say anything about where we're going. What do you think the skipper would say if we told him? You think he'd say, 'You and Teddy are headed down to Vegas together at the last minute? Nothing to do with that little matter we discussed a few days ago, of course. I think that's great, go ahead.' You think he'd say that?"

"Nooo," Teddy said. "But we don't even know for sure that's where they went. They could have gone anywhere."

"That's true, but even if they're not there, someone might know where he is."

"What are the chances of that?"

"Better than our finding him by hanging around here."

"Yeah, but . . ."

"But what?"

"If someone tries to contact us, and we're not around, we could get into some serious trouble."

"I don't believe it—Theodore McDonald being cautious."

"I like my job," Teddy defended himself.

"Ellie liked hers too," Sam said.

CHAPTER 36

"Good Lord, it's hot. You know, I thought I'd do anything to get out of that rain, but rain is sounding pretty good right now," Teddy said.

"Find it yet?" Sam asked.

"No. I give up." Teddy tossed the map over his shoulder into the backseat of the car. "I can't find this place anywhere on the damn map. What if it doesn't exist? What if he put down a false address on his driver's license to throw us off? You didn't think of that, did you?"

"I did, actually. I called information and checked." Sam eyed the flat, empty desert that stretched out on either side of the road. "It's out here somewhere."

"Maybe it is, but I still think we should have stayed in Sitka and tried to phone first," Teddy insisted.

"And risked scaring him off?"

"We could have pretended to be one of those annoying solicitation calls."

"Calling from the Sitka area code? Don't you think that would be a little suspicious?"

"How could he tell?"

"We couldn't take the chance he has one of those call-identifier things."

"I think you can sign up for some service that blocks that," Teddy said.

"We're here, all right? So why don't we stop arguing about whether or not we should have come."

There was a gas station up ahead on the right, and Sam pulled into it.

"What are you doing?" Teddy said.

"I'm going to ask."

"We've asked in three places already."

"I'm going to ask again." Sam got out of the car but then leaned over and said, "You want anything?"

"Get me a ginger ale." He watched Sam walk toward the store, then he called out the window, "And some Twinkies if they have them."

Teddy pulled his head back into the car and wiped his forehead with his sleeve. He recovered the map from the backseat, and when Sam returned, he was using it as a makeshift fan.

"Hey, I finally found what this thing is good for."

Sam dropped a bag through the window onto Teddy's lap, then rounded the car, got in, and started the engine.

"So are we going to drive around aimlessly for another couple of hours?" Teddy said.

"That sounds like fun, but I've got a better idea."

"Yeah?"

"Why don't we find Ellie?"

Teddy threw his hands up. "Brilliant. I knew you were a genius. So where is this place? Mars?"

"The attendant says two miles back," Sam said.

"I'd swear we haven't passed anything for twenty miles."

"It's a dirt road, unmarked. Easy to miss."

"Tell me something I don't know. And where's the house?"

"Another fifteen miles down that road," Sam said. "And from what this guy says, it's more like a palace."

"I guess the drug trade pays pretty good."

"He seemed to know a lot about it, and I found out that the place doesn't belong to Nicolas Andreakis."

"Great, so we came down for nothing."

"It belongs to Alexi Andreakis. His father."

"Did this gas station guy happen to know if the son is home for a visit?" Teddy asked, half sarcastic, half hopeful.

"No, but he did know that there's some big party there tonight. His niece works for the catering company they use, and if I had to guess, I'd say there's a good chance that our man will be there."

"And where he is—hopefully Somers is too."

"Hopefully," Sam echoed, but there was a catch in his voice as he said it.

Teddy looked over at him but tactfully let it pass. "So what now?"

"We go back to the city and buy a good pair of binoculars and some supplies. Then we come back and watch the road."

"Can we at least go back to the rental place and get a car with air-conditioning that doesn't feel like a tropical breeze?"

"We won't be able to keep the car running anyway. It would look strange, sitting there with the engine running. But it should be cooler at night."

"You're planning on spending the night?"

"You will too," Sam said. "That is, unless you're intending to walk back."

Ellie emerged cautiously from her room the next morning to find Nicolas lying on the sofa, just as usual. He was dressed in the slippers and cotton robe provided by the hotel, flicking through the channels on the TV.

"Good morning," he said when he spotted her.

"Unfortunately I can't agree with you there." She pressed a hand to one temple.

"I didn't wake you, did I?"

"Don't be stupid. It's," Ellie checked her watch, "it's afternoon. It's about time I got up."

She sat in the armchair, and there was a moment of silence. It was the first awkward silence she'd noticed between them in a long time. She thought of the conversation of the night before and felt her face getting hot again with embarrassment. Was he thinking of it too? Was that why he wasn't saying anything? Was he laughing at her? Or worse, pitying her?

She said the first thing that came to mind. "You been up long?"

"You could say that—I don't know that I ever properly went to sleep."

"You must be exhausted."

"I'm used to it. I'm a chronic insomniac."

She stared at him.

"That means I have trouble sleeping," he said.

"I *know* what it means. I just didn't take you for the type."

"What type is that?"

"Driven, uptight, ambitious."

"You mean like you," he said.

"Very funny," she smirked. "But I don't have trouble sleeping. Waking up, that's another thing, and speaking of, where's the coffee?" He'd had coffee waiting for her since discovering she couldn't face the morning without at least three big mugs, though he couldn't resist teasing her about substance abuse. He, of course, didn't drink caffeine.

"I ordered it ages ago. I'll call them," he said, starting to swing his legs off the couch.

"No, don't. I'm sure it will be here soon."

"You sure?"

"I won't go into caffeine withdrawal convulsions for another, oh, twenty minutes or so."

He lay back down and, picking up the remote, he said, "You mind if I turn this up for a second? I want to hear the news."

"You don't have to ask me—it's *your* room," she said.

He aimed the remote, but instead of turning up the sound, he turned the TV off. "What's wrong?"

She answered his question with a question. "How much did I lose last night?" She remembered the sense of willful destruction. When she started losing, it was like she couldn't get rid of it fast enough.

"Maybe we should wait until the coffee comes? Or should I get you something stronger?"

"You can tell me," she said. "I'm not some delicate, pampered female who needs to be coddled."

"I know you're not that." He smiled at the incongruity of the image.

"So spit it out. How much did I lose?"

"I don't know exactly—"

"Then approximately," she cut in, starting to think that he was drawing it out on purpose. Was it possible that he was enjoying this?

"All right. Approximately one-fifty, one-sixty."

"Hundred thousand?"

"Yes. Around there. Maybe a little more."

"How much more?"

"Ten, fifteen thousand at most."

"So one hundred and seventy-five thousand?"

He looked at her. "Are you all right?"

"How am I going to pay you back almost two hundred thousand dollars when I don't have a job, and I don't have any prospects for one? Hell, I'll be lucky if I get minimum wage."

"Don't worry about it—"

"Don't give me any crap about how I don't have to pay it back," she interrupted him.

"I wasn't going to," he said.

That silenced her.

"I was going to say that it's not as if I expect you to turn around and pay me back tomorrow, and I'm not going to crush you with crazy interest or anything."

Ellie realized she hadn't even thought about interest.

"But I have some good news—something that might go part of the way to solve your problem. I was starting to tell you last night, but then it didn't seem like the best time."

The embarrassment, forgotten in the shock of how much she had lost, came flooding back. "I'm sorry about that. I was really out of it. Someone should tape my mouth up when I've had that much to drink."

"Don't worry about it."

"I'm going to have to start making a list to remember all the stuff I shouldn't worry about."

"Like I started to say, there's something that you could do that—"

Nicolas was interrupted by a knock at the door. He glanced up.

"Breakfast, I guess. It's about time." Then he called out, "Come in."

The door didn't open. Instead, the knock came again. Nicolas heaved himself off the sofa, disappeared down the short hallway, and Ellie heard him saying, "Why didn't you just come—" when he stopped abruptly in mid-sentence. Then, "What the hell are *you* doing here?"

Ellie looked up. At first, she couldn't figure out what was wrong because all she saw was the front end of the cart, but then she saw the person who was pushing it, and it wasn't one of the hotel staff. The man who stepped into the room was dressed in a suit that even Ellie, knowing as little as she did about clothes, could tell was expensive. The man was taller even than Nicolas, with wide powerful shoulders and black hair streaked with gray.

"Who is he?" Ellie asked Nicolas when he reappeared.

The man hadn't noticed Ellie. Now he gave her a look that swept from head to toe and back again, then glanced back at Nicolas.

"Aren't you going to introduce us?" he said to Nicolas.

Nicolas shrugged. "If you insist. This is Ellie. Ellie . . . this is my father."

Nicolas's father looked around the room, noting the dirty dishes on the coffee table, the scattered newspapers, Nicolas's battered sneakers, and a pair of Ellie's socks, and then came to rest again on Ellie herself, sitting motionless in the chair. "Call me Alexi. I'm sorry for barging in on you like this."

Ellie didn't think he looked very sorry, but she said, "Don't worry about it."

"Can I pour you some coffee?" he offered, still ignoring his son.

"Sure."

"How do you take it?"

"She likes it with milk, no sugar," Nicolas said, passing his father and perching on the arm of the sofa.

Alexi poured, and Ellie got up and received the cup. "Thank you."

Alexi poured another cup and held it out to Nicolas. "Black for you."

Ellie noticed that when he spoke to his son, his lips seemed to tighten around the words, as if he had to force the pleasantries out.

"He doesn't drink coffee," Ellie informed him.

"You must be joking. The only solid food he eats is coffee. That's the way he likes it—practically solid it's so strong. Don't tell me my son doesn't drink coffee."

"I don't . . . anymore," Nicolas said.

"And now you're going to tell me you've given up smoking and drinking too?"

"It's been a long time—" Nicolas started to say.

"You don't need to tell me that. Take the damn coffee."

"No thank you. No coffee for me."

"Reformed?" Alexi said with raised eyebrows that suggested, at least to Ellie, skepticism if not outright disbelief.

Alexi took a sip from the cup he'd been holding out to Nicolas. "Don't try to convince me you've given it all up and gone the straight and narrow because I know better."

"No, you're right. I'm still your same old useless son," Nicolas said with a smile.

"If useless were the worst of it, I'd consider myself lucky."

Ellie was watching the exchange, and she saw that Nicolas's smile faded at his father's words, but when he caught Ellie looking at him, he tried to summon it up again.

"I came by because I need to speak to you," Alexi announced abruptly. "I'm sure you're well aware about what." He fixed Nicolas with a hard look, then shot back his cuff and checked his watch. "We won't go into it now because I've got a meeting, and I'm having people to the house this evening. I'll send the car for you at six, and I expect you to look presentable." Tilting his head back, he drank the cup of coffee in one long swallow. When he turned to Ellie, instead of the hard, impassive face he had shown his son, he was smiling. He set down the cup and took a couple of steps to where she sat, holding out his hand. She took it, but instead of shaking it he held on, covering it with his other hand, and fixing her with eyes that were just as dark and intense as his son's. "I look forward to seeing you this evening as well."

"You didn't even ask her if she wanted to come," Nicolas said. "She might not want to."

"Of course she wants to come." Alexi's eyes were still fixed on hers. "Don't you?"

Ellie didn't know how to respond. She had the feeling that Nicolas wanted her to decline the invitation, but she found that Alexi had put the question in such a way it was almost impossible to say no. She compromised, saying, "I'm afraid I didn't bring anything presentable to wear."

"Don't be silly. You don't have to worry." He paused and turned to Nicolas. "But you do. You should worry."

When Ellie heard the door close behind Alexi, she turned to look at Nicolas, but he was over by the cart, calmly retrieving his breakfast. She watched as he took the plate full of food and a glass of orange juice over to the coffee table. He set them down, then sat and fixed his eyes on the television.

She got up and refilled her coffee, took a croissant, and returned to the armchair. Nicolas didn't even look at her.

His silence was formidable, like a wall he had erected to discourage questions, but she asked one anyway. "Do you know what he wants to talk to you about?"

"Maybe," he replied, still staring at the television.

She took a bite of the croissant and wiped her fingers on her shirt. "It's the money, isn't it?"

This time he looked at her with a strange expression she couldn't interpret.

"If you want, I'll talk to him," she said. "Tell him it wasn't all you. I lost a good chunk of it."

"Just stay away from him. I'll handle it."

"But I want to help. I feel responsible."

"You can help by staying away from him." He looked down at his untouched food, then added, "And by not sleeping with him. That would help."

Ellie almost laughed, but he looked so serious that she managed to hold it back. "Okay. I won't sleep with your father."

He nodded.

She wanted to jolt him out of that blank stare, so she said conversationally, "How many of your girlfriends *has* your father slept with?"

"Seven."

"You're joking, right?"

"I wish I were."

She was shocked into silence. Then she managed to ask, "But . . . why?"

"Why does he do it, or why do they?"

"I don't know. Both, I guess."

"Well, you could get into the whole psychological thing with my father—like a reverse Oedipal complex or something, but if you ask me, it's simple. He does it because he can—to show me he can do just about anything better than I can."

"Why do they go along with it, the women?"

He shrugged. "You'd have to ask them that."

"Sounds like you're dating the wrong women."

"Now that's insightful."

"Sorry."

There was a small silence.

"He married one of them," Nicolas said.

She looked up and found, to her surprise, that he was smiling. "One of your girlfriends?"

"Yes, one of my girlfriends."

"Is he still married to her?"

Nicolas's smile widened. "No. It didn't last long, though it was memorable for all that."

"I'm guessing it wasn't true love."

"No. Not true love."

"Did he get her pregnant?"

"Oh, that's happened before. He wouldn't marry a woman just because of that."

"Then why?"

Nicolas laughed. "Because I was engaged to her."

It was so unexpected that Ellie didn't know what to say for a minute. "I don't see what's funny about that," she said finally.

"Then I'll tell you what's funny about that. I wasn't really engaged to her. I just pretended to be, and Alexi fell for it hook, line, and sinker. She made my father miserable for a solid six months, though in front of me he pretended that it was marital bliss."

"Did you tell him . . . ?"

"Of course I told him. Where's the fun if he doesn't know? He filed for divorce an hour later, but it cost him a small fortune to get rid of her. Now he's a lot more cautious. He managed to avoid the hooker I pretended to be dating who also happened to have the clap, but I think it was a close thing."

"You didn't," Ellie said, starting to laugh.

"The hell I didn't. And I could tell his brain was working overtime trying to figure you out."

"What's to figure out?"

"You don't fit the profile."

"Not pretty enough?"

He shot her a disgusted look. "No, that's not what I meant. No, you don't fit because usually—for some reason—I tend to pick them dumb and flashy."

"For some reason," she scoffed. "You mean for a very specific reason."

"What reason?"

"You know exactly what the reason is. You pick them dumb and flashy—and safe."

"Safe?"

"Playing it safe all the way," she nodded sagely. "No danger of your father stealing something that you cared about. No danger of getting hurt. What do you say to that?"

When he spoke, his voice was soft, almost gentle. "You could hurt me."

She felt as if her heart stopped for a second, then started beating again, faster than it should have. "How could I hurt you?" she said, trying to sound normal and, she suspected, failing.

"Now you're playing dumb. Just like my other girlfriends."

"But I'm not your girlfriend."

"I know." He paused, and she thought he was about to add something. He must have changed his mind because he stood abruptly, saying, "I've got to do some errands before we go tonight. Could you be ready by six? My father has a thing for punctuality."

"Your father," she said, "has a thing for your girlfriends."

"And I indulge him in those two things, and those two things only," he replied, moving toward the door to his room. He delivered his parting shot over his shoulder. "And, as you pointed out, you're not my girlfriend."

"Thank God for small blessings," she shouted after him.

About an hour after Nicolas left, a package was delivered to the room. Ellie was watching TV while doing sets of push-ups on the floor next to the coffee table. She'd started doing push-ups when she was fifteen and bone skinny, having read somewhere that you need to be strong to fly jets. In the course of time she had switched her sights from jets to helos, but she hadn't given up the push-ups or the belief that the extra strength was an advantage. She'd never managed to put any bulk on her thin frame, but by now she was so good at them she dipped and rose with an effortless swoop, as if her body were weightless. She didn't think about the fact that the whole reason for doing the push-ups was now gone.

Her nose was brushing the carpet when the knock came at the door.

Ellie abandoned the push-up and knelt, brushing her hands on her jeans. Her first thought was that it was Nicolas's father back again. She approached the door warily and called out, "Who is it?"

"Hotel service. I have a package for you."

She opened the door cautiously and saw a bellboy holding a flat rectangular box.

"Are you Ellie?"

She nodded, signed for it, then took the box back into the room. It had a note taped to the lid, but all it had written on it was her first name and the room number scrawled hurriedly. She removed the cover of the box and lifted out a dress.

So that was the errand that Nicolas had to do, she thought, smiling. The dress didn't look like much—it was black and very plain, with a high neck and a low back—but it had been thoughtful of him, and it was certainly more suitable than the stuffy black wool, which would have been her only other option.

She draped it over her arm and headed into her room to shower. She washed her hair, then almost panicked when she realized she didn't have a razor. She found one in the complimentary basket, underneath the shower cap, but she left a lake-sized puddle on the floor of the bathroom retrieving it. Then she dried off, applied deodorant, brushed her hair and twisted it into a knot, and slipped into the dress. She stared at herself in the mirror. She'd thought it was a rather plain dress, but it didn't look plain on. She'd certainly never looked like this in her flight suit.

The neckline was straight across and reached almost to her throat. Spaghetti straps arched over her shoulders and were attached to fabric along the side. She turned around to look at the back and stared, this time in horror. She immediately started to take it off. There was no way she was going to go out wearing a dress like that.

Then she paused, wondering if Nicolas had known when he picked it out that it was cut so low in the back, it was virtually impossible to wear anything underneath. Had he known how much would show? She concluded that most likely he had, which made the dress tantamount to a challenge.

It was five forty-five when she emerged from her room, and she found Nicolas waiting, stretched out on the couch as usual. He looked like the same Nicolas, but different at the same time. He was dressed in a tuxedo, pressed and crisp, the lines in the pants like a razor's edge. He looked wealthy and assured and incredibly good-looking. In the last week she'd almost gotten used to him, but now she felt intimidated all over again.

"You look . . . nice," she said.

"Thanks." He squinted at her. "So do you. Have I seen that dress before?"

"Ha ha, very funny."

"What's funny?" He looked genuinely confused.

"You picked it out."

"I did? When?"

"This afternoon. I mean . . . it was delivered to the room this afternoon and there was no note, so I thought . . ."

"My father," Nicolas said.

"Your father," Ellie echoed, with sudden understanding.

"He's shown remarkable restraint. It's certainly not as revealing as I would have expected."

She took a step backward, toward her room. "I'd better change."

"Why? You look great."

"I just need to." She took two more backward steps and her heel hit the wall.

"Hold on a second."

She froze.

"Turn around," he directed her.

She hesitated, then turned reluctantly.

"Holy—"

She spun back around, feeling the blood start up again in her cheeks. Nicolas began to laugh. Ellie retreated down the hall, yanked open her door, and stalked through, slamming it behind her.

She was rummaging through her duffel bag when she heard the door open. She ignored it and continued to pull out clothes, strewing them all over the floor. She found the black wool crumpled into a ball at the bottom. She pulled it out and tossed it on the bed.

"Do you mind?" she said, turning to face him.

He was looking at the black wool. "Is that what you're going to wear?"

"Yes, it's what I'm going to wear. What's wrong with it?"

He looked at it. "Um . . ."

"What?"

"Well, it looks like something you'd wear to a funeral."

"That's because my mother bought me this dress to wear to my uncle's funeral. I didn't have much use for dresses at the air station," she informed him.

Nicolas glanced at his watch. "Could I ask you a big favor? Before you said you wanted to help. Well, tonight might be tricky for me and anything that might help put my father in a better mood . . ."

She *had* said she wanted to help.

"Fine," she snapped. "I'll wear the dress, but only if you keep your big mouth shut."

His lips started to twist into a smile, but he pulled his face into a mock serious frown. "I promise. No wise . . . cracks," and he broke into a grin.

She leveled a finger at him. "You want me to change into the funeral dress?"

"I'll be good." He managed, though with considerable difficulty, to keep a straight face.

"You owe me for this. Big time."

"We're going to be late," he said with exaggerated mildness.

"You first."

He obeyed, leading the way out into the corridor. There was no one in the elevator when it arrived, but when it reached the lobby, there was nothing for it but to leave the protection of the wall and follow Nicolas out. She could sense the heads turning as she passed by.

"I feel like everyone's staring at me," she whispered.

"They are," Nicolas whispered back. "Because you look fantastic."

The car was waiting outside, and she slid in with a sigh of relief. Nicolas climbed in beside her.

"Thank God that's over," she said.

"What's wrong with a little honest admiration? Most women enjoy it."

Ellie kept her head turned away from him, gazing out the window at the neon lights of the Strip, cheap and garish in the daylight. "There's nothing wrong with honest admiration," she said. "Only I'm used to doing something to earn it."

"This detective thing sucks," Teddy said, and Sam, for once, didn't contradict him. They had been sitting in the car for several hours, a couple hundred yards away from the turnoff, staring out over the scrub brush and packed earth. The air was so dry it seemed to suck the moisture right out of them. Consequently, the backseat was littered with bottles—all with a single swallow of liquid still in the bottom—alongside the silvered insides of candy wrappers.

"In the movies, we'd only have to wait about five minutes for Somers to show," Teddy said.

"At least there's some activity," Sam responded.

"Sure, we've seen half a dozen delivery vans, and now we've got the limo parade. I've never seen so many rich people in one place before."

"They tend to hang out together," Sam said.

"The richest guy I ever knew was a kid I grew up with. His father owned a bunch of strip clubs in Minneapolis, but they weren't limo rich. They were only Cadillac rich. Guess that isn't the same league."

"I picked up a rich guy once on a SAR," Sam said. "We got a call that he was getting pain in his chest and down his arm, so we went out and picked him up, right off his yacht. The ambulance was waiting when we got back, took him to the hospital, but they tested him and didn't find anything wrong. We didn't think anything of it until a different story made its way back to us a few weeks later. One of the crew of the yacht told someone, and they told someone, and so on, until it got to a Coastie. This guy had been taking a weekend cruise on his yacht when the engine crapped out halfway into the trip. It wasn't really a problem because they could just sail it back in, but there wasn't much wind, and the owner was worried he wasn't going to make it back for some meeting on Monday morning. He told the captain to call the Coast Guard to come and get him, but the captain said that he couldn't do that. He tried to explain to the man that the Coast Guard was only for emergencies. I guess he explained too well because an hour later he got the message that the owner had pains in his chest and down his arm. The captain had his doubts, but he couldn't take the chance that it wasn't real, so he called us in. We were just a glorified taxi service for this guy. It was like he thought he was different—more important—than regular people, and the rules didn't apply to him."

"Hey, no offense, but wake up," Teddy said. "The rules *don't* apply to them. You can buy almost anything if you have enough money."

"That's what they want you to think, but you can't buy anything that's really worth having. Give me a nickel for every unhappy little rich kid, and I'd be rich too."

"I don't know. I'd be willing to give it a try. I think I could be rich and happy."

"Maybe you could, but you're not rich now, right?"

Teddy snorted, "Hardly."

"But you're happy for all that. If you suddenly won the lottery, what would you change? Would you quit your job? Move to Florida and start playing golf? Would you start going to parties in your limo?"

"Okay, you have a point. I don't see it happening." Teddy bent and rummaged around at his feet, then said, "You got any water left?"

"Didn't you buy a six-pack of Coke? Did you drink the whole thing already?"

"No, but it's warm now."

Sam sighed. At the time he had questioned the wisdom of Teddy only buying soda, but now he managed to refrain from saying, I told you so. He handed over his bottle of water.

Teddy unscrewed the cap and took a grateful slug. Another limo turned down the road, and they both followed its progress until all they could see was the cloud of dust from the wheels.

"You know what's weird?" Teddy said. "The idea of Somers at this party—that she's hanging out with these people, like she's one of them. I can't seem to get my head around that."

"I know what you mean."

"She might have been in one of those limos that went by, for all we know. She could be in that one," Teddy gestured to yet another car heading up the drive, tinted windows shut tight. "She could leave in one too, and we'd have no clue."

"I know," and Sam raised the binoculars as if he could see through the darkened windows.

In fact, it was only a few minutes later that the limo carrying Nicolas and Ellie turned down the dirt road leading up to the house.

Once in the limo, it didn't take long to get out of the city; ten minutes and they were surrounded by desert. The sun had just dipped below the mountains to the west, and the remaining light was shading softly into evening. There was a husky quality to the desert twilight that made Ellie want to hold her breath. This wasn't something you could see from a hotel room, with all that blinding neon burning day and night.

When they turned onto a two-lane road headed west, the partition between their portion of the limo and the driver rolled down.

"Yes? What is it?" Nicolas asked.

"I wanted to say hello," the driver said, glancing quickly over his shoulder, and Ellie caught a glimpse of a beaky profile, sparse tufts of white hair, and leathery, age-spotted skin.

"Anthony? Why didn't you let me know it was you up front? How are you?"

"Can't complain. Can't complain."

"You never would complain anyway," Nicolas said. "What are you doing picking us up? Doesn't my father need you at the house to get ready for the party?" Nicolas turned to Ellie. "My father usually doesn't let Anthony farther away than the next room, in case he might need him for something. I don't remember a time when Anthony wasn't around. He used to run interference between me and Alexi."

"What do you mean 'used to'?" Anthony said.

"Point taken. So why did he send you? Did he think I might try to duck out, and he wanted you to make sure I showed up?"

"No. I asked if I could come pick you up."

"You did?"

"I told your father that I needed to go into town."

"And he bought that?"

"Probably not, but he didn't say anything."

"So why did you come?" Nicolas said.

"I wanted to prepare you for tonight—give you some warning. Your father is very angry with you about something. I wanted to find out for you what it is, but I thought it was best not to try."

"It's all right. I know what it is."

"Did you do something you shouldn't have?" Anthony said, his voice somehow containing both amusement and rebuke.

"That's the story of my life. So you say he's really angry?"

"I haven't seen him this worked up in years."

"Good," Nicolas said, but watching him, Ellie thought he looked uneasy if not outright nervous.

Anthony slowed the car and turned from the two-lane highway onto a narrower, rougher road, and then onto a packed dirt road marked with a sign that said PRIVATE ROAD. NO TRESPASSING. They passed through several miles of sand and scrub before Ellie spotted a house in the distance. About a quarter-mile from the house, they passed abruptly from sand to thick grass. Tall, thin palm trees flanked the last hundred yards.

"Good luck," Anthony said as a uniformed man opened the car door for them. There was another man to open the front door as well. Nicolas and Ellie were directed to go through the house to the back patio. As they passed through, Ellie took note of the fountain in the hallway and the vaulted glass ceiling above.

"Did you grow up here?" she asked Nicolas.

"I spent vacations here," he said. "But I mostly did my growing up elsewhere."

Beyond the patio there was a gentle slope of lawn and a pool filled with hundreds of floating candles. The party was already in full swing, there was a string quartet playing and waiters circulating among the clusters of guests. She saw immediately that the dress wouldn't be a cause for attention here—every woman she saw was more scantily clad than the last.

"Ready to mingle?" Nicolas asked her.

"I guess."

He must have heard the uncertainty in her voice because he said, "Don't worry. Nobody's going to expect you to talk or anything."

She laughed. She thought he was trying to be funny, but it wasn't long before she realized that he wasn't joking. She smiled and nodded when it was called for, but mostly she listened to endless talk about the business of shipping. There was always another woman across from her, on the arm of the man Nicolas was in conversation with, but they never spoke to Ellie, and she couldn't think of anything to say to them.

After about twenty minutes—which felt like an hour—they spotted Nicolas's father on the other side of the pool. Alexi saw them at the same time and beckoned them over.

"I should warn you," Nicolas said through a teeth-clenching grin. "My father loves an audience. It's easiest if you just go with it."

"All right," she agreed.

"Hold on tight, here we go," Nicolas muttered and led the way.

"Here he is, my son," Alexi's voice boomed out across the crowd as they approached. "A lot of people might say he's lazy, but that's not true. He works very hard . . . at spending my money."

There was a smattering of laughter from the crowd.

"So much money, so little time," Nicolas replied as they reached Alexi.

"He doesn't even buy anything with it. He loses most of it gambling, and he does it on purpose, you know," Alexi said to Ellie, but still loud enough for those around them to hear. His voice lost its joking tone and turned hard. "He does it to piss me off."

At that, the guests standing closest seemed to melt away until the three of them formed a small island, alone in the sea of people.

"He doesn't just lose randomly, like most of us," Alexi continued. "Have you ever noticed that?"

"I don't think—" Ellie started to say, but Alexi cut her off.

"No, it's not random. He loses systematically. I have to give him credit—he's phenomenal with numbers. Six decks, and he counts the cards. It's such a waste. He's got a brain like a fucking computer, underneath all that attitude. He could make money without even half trying."

"I've watched him play—"

"You mean watched him lose."

"I've watched him play and lose," Ellie said. "It didn't look to me like he was counting cards."

"Haven't you noticed that when he makes his largest bets, he invariably loses. He never ups the ante on any really strong hand. You see, he counts the cards, and then he makes his big bets on the hands where he knows the odds are against him." He must have seen the disbelief on Ellie's face because he said, "You don't believe me? Ask him yourself, then."

Ellie turned to Nicolas.

Nicolas rocked back onto his heels and tilted his head to look up at the sky. "I like to think of it as an act of faith."

His father snorted, and Ellie said, "What's that supposed to mean?"

"Isn't faith the triumph of hope over probability?"

"But you always lose," Ellie pointed out.

"Mmm. You've got me there. By the way," he turned to his father, "I need some more money."

Ellie saw Alexi's jaw flex, but then he forced a laugh. "How can I say no to my only son? But," and now his smile seemed genuine, "you will have to do something for it. I can't bring you up thinking that you don't have to work for what you get, can I?"

"Of course not," Nicolas said. "As long as it's not too strenuous."

"It's light work," his father assured him. "You can have as much money as you want . . . if you don't mind begging for it."

His voice was serious, but then he broke into a chuckle, and Nicolas laughed with him. Ellie almost laughed as well, with relief. It was a joke, she thought—a sick one, but still a joke.

But it wasn't. Ellie watched, horrified, as Nicolas lowered himself theatrically down on one knee, then on both. The people closest to them had been surreptitiously listening to the whole conversation, but now they forgot themselves and stared.

Alexi's eyes narrowed. "What do you think you're doing?"

"I'm begging," Nicolas said in a normal tone, and then in a voice that carried across the crowd, he said, "Father, I've spent all the money you gave me. Will you give me some more?"

Ellie could sense the heads turning.

"More? Did you hear him?" his father said to his guests. "He wants more. He's already wasted more than a small country's GDP." He turned back to Nicolas. "How much do you need?"

"Need?" Nicolas mocked the question.

"Want. How much do you want, then?" Alexi amended.

"Two or three."

"That's two or three million," Alexi announced. Then to Nicolas he said, "How long will it last you this time?"

Nicolas shrugged.

"Does anyone here think I shouldn't give my worthless son the money he wants?"

Ellie couldn't bear to look at Nicolas down on his knees, but watching the crowd was almost worse. Some people had the decency to look horrified, but a good many were smiling, and everyone was watching. No one else had turned away.

There was a moment of absolute silence, then Alexi said, "All right, you can have the damn money. Get up."

But Nicolas didn't get up right away. Instead, from his pose on his knees, he looked around at the people. "I don't know what you're all staring at," he said. "You're all doing the exact same thing here tonight—you're all here for my father's money. I'm just more honest about it." Now people turned away.

Alexi's abrupt, booming laughter made everyone nearby jump. He held his hand out to his son.

Nicolas took it, almost reluctantly, and his father hauled him up, and then pulled him into a one-armed hug. Ellie saw him whisper in Nicolas's ear, but she couldn't hear what he said.

Then Alexi released him, and Nicolas stumbled backward.

"My son," Alexi said, holding out his arm, as if presenting him to the crowd. "Who wouldn't be proud of him?"

Nicolas stood like a fighter who had taken a hit but was trying to keep his feet. He turned to her, as if for help, but she took a step back, then another, then she turned and fled.

Ellie pushed her way through the guests. She grabbed a drink from a passing tray and headed down the slope of the lawn. She stopped when she'd gotten a little way beyond the crowd to pry off her shoes. The grass felt cool and soft under her bare feet.

Ellie continued until she reached the place where the lawn met the desert, and she settled at the edge, her butt on the grass and her feet on the hard-packed sand. The border was a marvel, as straight as if it had been drawn by a ruler, one side green, the other brown. She wondered how they did it—did someone come and weed the edge to get it that straight?

The sounds of the party floated down to where she sat as if from miles away, and she could see the place where the city lay from the halo of light it cast above the horizon. She dug her toes in, scraping away at the hard crust of sand and thinking about Nicolas. What he'd done had disgusted her, but she knew she still shouldn't have left him.

She sat until the sounds of the party grew fainter, and finally all she could hear was the occasional hum of a passing car from the road. She didn't catch the sound of the approaching footsteps, muffled in that thick, green carpet—the first she knew of his presence was when he spoke.

"Are you enjoying my party?" Alexi asked.

She managed to hold in the jerk of surprise. "Not much," she admitted.

"You're supposed to say, 'Oh, I'm having a great time—it's a wonderful party.'"

"I'm sorry," she apologized automatically.

"You know what? I don't believe you. I don't believe you're a bit sorry," he teased her.

"Do you want me to tell the truth, or do you want me to lie? Make up your mind."

Her annoyance only seemed to amuse him more. "I guess I want the former, but I'm used to the latter."

"You're going to have to choose. You can't have both."

"The truth then," Alexi said.

"The truth? I don't think you should have given Nicki the money. Not even if he begged."

The charming smile disappeared and was replaced by a glare. "Young lady, you should stay out of things that aren't any of your business."

She turned away from him and stared out over the desert. After a moment, he stepped forward and lowered himself on the lawn beside her. He was the one who broke the silence.

He said, "May I ask you a personal question?"

"You can try."

"What are you doing with Nicolas?"

She hesitated, formulating her answer so she wouldn't have to recount the whole story. She explained it by saying simply, "He brought me down here as a sort of return favor. I helped him, now he's helping me."

"Nicolas doesn't do favors. Not even return ones." He must have read the look on her face because he said, "You don't have to believe me, but I am telling you the truth. While I'm at it, I'll tell you something else. Nicolas is headed for trouble. You'd be a whole lot better off with me."

Ellie made a noise deep in her throat that was halfway between "huh" and "ha." "Nicki told me that you'd hit on me."

He plucked at the grass and tossed the blades out into the sand. "Don't be offended. You should consider it a compliment."

"It's not a compliment. It's a track record," Ellie said.

Alexi gave a short laugh. "Not many people would talk to me that way, you know."

"That's too bad. Everyone needs to have someone give them a hard time every once in a while."

"I've got Nicolas. No one can come close to him for that. In fact, I've had about enough of it, as he's about to find out."

He pushed himself up off the grass. "May I walk you back up to the house? Nicolas might not have told you, but we still have business to conduct tonight. Since it's late, I've asked the housekeeper to make up a room for you."

When they reached the house, Ellie found that she had been down by the desert for longer than she'd realized. All the guests had gone. The staff were the only people left on the lawn, and they were busy breaking down tables, fishing the floating candles from the pool, and gathering trays of dirty glasses.

She followed Alexi inside to the vestibule with the vaulted glass ceiling, where he stopped. "If you'll wait here, I'll send someone to show you to your room and make sure you have everything you need." Then he gave a small nod and left her.

She stood there a few minutes, watching the staff cleaning the lawn. Then she started to look around her. Curiosity prompted her to venture out of the atrium and through the doorway where Alexi had disappeared. She found a sitting room furnished in a style that had to be called Louis the Fourteenth, or Tenth, or something like that. It looked like it belonged in a palace, and she couldn't imagine anyone sitting there by choice. She wandered through into the room beyond, and that's when she heard Alexi's muffled voice, loud and angry. Ellie could just make out the words, "Did you think I wouldn't find out? If so, you're not as smart as I thought. When you commission a special container, it's going to get back to me. I sent a message to you, almost two weeks ago—I warned you that my ship had better be clean when it gets into port. And now I find that you've done nothing about it."

"I'm working on it," Nicolas answered.

"Working on it! You'd better work fast, then."

"It's not easy getting to a ship that's somewhere in the middle of the Pacific."

"I don't care how hard it is. Get it done, or I'll make sure you go down for it."

A soft voice behind her said, "Excuse me, miss."

Ellie spun around and recognized the beaky profile of Anthony.

"Ellie. My name is Ellie."

"Yes," he smiled. "Mr. Andreakis asked if I would show you to your room. I'm sorry if I kept you waiting."

"That's all right. I haven't been waiting long." Ellie only wished it had been a little longer.

CHAPTER 44

A soft rap on the door of her room woke her the next morning. She'd barely raised her head from the pillow when Nicolas opened the door. He said, "Be ready to go in five," tossed a pair of jeans and a T-shirt on the floor, and disappeared. She groaned and rolled out of bed. The clothes were a little big, but they were certainly better than putting on the dress from the night before.

When she went downstairs five minutes later, the hallway was empty and the house was dark. She thought she heard the idle of an engine, and when she looked out a window to the front, she saw Nicolas in the driver's seat of a convertible Porsche—his father's, Ellie had to assume.

She opened the front door. The sun was low in the east, sending long arms of light stretching out along the sand, but even this early in the morning the breeze felt hot—especially after the chilly temperatures of the air-conditioned house.

She descended the steps and climbed into the car, a little worried that Nicolas might be angry at the way she had left him the evening before, but he greeted her with a bright "Good morning." Then he added, "Did you sleep well?"

"Yes, great thanks. How did your talk with your father go last night?"

"Horribly," he said with a grin.

"I'm sorry," she said. "But you don't seem upset."

"Nope."

"What are you so cheerful about this morning?"

"It's a new day, and I've planned a little surprise for you—to make up for dragging you to that awful party last night."

He put the car into gear and started off. At the end of the private road, he turned left instead of right.

"So we're not going back to the city?" she said.

"Who says we're not?"

"It doesn't take a genius to figure out that we're headed in the oppo-site direction. Where are we going?"

"I told you, it's a surprise."

She saw that she wasn't going to get anything out of him, so with an effort, she managed to hold back her questions for the rest of the ride. Half an hour later Nicolas slowed and turned down an access road, then into a parking lot in front of a sheet-metal hangar.

Ellie leaned forward to look at the sign over the door. It read, BOBBY'S SKYDIVING CENTER.

She glanced over at Nicolas.

He said, "Ready to have some fun?"

Ellie followed Nicolas into the reception room. One wall was lined with cubbies that held packs. Another wall had a row of laundry baskets filled with gear: helmets, goggles, jumpsuits. There were a couple of old couches and, in the corner, a desk.

"Hey, Bobby," Nicolas said to the woman sitting behind the desk.

Bobby looked up. She was somewhere between forty and fifty, with short blond hair and a lean, sunburned face. "Hey there, Nico. Haven't seen you in a while."

"Miss me?" Nicolas leaned an elbow on the counter.

"I missed your money."

"A little slow?"

"It tends to be slow over the summer, but it's starting to pick up now. I've got a full roster today."

"That's why I wanted to get here early. I was hoping I could get up before the crowd."

"Who's the whuffo?" Bobby jutted her chin at Ellie.

"Friend," Nicolas said briefly.

"Uh-huh." Bobby looked her up and down, and Ellie returned her stare. "You taking her up tandem?"

"I was thinking she'd jump on her own."

"She certified?"

"She's been up before." Nicolas turned to Ellie, "Haven't you?"

"Yes, I have." She'd done quite a few jumps when she was younger, before she had started flying.

"Anything to prove it?"

Nicolas answered for her. "Yes, as a matter of fact, I've got it right here."

Ellie turned to him, startled, and saw him taking out his wallet. He started counting bills onto the desk.

He paused. "Enough proof?"

"I think I'll need a little more," Bobby said, her eyes on the pile.

He started peeling off more, slowly placing them one by one on the growing stack. Finally Bobby said, "That's enough."

Nicolas stuck what was left back in his wallet and tucked it back in his pocket.

"She'll still have to sign the waiver—and you too. I can't have *enough* copies for you."

Bobby ducked behind the desk and reappeared with two sheets of paper. Nicolas signed his with a flourish and handed Ellie the pen. She stepped forward to sign.

Bobby whipped the sheets away and checked her watch. "You'd better go get your rigs. I'll tell the pilot."

"You haven't needed to borrow either of my rigs by any chance, have you?"

"The way you pack 'em? We'd have clients walking out of here black and blue where the straps grabbed them on the release."

"That means I don't have to repack the canopies."

"Good thing too 'cause you don't have time. As it is, you'd better move your ass if you want to go up before my first group." Then, suddenly serious, she said, "Hey, take it easy today, all right?"

"What's the fun of that?"

"If you hammer in, there's an awful lot of paperwork for me, not to mention what it would do to my business."

"And here I was, thinking you cared."

Fifteen minutes later they climbed into the Cessna. Then it took about twenty minutes to circle up to thirteen thousand feet. When they were almost at jump altitude, Nicolas leaned in close so Ellie could hear him over the noise of the engine. He said, "Let's make this interesting, shall we? You ever heard of a low pull contest?"

She hesitated, then nodded.

"Rules are simple. First person to go for their rip cord loses."

She turned, put her mouth to his ear, and said, "You're on."

The pilot called out, "You ready back there?"

"Sure are," he said. Then to Ellie, "You ready?"

"Ready."

He opened the plane door, and Ellie felt her heart pounding to a familiar rhythm.

Nicolas climbed out onto the strut under the wing, his hands on the wing support bar, and as soon as he was in place, Ellie climbed out after him, feeling the rush of the ninety-mile-per-hour wind whistling past and staring down at the brown carpet of desert spread out below. She sucked in a lungful of air and let out a laugh in the rush of excitement. She glanced over at Nicolas. His teeth were bared in a grin that looked to Ellie to be closer to pain than pleasure.

"READY . . ." Nicolas yelled.

"SET . . ."

"GO!"

They both let go of the wing support and fell into space.

Ellie arched her back, keeping her arms and legs evenly spread. The ground was a flat sandy expanse with spiderweb lines of road, impossibly far away.

She knew she was falling—she could hear the wind rushing by, and her ears were popping—but she had almost a feeling of being suspended. For a moment Ellie forgot the contest, she forgot that Nicolas was in the air beside her, she forgot everything. Shutting her eyes, she felt the pressure of the wind against her body. The sound of it was the only thing she could hear.

How long did she keep them closed? Ten seconds? Fifteen? It seemed to her just a flash, but when she opened her eyes again, she was startled by how much closer the ground had come. She could see the cars on the roads now, the sun glinting off the bumpers and windshields. The buildings were Monopoly-sized and not mere specks. She checked her altimeter and it showed that she was flashing past five thousand feet, the height at which most jumpers pulled their parachutes.

Ellie glanced over to check on Nicolas and found him almost exactly parallel to her, only twenty feet away. At a glance, she could tell he knew what he was doing. He was busy making tiny adjustments in his body position to keep his fall rate identical to hers.

She glanced at her altimeter again and saw that they had passed below four thousand feet. They were punching through a thousand feet approximately every six seconds. All she did was look over at Nicolas again and back at the altimeter, and it read three thousand.

She started to get a sense of her own speed. She was hurtling toward the ground at a hundred and twenty miles per hour. Now she could make out details in the landscape. She could see the scrub brush and the corrugated tin of the rooftops.

Another look showed her just shy of two thousand feet, where even the professional sky divers deployed their canopies. The sense of joy had evaporated and she was aware of a tightening in her stomach. Nicolas would deploy soon, she thought. Any time now—but when she looked over, it seemed like his arms were stretched out as if reaching for the earth, ready to embrace it.

A thousand feet.

The feeling of being suspended in air was gone. She was falling, rushing toward the ground, and the stretch of sand appeared to rise up as if to meet her. Ellie moved her hand to her rip cord, and out of the corner of her eye, she saw Nicolas do the same. She expected him to pull, but he didn't.

She was at the point that she could see the individual stalks of the long desert grass when she convulsively jerked the cord. The canopy deployed, and as it filled, she was jerked upright just in time for her to be able to land on her feet. The parachute had arrested free fall, but she still hit hard enough that her knees buckled, and she rolled to absorb the impact, ending up with a thud on her back.

She lay on the ground, motionless, staring up at the stretch of blue sky. Everything was almost unnaturally quiet now, and her breath sounded loud and ragged in her ears.

Ellie pushed herself up, her arms feeling shaky. Her red canopy spread across the sand in front of her, rippling in the slight breeze.

She stared at it, her mind a blank. Then she remembered Nicolas.

She twisted and saw the blue of his canopy about thirty feet behind her. She scrambled, half on her hands and knees, to the edge of it. She couldn't see him, but she thought she saw a lump beneath the settling folds. She grasped the edge of the fabric, but her courage failed her for a second. Then she started rolling back the canopy.

She said, "Nicki," but it came out as a whisper.

Ellie gathered up fabric by the armful until she finally reached him. She dragged the canopy to one side, dropped it, and got down on her knees. His face was turned toward her, and his eyes were open.

Oh God, she thought. He's dead.

Then he blinked.

 Ellie let out a half laugh, half sob.

Nicolas blinked again and his eyes focused on her. He muttered something.

"Don't try to talk. Just stay there. You're going to be okay," she said, though she had no idea if he was.

He closed his eyes for a second, then opened them again, and moved one arm.

"Don't—" but even as she was about to tell him not to move, he managed to flop over onto his back.

"Ellie." His voice was hoarse and low.

"I'm here," she bent over him. "Are you okay? Does it hurt? What is it?"

"I'm fine," and to prove it he pushed himself up into a sitting position. "I'm fine," he repeated.

"What can I do? Can I do anything? I can go call an ambulance. What do you want?"

He took an experimental breath. "Whiskey," he said. "I want a whiskey."

She sat back on her heels. "Whiskey?"

"If there's no whiskey, I guess I'd settle for vodka." He tried to get up, but groaned and instead held out a hand to be helped up.

"There's only one problem," she said, giving him a heave up to his feet.

He managed to stand, but he kept a steadying hand on her shoulder. "What's that?"

She grinned. "You don't drink."

■

Ten miles down the road they found a cluster of buildings, among them a gas station, a diner, a motel, and a bar. Though it was early, a neon sign in the window on the bar read OPEN.

When they entered, it took a moment for their eyes to adjust. The only light came from what managed to penetrate the cloudy windows, helped out by a TV that flickered silently in the corner behind the bar. The chairs were all still up on the tables from the night's cleaning— except for one, which was occupied. There was a man sitting at the bar, his hand curled possessively around a beer, watching their approach. When they reached the counter he called over his shoulder, "Mary. Comp'ny." Then he switched his attention back to the television.

A woman appeared through a door behind the bar, wiping her hands on a corner of her apron.

"Sorry, I'm doing some Sunday baking," the woman told them.

"Is it Sunday?" Nicolas said. "I hadn't realized."

"Comes around quick, doesn't it? Just take a couple of stools down and make yourselves comfortable. What can I get you?"

Nicolas ordered six whiskeys, saying that he would just order them now to keep from having to make her run back and forth. She nodded, as if that were the most natural thing in the world, set the glasses along the counter, and poured each one nearly to the brim. "You want me to leave you the bottle too?" she suggested. "You can keep track of how many you drink and let me know."

"That's an even better idea," Nicolas said. "I shouldn't have made you dirty all those glasses."

She waved it away. "What do you think dishwashers are for? Call me if you need anything." She turned to the other man at the bar. "Henry, you okay?"

He grunted.

"I'll bring you a biscuit when they're done," she said.

"Don't want a damn biscuit," the man muttered as she disappeared back through the door.

"Cheers." Nicolas raised his glass to Ellie with a smile, but she noticed that his hand was trembling slightly.

"Cheers," Ellie echoed his salute and tossed back the shot.

"I told you we were going to have some fun, right?" Nicolas moved another shot glass over in front of her and took one for himself.

"Yeah, fun," she said a little weakly. "How do you feel?"

"I feel pretty good. I'll probably be stiff tomorrow, but this should help." He picked up his second glass.

"I guess you do this sort of thing all the time," she said.

"Not all the time. Only on very special occasions."

"What's the special occasion?"

He looked at her. "You. You're the special occasion."

◼

They were well into the bottle when Ellie noticed a dartboard over on the far wall and challenged Nicolas to a game. She beat him soundly the first time, by a narrow margin in the second, and lost the third and fourth. It wasn't that he got better but that she got progressively worse. By the time they started the fifth, they found they could barely hit the target; the darts kept bouncing off the concrete wall. They abandoned the game when the proprietor emerged with a tray of biscuits. Henry's sat untouched in front of him, but Ellie and Nicolas ate four apiece.

Ellie had half a biscuit in her mouth when she said, "I want to ask you something," but it came out more like "Iwunasusmthn."

Nicolas laughed. "Is that a new language?"

She swallowed the biscuit and took a mouthful of the whiskey to wash it down. "I want to ask you something," she said again, though even without a mouthful of biscuit her speech wasn't quite clear.

He turned, his face very close to hers. She could smell the whiskey on his breath as he said, "Fire away."

"How did you pull that off this morning?" she asked.

"Pull what off?"

"Winning. How did you time it? I still can't figure it out."

He took the bottle and managed, with a relatively steady hand, to top off their glasses. He set down the bottle and said, "I didn't have it timed."

"What do you mean?"

"I wasn't going to pull until you did."

"And if I waited for you?"

"It would have been a tie."

Ellie felt a chill raise the hair on her arms. "You're lying."

He smiled a little at that.

"What's so funny?" she said, suddenly angry. "You crazy son of a bitch. You almost died out there today. I don't see what's funny about that."

He set his glass down hard on the counter. "I'm a crazy son of a bitch? What does that make you? Why do you assume I'm the only one who almost died? Let me tell you something. I've been doing this for ten years, and I have never seen someone pull that low. I thought it was over—for both of us. Tell you the truth, I was sure of it."

"Jesus," Ellie breathed. "Do you have a death wish or something?"

"No."

"But you're not afraid of dying?"

He fixed his gaze on the counter, working at a chip in the wood with a fingernail. Then he looked up at her and said, "There's nothing that terrifies me more."

CHAPTER 46

Nicolas and Ellie emerged from the bar, squinting in the hard afternoon light. They wandered over to the car, and Ellie stood with her hip propped against the hood. She could feel the hot metal through the fabric of her jeans.

"You're in no shape to drive," she said to Nicolas.

He stood without support, but not steadily. He shaded his eyes as if the light hurt them. "Neither are you," he pointed out.

They looked around aimlessly. Ellie noticed it first.

"Motel," she said, pointing across the deserted intersection.

"You're a genius. I could use a siesta."

They made their way across the street, into the registration office. An old man wearing suspenders over an undershirt sat in an ancient leather recliner with his eyes closed.

"I hate to wake him," Nicolas said.

"I don't," Ellie replied and rang the hand bell.

When the man opened his eyes and looked at them, it was obvious he hadn't been asleep at all. He heaved a sigh and pushed himself, with a bit of difficulty, out of his chair. Ellie could see where the seat was slick and shining with sweat. Who would use a leather armchair in the desert, she wondered.

The man picked a key off the board behind him and slapped it down on the counter. "Forty-nine, ninety-five." He eyed them up and down and added, "Cash."

"We'd like two rooms, actually," Nicolas said.

"That'll be one hundred even."

"Hey," Ellie protested. "That's not right. It should be ninety-nine dollars, ninety cents."

Nicolas reached for his wallet and sorted through the bills. "I only have eighty." He turned apologetically to Ellie, "I gave so much to Bobby, and then there were the drinks . . ."

"You got eighty, you get one room," the man said.

"I have a credit card," Nicolas offered.

The man didn't even blink. "Cash."

Nicolas looked at Ellie.

"What's the big deal," she said, reaching for the key.

Nicolas handed over the money.

"Which one is it?" Ellie asked.

"Number's on the key," the man said, returning to his chair.

Nicolas laughed and pulled Ellie out by the arm before she was able to reply.

CHAPTER 47

Sam and Teddy were in the motel's parking lot across the street when Ellie and Nicolas emerged from the bar. But for a lucky break, Sam and Teddy might still have been sitting by the turnoff. They had both been fast asleep when Nicolas and Ellie pulled out that morning. If Nicolas had turned right and headed back to the city, they would never have seen them, but he had turned left, and Sam, roused by the sound of the car, woke just in time to catch sight of Ellie's profile as the Porsche flashed by.

Sam had fired up the engine and pulled onto the road after them, slamming Teddy—who was sleeping soundly—hard against the passenger door. With the straight Nevada road, they had easily kept the car in sight without needing to stay too close. They had followed the Porsche to Bobby's Skydiving (though they hadn't witnessed the jump) and then to the bar . . . where they sat across the street, watching the entrance from the car. As the morning passed, the sun beat on the roof, bringing the heat inside the car to the level of an oven. They slumped down in their seats, sweaty and exhausted after almost twenty-four hours in the Pontiac. Teddy dozed, but this time Sam kept his eyes open. He saw when Ellie and Nicolas left the bar, and he shook Teddy's shoulder to wake him.

"Looks like they're about to move." Sam fitted the key into the ignition.

"Looks like they can barely move," Teddy observed, sitting up and stretching. "Holy shit." He froze as Nicolas and Ellie turned and looked directly—it seemed—at them.

"They're headed over here," Teddy whispered, out of the side of his mouth.

"I can see that," Sam whispered back.

"Shit, what do we do?"

"Just don't move," Sam said. "Don't do anything to draw attention."

Ellie and Nicolas made their way across the street, and when they passed, they were only a car length away, but neither of them even glanced toward where Sam and Teddy sat rigid and motionless. Sam watched in the rearview mirror as they disappeared into the office.

"Scrunch down in the seat," Sam said. He slid down as well, but reached up to adjust the rearview so he could see when they came out. He didn't have long to wait. A few minutes later Ellie and Nicolas emerged and walked along the concrete pathway to the last room at the end of the row. Ellie opened the door, they both disappeared inside, and the door swung shut.

"We're clear," Sam said.

"Where—?"

"The last room on the end."

"Oh." There was a short pause, then Teddy said, "Hey, I'm sorry."

"What for? They've been together in Vegas for more than a week."

"I guess, but when they're renting a motel room in the middle of the afternoon—"

"All right, now you can shut up," Sam said.

They were silent for a minute. Then Teddy spoke. "What do you think about renting a room so we can get cleaned up? I know I'm getting pretty ripe—and we can take turns keeping an eye on their room. We should have plenty of time—they'll probably be in there awhile."

"You're killing me, Teddy," Sam said.

"Shit. I didn't . . . I'm—"

"—sorry," Sam finished for him. "I know."

"I am. It's not fair. The chicks always go for the dangerous ones. Nice guys finish last."

"Who says I'm a nice guy?" Sam said.

"Come on, Commander."

Sam sighed. "Oh, screw it. I'll flip you for the first shower."

C H A P T E R   4 8

 When Ellie opened the door, her first thought was that the room smelled like a mix of stale cigarette smoke, disinfectant, and old sheets. Then she saw the queen-sized bed.

"We forgot to ask for twin beds," she said.

"We can go back," Nicolas offered.

"I'm too tired." Ellie crossed to the bed and collapsed on top of it.

"Hold on. Let me take the bedspread off," Nicolas said.

"I can't get up."

"They never wash that top cover, you know."

She groaned but managed to push herself up.

He pulled back the cover and the blanket underneath, and let them pool on the ground at the end of the bed. Ellie flopped back down and closed her eyes. She felt the mattress bend under his weight as he sat on the edge. When she cracked an eye open, she saw that he was taking off his shoes. She closed her eye again, and a second later she heard the creak of the bed as he lay down.

They lay there, side by side, in what felt to Ellie like dead silence.

When she couldn't stand it anymore, she opened her eyes and looked. Nicolas was lying there, staring back at her.

"What?" she said.

He smiled. "Nothing." He closed his eyes.

She waited for him to say something else. They were, after all, lying on a bed together. He made a noise, but it wasn't one she expected. She didn't believe it until it came again—Nicolas was snoring.

Annoyed, she rolled onto her side, away from him, but she wasn't able to stay angry long because, within minutes, she was asleep as well.

"Hey, Ellie. It's okay. Hey, it's all right."

Nicolas's voice pulled her out of her nightmare. Ellie's eyes flew open, her heart racing.

Nicolas had his arms loosely wrapped around her. "You're okay," he said again. She started to sit up, but he didn't let her. Instead he pulled her closer; her head was tucked underneath his chin, her nose pressed up against his shirt, smelling sweat and alcohol and what she recognized as his scent. He stroked her hair, murmuring, "I'm here. I'm here."

She sighed and wound her own arm around his waist, clutching a handful of T-shirt in one fist and nestling her cheek against his chest.

It wasn't until she had mostly recovered from the aftereffects of her dream that she noticed his heartbeat had quickened from the slow, regular thud it had been when she had first awakened.

She drew back a little and looked up at him. His face was close, but she couldn't read his expression in the dim light.

Neither moved for a long breath.

Then he lowered his head, and his lips touched hers. His kiss was softer than Ellie had imagined, and she felt it like a live current through her body. She didn't know what had been holding him back, but with that kiss, she knew he had wanted this as much as she had.

Ellie woke naturally the next time. It was dark in the room—dark outside too; there was no light filtering in around the edges of the curtains. She had shifted in her sleep so that now she was curled away from Nicolas, but he had an arm draped around her middle, and they were both sticky with sweat where skin touched skin. She had a pounding headache, and her mouth felt like it was filled with sawdust, but she had no desire to move. She tried to lie as still as possible, but he said softly in her ear, "You awake?"

"Yeah." She expected him to lift his arm, to move away, but he didn't. Instead he dropped a kiss on her neck.

"Have you been awake long?" she asked him.

"A while," he murmured, his mouth against her hair.

"You should have gotten me up."

"Not for a million bucks."

"That's not saying much, coming from you," she observed.

He laughed, and his arm tightened around her. "You were sleeping so peacefully." He paused, then asked, "When you woke up before—what was it you were dreaming about?"

When Ellie didn't answer right away, he said quickly, "It's all right. You don't have to tell me."

"No, I'll tell you." But again she didn't speak immediately. Finally she said, "It was about my father mostly, I guess."

"Is he still alive?"

"Oh, he's alive, all right."

"What was he doing in the dream?"

"Flying. He was flying. He was a pilot in the Korean War, you know. Decorated war hero. In my dream, he was in his fighter, and there were planes all over the sky—like fireflies—and my father was firing at them. Some of them exploded in a ball of flame. Some of them went into spiral dives. Some just went straight down as if they were gunning for the ocean floor. I was in my helo with my crew, and every time a plane went down, we tried to save them, but all we were pulling in were bodies. One was Dave's. Another was yours."

"Look at me for a second," Nicolas said.

She rolled over on her back, and he propped himself up on one elbow.

"Let me ask you a question. How many people did you save while you were in the Coast Guard?"

"Fourteen."

"That's a lot of people who owe their lives to you. I happen to be one of them."

"But fourteen is my grand total," she said. "That's it. Career over. No awards, no medals, no distinctions. Well, wait. One distinction. I have the distinction of getting my wings jerked, and you can't forget, I also have a death on my conscience as well, and I'm not so sure that one doesn't cancel out the fourteen saves."

"What's this death you're talking about?"

"Dave. My copilot."

"Whoa. Who says you're responsible for your copilot's death?"

"Don't you think jerking my wings was a good hint? But no one has to tell me. I know it was my fault. It's a miracle something like that didn't happen earlier. I deserved everything I got . . . and then some."

She rolled onto her side again, gathered the pillow to her chest, and said in a low voice, "Nicki, I'm scared."

"You?" She felt him pull back from her then. "I didn't think you were scared of anything."

"Of course I'm scared of stuff. Right now, I'm scared of the rest of my life. What am I going to do?"

"Who says you have to do anything?"

"I do, Nicki. I can't live in a hotel room with you forever, gambling away your money, wearing skimpy dresses, and fighting off your father."

Nicolas swung his legs over the edge of the bed and leaned forward, his head between his hands. "What if I told you . . ." but he trailed off before he finished.

"What if you told me . . . what?"

She saw him lift his head, curl his hands into fists, then release them. He twisted to look at her. "What if I told you I had a job for you?"

"Thanks, but I don't want a pity job."

"It's not a pity job."

"Oh right. What can I do? What am I qualified for?"

"You can fly."

"Fly?" she repeated. The thought of flying again should have been the best possible news she could have heard, but Ellie was conscious only of a sickening lurch—something close to fear. "I don't have a license."

"If you put it that way, you can't." He paused and, in that second, the relief she felt disgusted her. Then Nicolas qualified his sentence, adding, "At least not legally."

She frowned. "What . . . what would I be doing for you?"

He didn't answer right away.

"That part isn't legal either, is it?" she said.

"No. It isn't."

"Jesus, Nicki." She sat up, pulling the sheet around her. "What exactly is this job?"

"I can't tell you what it is. Not yet."

"How can you ask me to do something when I wouldn't know what I'd be agreeing to?"

"I can tell you a little. For the rest, you'll have to trust me."

"Oh great," Ellie groaned and flopped back on the bed.

"I know. That's the worst thing I could ask, right?"

"It's close. So what *can* you tell me?"

"We'd be picking something up."

"Picking something up? From where? And how far would we be taking it? And why do you specifically need a helicopter?"

He grimaced in apology. "I can't tell you much, but I need a helicopter because the package is being stored someplace that's hard to get to."

She wondered if it had something to do with the conversation she'd overheard the night before. "This is not a lot of information you're giving me here," she said.

"I know."

Was she imagining things, or did Nicolas look nervous?

"This thing," she said. "It's important, isn't it?"

"Yes. It's important. It's important to me. I wouldn't ask you otherwise."

She voiced her concern in a half joke. "You're not afraid to fly with me? I mean, the last time I was up, I crashed."

She was startled at his response—he turned on her, saying fiercely, "That wasn't your fault."

At that moment, she almost loved him for it.

"You're the only one who thinks it wasn't," she pointed out. After she said it, she remembered Sam and his visit to her apartment.

"I would only ask someone who I was absolutely sure could do it. In fact, I can't think of anyone else who I'd trust with this."

"So it's me or no one?"

"That's about it."

"What will you do if I say no?"

"I don't know. Haven't thought that far ahead yet."

She wanted to say no. She knew she should say no, but she found herself saying, "Can I think about it?"

"Yes, but not for too long, okay?"

"How long do I have?"

"Till tomorrow. I meant to ask you before this—I started to bring it up a couple of times, but I didn't want you to feel like you had to . . . because the money . . . even though I should mention that if you did it, we'd be square and then some."

"I wouldn't be doing it for money," she said. She wouldn't be doing it at all, she thought to herself. She'd tell him no tomorrow.

CHAPTER 49

 "Commander!" Teddy poked his head into the motel room. "Pantano," he said urgently.

Sam emerged from the bathroom, rubbing his hair with a towel, fully dressed except for his socks and shoes.

"He's gone," Teddy hissed in a stage whisper. "Somers is alone in the room."

"What?" Sam dropped the towel. "Well, why didn't you go in and talk to her?"

"I thought it would be better if you did it. If he came back he might recognize me, but he doesn't know who you are."

"All right, where did he go?"

"I didn't stay to see," Teddy said. "I came right in here to tell you. It looked like he was crossing the street."

"Then we don't know how much time we have. I'd better get going." Sam slipped out, still in his bare feet, and padded down the cement walkway to the door at the end of the row. He checked that Nicolas wasn't in sight, then he put his hand on the knob. It was unlocked.

He heard Ellie start to say, "That was quick. Were they out of . . ." but she broke off when she saw him.

Sam stepped in and closed the door behind him. Ellie was half sitting up in the bed, staring at him. She had the sheet pulled up and pinned underneath her arms like a toga. Seeing her like that, he flushed and quickly looked away. He spoke rapidly, keeping his eyes fixed on the wall just above her head. "Where did he go? When will he be back?"

"Who?" she said, rather stupidly. She was still trying to recover from the shock of seeing Sam so badly out of context.

He managed to look at her. "The guy. Nicolas."

"Um . . . he went for some Gatorade. What are you doing here, Sam?" Her eyes slid to his bare feet. "And where are your shoes?"

"Listen, you need to call us as soon as you can, but don't tell him about it. It's very important. We'll get a room at . . . name a casino."

"We're staying at Caesars."

"No, not the one where you'll be. Another one."

"The pyramid one," Ellie said. "I think it's called the Luxor."

"We'll be there, under my name. One of us will be in the room until you call."

"Who's us?"

"Teddy's here too," Sam said. "I'd better go. Remember, call as soon as you can, but whatever you do, don't let him know." Without waiting for an answer, he turned and slipped back outside.

He was just in time. He saw Teddy standing at the door of their room, pointing desperately across the street. Sam resisted the urge to look over his shoulder. He walked quickly to where Teddy stood at the door to their room and ducked inside. Teddy slammed the door behind him.

"Did he see me?" Sam asked.

"I don't think so. He was just coming out of the store, but he wasn't looking over here."

"We'll find out soon enough. If he did see, he'll come to check it out."

They stood there, waiting for the knock. Finally Sam relaxed. "He didn't see me. We'll wait a few more minutes to make sure, then we can get out of here."

"Get out of here? What do you mean? Did you talk to her?"

"I told her we'd check into the Luxor, and that she should call us there as soon as she could."

"What did she say?"

Sam smiled. "She said, 'Where are your shoes?'"

"That's Somers for you. Always coming up with something profound on the spur of the moment. Did she say anything else?"

"That's all we had time for."

"So of course you stuck to important things, like footwear. What are we supposed to do now?"

"We go check into the hotel. Then we wait."

Teddy sighed. "We should certainly be good at that by now."

It wasn't hard to find the Luxor—it was the only giant Egyptian pyramid on the Strip. Sam and Teddy parked in the back and approached along a raised walkway, past the deserted lake-sized pool surrounded by hundreds of unoccupied deck chairs. When the doors to the casino slid open, they were greeted with a rush of cold air and the clanging, ringing noise of the slots. At first it was like any other room, but as they walked along, they reached the section where it opened up, and there was no real ceiling—just the inside of the pyramid rising to its point.

As they headed over to the registration desk, Teddy craned his neck, like a tourist, but Sam seemed unimpressed.

"You don't get this kind of thing where I'm from," Teddy said.

They found registration and got in line.

"Where *are* you from?" Sam asked a moment later.

"Small town in Minnesota. What about you?"

"New York."

"Where in New York?"

They were interrupted as it was their turn. The woman behind the counter handed over a registration form. Sam answered the question as he bent to fill out the registration form. "I'm from the city," he told Teddy.

"What, New York City?"

"Mmm," Sam said, writing.

"You're kidding."

Sam signed the bottom of the form and handed over his credit card. "No. Why would I be kidding?"

"No reason, I guess. I'm surprised is all."

"I don't seem like I'm from New York?"

"I don't know. I've never been, but I guess I thought that would be something you would've mentioned. Something I would've known."

"I didn't know you were from Minnesota."

"Yeah, but that's different, isn't it?"

"I guess it is," Sam agreed.

The woman who was checking them in handed over a plastic card. "This opens your room. You're in number 826, and the inclinator is over to your right."

"The what?" Teddy said.

"The inclinator. It's an elevator that goes up and sideways. It's over there." She pointed the way, then called out, "Can I help the next person?"

They moved away from the desk. "So this is all ho-hum stuff for you?" Teddy said. "Being from New York City and all."

"I've never been in an inclinator before," Sam replied.

"I've never *heard* of an inclinator before."

"Makes two of us."

They crossed the floor of the casino and pushed the button for the inclinator.

When they got in, Teddy said, "Looks like an elevator to me," but by the time they got off on their floor, he'd changed his mind. "That thing is weird," he announced.

"A helo's the only other thing I've been in that can go up and sideways at the same time," Sam said.

"Maybe so, but I've never felt seasick in a helo."

Their room was like any other standard hotel room, with twin beds, a table and two chairs in the corner, and a TV. The only difference was that the far wall of the room was slanted to form the outer wall of the pyramid.

Teddy crossed to the window and pressed his forehead against the glass. "Vegas doesn't look like much from up here," he said.

Sam had collapsed on the bed. "That's perspective for you."

They were silent for a moment, Teddy staring out at the Strip, and Sam staring up at the ceiling.

"You should get some sleep," Sam said.

"What if she calls?"

"We'll wake up."

"Right."

There was another stretch of silence.

"How are we gonna tell her?" Teddy said.

Sam closed his eyes. "I don't know. Start with the good news, I guess, and then we just . . . tell her."

"Right."

"Get some sleep."

Teddy turned away from the window. "Yeah."

"My guess is, she won't call tonight. Tomorrow maybe."

"I guess that'll come around soon enough," Teddy said.

The next morning dragged. Teddy and Sam watched a news show, then SportsCenter, and then two talk shows. At that point Sam said, "Turn it off. I can't stand it anymore." So Teddy went downstairs and bought a pack of cards at the gift shop. They were playing gin rummy in the room when the phone rang. Though they had been waiting for it, they both jumped at the sound. After a pause, Sam rose to answer it.

He lifted the receiver and said, "Hello?" and then quickly, "Where are you?"

Teddy, watching closely, thought he saw Sam blanch slightly.

"Right now? Of course. Right. Room 826. See you in a minute." Sam put down the phone and told Teddy, "She was calling from downstairs. She's coming up now."

Teddy half rose, started to sit back down, then changed his mind again and stood.

Sam started collecting clothes that were strewn on the floor—most of them Teddy's. "What should I do with these?" Sam asked when he had gathered them all up.

"Just stuff them under the bed."

Sam dropped them and shoved them underneath the bed with his foot. Then he pulled the coverlets up over the unmade sheets, and that was all he had time for before there was a knock on the door.

Sam jerked his head at Teddy to get it. Teddy shook his head. "What?" Sam said. "You planning on hiding in the bathroom or something? You're gonna have to see her."

She knocked again.

"Oh, all right." Teddy heaved himself out of the chair and went to open the door.

Ellie stood in the hall. They stared at each other for a moment. Teddy, for once, seemed to have nothing to say. Ellie was the one who broke the silence.

"Hey, shortie, heard you were here." She gave his shoulder a sock with her fist.

Teddy laughed in relief and shot back, "Yeah? I had no idea you were here. You following me or something?"

"How did you guess? You gonna let me in or what?"

"You know the password?" he said.

"Yeah. 'Fuck you.'"

He grinned and stood back to let her by.

"Hey, Sam," she said.

"Hi, Ellie."

Teddy shut the door.

"You want to sit?" Sam indicated one of the chairs at the small table.

"Sure. Thanks." Ellie sat down, Sam perched on the edge of his bed, and Teddy took the other chair. There was a pause. Neither Sam nor Teddy managed to meet her gaze.

"So what the hell are you two doing down here?" she said.

Neither man responded immediately. They had traveled several thousand miles to tell Ellie about Nicolas and the helo, but they both discovered that it seemed suddenly impossible to just blurt it out.

Teddy evaded her question with an accusation. "You left without saying good-bye."

"Yeah, on purpose," she responded. "And that's another thing. How on earth did you find me?"

"It wasn't easy," Teddy said. "We didn't have a clue where you'd gone. We even called your parents, until I remembered the car—"

"Teddy," Sam interrupted. "Skip it. It doesn't matter."

"You called my parents?" Ellie sounded horrified.

"I talked to your father," Sam admitted.

"He told him off pretty good," Teddy said.

"I want to apologize . . ." Sam began, until Ellie started to laugh.

"I wish I'd been there. What was so important that you braved my father—not to mention coming all the way down here?"

There was another awkward pause. Finally Teddy spoke. "I tried to tell you that night I saw you at Marcy's."

"Tried to tell me what?"

"I wanted to tell you . . . they brought up the helo."

For a moment she felt nothing . . . no, that wasn't exactly right—she felt suspended. It was the feeling she'd had when she was skydiving, when she knew that she was falling at terminal velocity toward the ground, but she had the sensation of stillness, as if she were hanging in midair.

"It was Commander Pantano that got it going," Teddy hurried on.

Ellie looked at Sam, but he was staring at the carpet.

"The helo was in good shape," Teddy continued. "There was some damage, but not so much that . . . I mean . . . Shit, Somers, it wasn't your fault."

They waited for her to say something, but Ellie didn't make a sound.

"I'm really sorry," Teddy said. "I can't tell you how sorry . . ."

Ellie covered her eyes. "They're going to reinstate me?" she asked from behind the shield of her hand. She should have been ecstatic. She should have been out of her mind with joy—she'd just discovered that it hadn't been her fault—but somehow the idea of flying again wasn't any less frightening.

"They'll have to," Teddy said.

Ellie raised her head at that. "What do you mean, 'They'll have to?' Didn't they send you? Isn't that what you're here for?"

"Well, no," Teddy said, but he stalled there and couldn't go on.

Ellie looked to Sam. "Sam? What is it?"

"We're not really supposed to be down here. And we're definitely not supposed to be telling you about all this."

"Why not? They're not going to try to cover it up, are they? Pretend like they didn't find anything?"

"No, nothing like that," Sam said. "No, they're not going to cover it up. They just don't want anyone to know about it yet. I mean, they don't want anyone to know why the helo went down."

"I don't see why. Was it . . . oh no." She looked at Teddy.

"No, it wasn't Teddy," Sam said.

"Another of the guys who worked on the helos? John? Was it—"

"It wasn't John."

"Paul?" she guessed.

"No, not Paul."

"Who was it then? I'm not going to hold it against them. People make mistakes. I understand that. You can tell me."

"Nobody made a mistake," Sam said quietly.

"I don't understand. Then how . . . ?"

"It wasn't a mistake," Sam repeated. "Someone did it on purpose."

Ellie's mouth opened, as if she were about to speak. Then she closed it again.

"It was a zip gun rigged to puncture the tail rotor gear box."

Ellie got a flash of memory. She felt the helo yaw beneath her, and then she was back in the hotel room, holding on to the arms of the chair, and Sam was still talking.

"They don't want us telling anyone because they don't want it to interfere with the investigation."

"We're not even supposed to know," Teddy said. "Well, I'm not supposed to know, but the skipper gave Commander Pantano the okay to tell me."

"So the skipper sent you down here to tell me?"

"Not exactly."

"Then how did you get permission to . . ."

"We just came," Teddy said.

"We were authorized for leave," Sam amended. "Until tomorrow."

"You could be in serious trouble," Ellie said. "What if you can't get a flight? Then you're talking about Unauthorized Absence. You could be court-martialed for that."

"We'll be fine."

Ellie ignored Sam's comment. "You did all this to find me and let me know that it wasn't my fault? Christ. I . . . I don't know what to say."

"Don't say anything yet," Teddy said. "That's not the reason."

"It's not? Then what's the reason?"

"Because . . ." Teddy hesitated. "The commander was the one who figured it out."

Ellie looked to Sam.

Sam shot Teddy a deadly look, then faced Ellie reluctantly. "Ellie," he said. "Ellie, the person who did this had to have access to the helo, right? And there were only a few weeks between the accident and the last overhaul, and you know we don't let just anyone near the helos."

"Tours?" Ellie suggested. "We show people around sometimes."

"We checked."

"I showed that reporter around," she said. "He sat in the pilot's seat."

"But you didn't leave him alone there, did you?"

"Of course not."

"And this was rigged in the cabin. Did he climb back there?"

She shook her head. "But I can't believe anyone on base would . . ."

"Neither did the skipper," Teddy said. "That's why he told us. To see if we remembered anybody who got near the helo."

"Did you?"

"Not at first," Teddy said.

"But eventually you did?"

"Yes," Sam answered her.

"And?"

"The only other unauthorized personnel that get near the craft are the SARs," Sam said.

Ellie was suddenly very still.

"We only had one SAR where we took someone on board in those few weeks," Teddy said. "Do you remember?"

"Yes," she responded tonelessly, though what she really wanted to say was no. No, it isn't possible. No, you can't be right. But she knew that it was possible, and that they were right.

"Do you know why?" she asked.

"It was because of the drugs," Teddy said. "Remember we were tailing that boat—his boat."

His boat, she echoed, but not out loud. His drugs. She thought of the "job" he needed her to do that wasn't quite legal and everything fell into place.

"And then I remembered that I'd seen you with him," Teddy continued. "I didn't recognize him at the time, but as soon as we figured it out, I put it together. That and the fact that you'd taken off that same night, and we thought there was a good chance you went with him. We didn't tell the skipper because we knew how it would look if they found you guys together . . ."

Ellie barely heard what Teddy was saying. She was reliving the last few weeks—their first meeting, that dinner on the boat, the trip to Vegas, yesterday. Oh God, yesterday. She saw it all from a different angle now. The supposed "coincidence" of their meeting—that had been a lie. He must have been following her, waiting for an opportunity.

The "why" might have been a mystery but for yesterday's request. He needed her for something. Now she saw that everything since that first meeting had been geared toward achieving that goal. How could she have been so stupid? How could he . . . "I'll kill him," she said softly.

Teddy stopped talking. "What's that?"

Then, as Teddy and Sam watched, a strange, disturbing smile lifted the corners of her mouth. "No," she said. "I take it back. I won't kill him. I'm going to do better than that."

Sam and Teddy stood in a line that snaked around in roped-off switchbacks, waiting to check in for their flight.

"At least we'll be back home tonight," Sam said, but he didn't sound happy about it.

"In a mere eight hours," Teddy replied. "What with the flight down and back, and all the time in that godawful car, it feels like I've spent more time sitting on my ass over the last three days than I have in the last year. Can you tell? Does my ass look flat?" Teddy pivoted as if to give Sam a good view.

"That's great, Teddy. Thanks, that's just what I needed. It's a fitting end to this nightmare. Me looking at your ass."

"Hey, it's not that bad," Teddy said.

"We came down here to get Ellie out of this mess, and all we've managed to do is get sucked in ourselves. Who knows what kind of craziness she's getting herself into, and chances are, we'll go down with her. That is, if we haven't already. I don't want to know what the skipper is gonna have to say about our little disappearing act."

"So why did you agree to this thing in the first place?" Teddy asked. "Why didn't you tell her that you didn't care what she wanted—that you were going to go back and report everything you knew. If you'd said that, there wouldn't have been a damn thing she could have done about it."

"I didn't say it for the same reason you didn't," Sam said. "Ellie had a point—if she doesn't go along with his plan, there's a good shot he'll get away clean. What evidence do we have? How are they going to prove anything in court, especially with the kind of lawyers this guy would have on his side? This way at least there's a chance we can catch him in the act. Do you think I would have agreed to this madness otherwise?"

Teddy nudged his bag forward with his toe as the line moved. "Yeah, I think you would. I'm not buying your Mr. Responsible act anymore. Before this, maybe, but not now. Consider yourself busted. You know this is a long shot—at best. I won't even say what it is at worst."

"Then why are *you* going along with it?"

"Why do I go along with any of these stupid ideas? I don't know." Teddy gave his bag an unnecessary kick. "I guess I figure if anyone can pull this off, Somers can. I've seen her do it before."

"Ordinarily I might agree with you, but this time there's one thing that worries me."

"Only one thing?"

"It's a big one," Sam said.

They moved up in the line, and now there was only one group ahead of them. "Do you have the tickets?" Teddy asked, checking his pockets.

"We have e-tickets," Sam reminded him.

"Oh right." Teddy shouldered his bag. "So what's this big thing you've picked out among the several thousand of things that could go wrong?"

"I'm just not sure that Ellie's going to follow through with it."

"What do you mean? After what he did to her, she wants to tear his guts out. Why wouldn't she follow through with it?"

A ticket agent beckoned to them to step up to the counter, but Teddy didn't even notice. He was waiting for Sam's answer.

"Well," Sam said. "Because I'm pretty sure she's in love with him."

CHAPTER 53

As Ellie walked back along the Strip, the neon lights looked bright and gaudy, like the decorations for a children's party. There were huge herds of tourists on every corner, and she marveled at all the people who had come to this improbable fantasy land in the middle of the desert to forget their lives and gamble away their responsibilities. But wasn't that what she had done as well?

The walk back seemed long, and when she reached Caesars she was dripping with sweat and tired of the jostling crowds. Yesterday, when they had returned to the casino, she had thought of it as coming home. Now as she turned up the drive and pushed through the doors into the lobby, it was with the feeling of having awakened from a dream.

She started toward the elevators, then hesitated. Nicolas would most likely have returned to the room. He would be there, waiting for her. At the thought, she changed course and went instead into the perpetual dusk of the casino.

She walked through the chain of small, dark rooms. Even the tourists with their Bermuda shorts, sneakers, and knee socks couldn't completely kill the atmosphere given off by the low hanging chandeliers, the blood red carpets, and those intimate, glowing circles of green felt.

Ellie wandered among the tables, stopping occasionally to watch, but she found her eyes were drawn away from the cards, or the dice, or the bouncing roulette ball, and up to the bright, flushed faces. She discovered, curiously, that she couldn't tell from the face whether the player was winning or losing—they all looked the same. They were all on the same drug; they were high on risk.

Eventually she made her way over to the high-rollers' section. Vicki was presiding over one of the tables, and she had three players who either didn't know, or didn't care about her reputation. There were two glum-looking thirtysomething men and a small, middle-aged Asian woman. The woman was on a streak, and as Ellie watched, she kept on winning. Doubling down, splitting the hand, hitting on seventeen, it seemed like she couldn't lose. She started playing two hands, and she won steadily on both. The woman's pile of chips grew until it formed a little wall in front of her.

Ellie had always looked at every bet only in terms of what she could win—the money, the medals, the recognition, the lives. Now suddenly she looked at that pile of chips, and she didn't think about how much more the woman could win but of all she stood to lose.

Ellie watched her play and all she could think was, Why don't you quit while you're ahead? It was a question she knew she should be asking herself. Here she was gambling again—only she wasn't gambling with a pile of plastic chips. This time she was risking the opportunity to get her old life back. Sam and Teddy had offered it to her, like a gift. All she had to do was buy a ticket and fly back to Sitka. Then it was just a matter of time before she'd be reinstated, and then everything could go back to what it had been.

The only problem was that she knew it could never be what it had been.

When Teddy told her that the crash wasn't her fault, after the first second of stunned surprise she had waited for the relief . . . but it hadn't come. She waited for the weeks of doubt and fear to disappear, but they had stayed stubbornly in place. She waited for the guilt to lighten, but even that yoke still hung on her shoulders, and now, having had the last hour to think about it, she thought she knew why.

Before the accident, she had never imagined that flying could be any-thing but fun. Flying for her had been as natural, as instinctual as walk-ing. But there was no going back to that easy assurance, that naïve, reckless confidence. It was like watching this woman with her pile of chips; all Ellie could see now was what she had to lose.

Dave had been a hard part of that lesson. It didn't matter that the crash hadn't been her fault—Dave's death was. Sam had skirted the topic of a warning light. She still couldn't remember the moments before the crash. Had they missed a warning light because they'd been concentrating on her little stunt? If that were the case, that meant if she hadn't tried bumping the boat, they would have seen the light, and she probably would have had time to bring them down safely on Dall Island—only a hundred yards away—before all the oil leaked out and the gears were stripped. Everything would have been different. Dave would be alive. That was one burden she couldn't lay at Nicolas's doorstep.

For the rest of what had happened to her, she could blame him. She did blame him. He'd taken away her job, and with it, her life. Then he had returned to Sitka for the express purpose of using her for this job of his. But somehow, worse than all that, was the memory of the day before in the motel. She acknowledged to herself that she might not have been so bent on revenge if they hadn't slept together. Not only that, he'd made her believe he really cared about her. She'd confided in him, and all along it had only been about his drugs. There was no way she was going to get on that plane to Sitka knowing that he might go unpunished. The thought of getting back in the right-hand seat of a helo might terrify her, but she would do it to nail him. The hardest task would be to act as if nothing had happened. She wasn't certain she could.

So instead of going back up to the room and facing Nicolas, she lingered by the blackjack tables. The woman with the pile of chips was losing now, and if anything, the crowd gathered around to watch was even larger than the one that had formed to see her win. Losing a small fortune, it seemed, was even more interesting than winning one.

Ellie glanced around, and her heart skipped. There—across the table watching her—was Nicolas.

From the steadiness of his gaze, she had the sense that he had been there for some time. He simply stood, looking at her with dark, heavy-lidded eyes. She thought that there was something almost melancholy in his expression. She felt a flash of . . . something . . . a split second in which she forgot the last few hours. It only lasted for that lightning moment, and then everything came flooding back, but that instant of sympathy was enough to give her the inspiration she needed for the pretense.

She rounded the table to where he stood and said, "Are you okay? You look awful."

"I came back to the room and you weren't there," he said, ignoring her question—or possibly answering it.

"I went for a walk."

"A walk," he repeated. "I thought . . . never mind." He shook his head, as if he could shake the thought from it. "You never went out for a walk before."

"I never had so much to think about before." That at least was true.

"Yes, well, I was thinking too," he said. "I was thinking maybe we'd better just—"

She didn't want to hear what he was going to say. She didn't want to know if he was planning on letting her off the hook—or pretending to.

"I'll do it," she said abruptly.

He broke off. "You'll do it?"

"Yes. I'll do it. Whatever the hell it is."

"You will." He tilted his head back and closed his eyes for a moment. Then his face split into a grin. "You'll do it," and he swept her up in a fierce hug.

It was so sudden, she didn't have time to react. In a moment he had her pressed up against him, his arms tight around her. Her hands were trapped against his chest, and she could feel the thump of his heart. Then, just as suddenly, it was over and he'd let go.

There was a smattering of applause around them.

Ellie lurched backward, into someone. She turned and there was an older couple, arms around each other's waists, beaming at her.

"Are you going to go do it now?" the woman asked.

"Have you got the rings?" the man said to Nicolas. "I'll sell you ours for a good price," and he laughed heartily at the joke, while his wife punched him in the arm and said, "Oh, Al."

"No, we're—" Ellie started, but Nicolas cut her off, saying, "Yes. We're going *right* now, actually. Ready, darling?"

She gritted her teeth, endured the arm he draped around her shoulders, and said, "Ready."

"Congratulations," the woman called after them.

"If you regret it in the morning, Reno's not too far," Al added.

Nicolas wasn't lying when he said they were going right away. In less than an hour they had boarded the jet and were in the air.

As they settled back into the leather seats, Nicolas looked over at her and smiled. "How 'bout it? You want to get hitched?"

"Now you're pushing it," she told him. She looked down at her lap, absently running her fingers over the ridges in the nylon strap of her seat belt.

"Seriously, thanks for agreeing to this."

"It's okay. I want to." She didn't even have to lie about that. "I want to do something to repay what you've done for me."

If she hadn't been looking for it, she would have missed the look. It was like a single frame inserted into a film, a flash of—was it remorse? No, more likely only a second of guilty self-knowledge.

He gave a little shrug, but otherwise ignored her remark. "All I can say is you're saving me from a fate worse than . . . well, not worse than death. If you ask me, nothing's worse than that, but about the closest thing to not living I can imagine."

"What's that?" She was intensely interested in his answer. That was what she wanted for him—that fate, that almost-death.

"A six-by-ten cell."

"You would have gone to jail?" She was thinking that she *could* have sat back and done nothing, but then, she told herself, she wouldn't have gotten the pleasure of sending him there.

"I don't know for sure. My father got wind of a little project of mine. He got the details wrong, of course, but he guessed enough."

"Was that what he was so angry about?"

Nicolas nodded. "He said that if I didn't remove my cargo, he'd make sure I went down for it. I'm not a hundred percent sure he'd carry through with his threat, but I don't want to test him."

This was sounding familiar to Ellie.

"It's definitely risky, but it shouldn't be a problem for you—not after what you've done in the past," he said.

That worried her a bit. What was he expecting of her?

"Don't you think it's time you told me a little more?" Ellie suggested. "All I know is that we're picking something up. Where are we picking it up from?"

Nicolas beat a nervous tattoo on his thighs with his palms. "A ship. One of my father's ships."

So she had been right. This *was* about the conversation she'd overheard. Then she remembered another detail that she'd forgotten. Nicolas's father had said that he'd sent Nicolas a message almost two weeks earlier, and he was angry because Nicolas had done nothing about it. Nicolas had replied, "I've been working on it." Two weeks, she thought.

He would have gotten the message right before showing up in Sitka the second time. That was no coincidence. He'd suddenly had need of a helicopter pilot, and he'd seen an opportunity in the ruin he had made of her life. She wondered why he hadn't just gone out and hired a pilot. For almost two hundred thousand, she would have thought that there'd be quite a few willing to do the job, even if it was illegal.

"And where is this ship?" she asked.

"It's en route to Vancouver. That's your specialty, right? Picking things out of the ocean."

"It was," she allowed. "What exactly are we picking up?"

"A cargo container. Off a container ship."

"One of those huge steel boxes? Like on a tractor trailer?"

He nodded.

"I don't have a lot of experience with sling loads," she protested. "I mean I could do it—if the winds are calm and the load is stable, but what are the chances of that? And we have a whole other host of concerns. I mean, what are the dimensions of this thing? How much does it weigh? What's the sling load capacity of the helo? And how far do you expect to haul it?"

"It's standard size—about eight feet high, eight feet wide, and twenty feet long. When we pick it up, the container is going to come in just over five thousand pounds. The sling load capacity of the helo we're using is six thousand pounds, and it's got a good range too. A couple hundred miles at least, and we won't be going anywhere near that far."

"Same as the Jayhawk," Ellie observed. "What kind of helo?"

"I don't remember the name of it," he said evasively.

"Is it one of those Skycrane helicopters they use for lifting lumber? Because it takes a while to adjust to a new craft. You need to get used to the controls, how loose or stiff they are, that kind of thing. It wouldn't be such a big deal, but if you're hauling something that size, you can't make mistakes. And what about pursuit? It's not like you can go very fast with five thousand pounds of sling haul. Jesus, Nicki," she said, falling back into the nickname without realizing it. "This isn't risky. This is crazy."

"It's not a Skycrane," he told her. "I did look into renting one, but they're booked up for months."

"It's not only that machine. Any aircraft takes time to get used to."

"Don't worry about it," he said. "It'll be fine."

"Don't tell me my job. It won't be fine."

He looked at her, as if gauging something. "I guess I should tell you. The reason you don't have to worry about the helo is because you'll be flying a Jayhawk."

"But how are you going to get a Jayhawk? You can't just go and rent one."

"Actually, we're going to borrow it."

"Borrow it? I doubt if even one of your father's rich friends has a Jayhawk sitting around in their backyard."

He smiled uncertainly. "We're not going to borrow the helo from one of my father's friends. We're going to borrow it from one of yours . . . we're going to borrow it from the Coast Guard."

She thought she was prepared for anything, but she wasn't prepared for this. She thought she knew what to expect. She had never been more wrong. She almost lost her nerve then. Nicolas must have seen it on her face. He must have expected it. How had he thought she'd agree to this? But at the same time it answered her question as to why he couldn't have gone out and hired a pilot for this job. It would have been nearly impossible to find a pilot with the skill to fly a Jayhawk with a five-thousand-pound sling haul, who was also willing to go along with a scheme this crazy. Especially with only two weeks to work with.

"You don't owe them any loyalty," Nicolas said, trying to answer her arguments before she made them. "They threw away one of their best pilots. You deserved better than that."

He'd made a similar comment before, and she remembered how pathetically grateful she had been. Now she knew that it wasn't blind faith that made him say that—it was hard knowledge. The reason he knew the crash wasn't her fault was because it was his. The thought renewed her determination to follow this thing through, but she had to pretend some reluctance. He'd be expecting it.

"The Coast Guard was my life," she said. "Even though I resigned, that doesn't go away. Not that quickly." Did she see a flicker of guilt over the fact that she had resigned because of what he had done? No, she was looking too hard, seeing things where there was nothing to see.

"Think of it as a prank," he said.

"They wouldn't think it was very funny."

"Then we'll be the only ones laughing. They'll get the helo back, and no one will be the worse for it."

"I could be very much the worse for it if they recognize me. There aren't a whole lot of women pilots around."

"You'll have something over your face, so they can't recognize you that way, and you're tall enough that if you dress in a bulky jacket, no one will know you're a woman. The only thing is, I haven't figured out how to deal with your voice. You'll need to talk, won't you?"

"Yes," she said. "I would, a little, but I wouldn't worry so much about that. The ICS isn't clear. It sounds more like one of the CB radios, and with the noise of the helo, I don't know if I could recognize someone's voice over it. If I don't talk too much that shouldn't be a problem."

"So you'll still do it?"

She pretended to consider. "No one gets hurt, right?"

"I swear," he promised. "No one gets hurt."

"You'll have to tell me what you're planning."

"Every step."

"Okay," she said.

"Okay?" he repeated, as if he didn't quite believe it.

"Yes, okay. I said okay. When do we do it?"

She had enough time to think that she didn't like the look of his smile before he said, "How does tomorrow work for you?"

Sam and Teddy had barely stepped inside the administra-
tion building at the air station when they saw Commander Traub in the hallway.

He spotted them and pointed, bellowing, "You two."

"Oh Lord." Teddy crossed himself as the CO strode
down toward where they stood.

"Where the hell have you been?" Traub demanded while he was still
ten feet away.

Teddy opened his mouth to answer but nothing came out.

"Well? Don't just stand there gaping. I've been trying to get a hold of
you since Sunday. Where have you been?"

"Fishing," Sam jumped in.

"Fishing? What the hell are you fishing for this time of year? Neither
of you even has a boat."

"We borrowed one," Sam said. "A sweet little twenty-footer."

"How nice," Traub drawled. "Catch anything?"

"We had a big one on the line," Teddy said. "But it got away."

Sam turned his laugh into a cough.

Traub eyed them both and then seemed to accept their story because
he said, "We've had a hell of a time around here while you two have
been off fishing. Have you heard the news?"

They shook their heads.

"They think they've figured out who sabotaged the helo. What do
you think of that?"

"Great," Teddy said. "That's great."

There was an awkward pause.

"Who was it?" Sam finally asked.

"I knew you'd be anxious to find out," Traub said with a sharp glance at them. "The SAR. The guy that you, Petty Officer McDonald, picked up a few days earlier. In checking up on him, they discovered that he'd bought the boat the day before and paid cash, and if that wasn't suspicious enough, he ducked out from the hospital. They don't have a name yet, but when they checked into airport records, they discovered a jet that flew in the day before and left the day after, registered to Andreakis Shipping Company. What do you think? You think that's a good lead?"

"Sounds promising," Teddy said.

"Could be," Sam agreed.

"At least they're not looking at air station personnel anymore. In fact, they made the announcement this morning. Everyone knows now. Well, everyone but Lieutenant Commander Somers. Does either of you two have any idea where she can be contacted?"

"No, sir," Sam said.

"I thought her family might know—" Traub started.

"I wouldn't recommend that, sir," Sam interrupted quickly.

Traub looked heavenward. "Now you tell me. Where were you yesterday?"

"Oh no," Sam said.

" 'Oh no' is right. I'm afraid I wasn't very polite."

"You too?" Teddy said.

"What do you mean, me too?"

"Commander Pantano called last week and pretty much told him off."

"You should have heard what he said about Ellie," Sam defended himself.

"I did," Traub replied. "And I didn't react much better than you."

They were silent for a moment. Then Teddy said, "Imagine what her father must think of the Coast Guard."

"Oh, he told me that too," Traub assured them.

Teddy was the first one to start laughing. Sam and the CO joined in a second later.

Sam was the first to try to recover. "It's not funny," he said, but he spoiled it by breaking into another set of chuckles.

"You're right, we shouldn't laugh," Traub said, still smiling.

"It's tragic." Teddy leaned weakly against the wall. "Poor Somers."

The thought of Ellie sobered them.

"If you hear from her, tell her to get her butt back here," Traub said. "She's had a long enough leave. It's time to get back to work. That goes for you two as well. I'll see you back here in the morning." He started to move past them down the hallway, then paused. "By the way, that's a nice tan you've got. You must have taken that twenty-footer pretty far out, seeing as it rained here . . . all weekend." Then he pushed through the exit and disappeared into the parking lot.

When he was sure the skipper had gone, Teddy turned to Sam and said, "Fishing? For God's sake, Commander, couldn't you think of anything better than that?"

"I didn't hear you coming up with anything," Sam replied.

"If I'd known you were going to say something so obviously stupid, I would have."

"I'm not going to listen to this. I'm going to my office."

"Well, I'm going to mine," Teddy said.

"You don't have one," Sam pointed out.

"Fine. I'm going to my desk, then."

They walked down the corridor without speaking. Sam's door came first. He stopped, and Teddy halted too.

"You gonna give me a lift home?" Teddy said.

"I'll come get you when I'm done."

Then Teddy headed off down the hall.

Sam entered the room, crossed to his desk, and settled into the old leather chair. He closed his eyes and finally faced the question that was running an incessant loop in his head—what did he think he was doing? He decided that if he'd been thinking, he wouldn't have gone down to Vegas in the first place, and he certainly wouldn't have agreed to let Ellie stay on with this Nicolas person in the hope of catching him in the act. Now, sitting alone in his office, he could see that clearly. The problem was, he seemed to lose all perspective whenever Ellie came into the picture. Insanity, love, he couldn't tell that there was much of a difference between the two.

Sam sighed, opened his eyes, and started in on his mail. He flipped through the envelopes. Then he noticed that the red message light was blinking on his phone. Picking up the handset, he punched in the code for his voicemail and found he had five new messages. The first two were routine, and he jotted them down on a pad. The next two were both from the skipper, the first was brief, merely saying to call him as soon as he got this message. In his second message Traub demanded, "What the hell do you two think you're doing?" Then Sam could hear him mutter "Damn it," as he hung up.

On the last message, for the first few seconds all Sam could hear was background noise. He was about to hit ERASE when the voice on the machine made him sit up, his free hand gripping the edge of the desk.

It was Ellie's voice, low, barely above a whisper, speaking quickly. "Sam. It's me. I don't know how much time I have. He wants to sling load a container off a ship, it's going down tomorrow, and he's going to use one of our Jayhawks to do it. You've got to get on the duty crew roster. I need you there. It's something like what he did . . . oh shit." The phone clicked and she was gone.

Sam sat, the receiver held tight against his ear. He didn't think he'd ever erase that message. She'd said she needed him.

CHAPTER 55

The call came into the command center at Juneau at eighteen hundred hours, just as the Arctic sun was sliding below the horizon. A vessel, identifying itself as the *Taku Queen* out of Vancouver, had radioed in a near collision with a small bargelike object. When the caller described it, the command center immediately identified it as a NOAA buoy, one of the incredibly expensive and complicated navigational and weather tracking stations. It appeared to have come unmoored and drifted in the current until it was only a few hundred yards from a rocky part of the coastline.

The *Taku Queen* was a small vessel and did not have the capabilities to rescue the five-thousand-pound buoy by itself, but the caller agreed to stay nearby and keep tabs on it until they could send someone to pick it up.

The ops center determined that the nearest Coast Guard cutter was at least five hours away, and in that time, according to the *Taku Queen*, there was a good chance the buoy would be washed into the rocks. A helo could pick it up in less than two. They made the decision, the call was relayed down to Sitka Air Station, and the mechanics on duty immediately started rigging one of the Jayhawks for a sling haul.

While the ground crew was working on the helo, the whoopee was sounded, and the duty crew ran for the operations center. Both Sam and Teddy were part of the four-man team.

On board the *Taku Queen,* Nicolas replaced the radio handset and turned to Ellie.

"It's done. They're sending a helo down. How long do you think we have before they get here?"

Ellie made some quick calculations in her head. "You have to allow time to rig the craft for a sling haul, mount the hook, determine the amount of fuel, and of course there's the flight time. At least an hour, maybe an hour and a half," she concluded.

"Then we've got some downtime. Everything's set to go, and there's no sense sitting here in this stuffy cabin. Let's go out on deck—we'll still be able to hear the radio if they call."

"Isn't it a little cold for that?" Ellie said.

"There should be a blanket around here somewhere." Nicolas opened a storage bin, and after a minute of searching, came up with two.

Ellie took the one he held out to her. Nicolas threw the other around his shoulders like a cape and led the way out onto the deck. There were no chairs, so Nicolas sat on the deck, using the wall of the cabin for a backrest. After a moment's hesitation, Ellie joined him. The night air was cold enough to chill the tip of her nose but no match for the heavy blankets Nicolas had found.

The sun had set but there was a full moon rising, and the stretch of ocean before them was calm. Six months earlier, the only thing Ellie would have noticed was that they had nearly perfect conditions for a night flight, but she wasn't thinking of the conditions now. She was thinking that in the moonlight the ocean looked lonely and desolate.

Nicolas seemed to share her melancholy—or at least the elation he'd shown when she first agreed to help had disappeared. He sat beside her quietly, his head tilted back, looking up at the sprinkling of stars.

They remained that way so long that Ellie was startled when Nicolas spoke.

"You don't know how much this means to me, your helping me with this," he said.

She glanced over at him, but he was still looking up at the sky.

"I know, you're used to saving lives," he continued. "After this, you'll have saved me twice, and I deserve it probably less than just about anyone."

"Now you tell me. I guess I should have thrown you back in that first time," she said, trying to lighten the mood.

But Nicolas answered her seriously. "Everyone would have been better off if you had. There's no one who would have minded very much. Well, except for me, and I wouldn't have minded for long."

"Don't be so melodramatic," she said. "I'm sure you're exaggerating."

"Am I? Have you seen any evidence of the close friends who would miss me? The loving family who would mourn me? You're the only one."

She wanted to close her eyes, to disappear, anything so long as she didn't have to listen.

"I don't mean to make you feel sorry for me. It's my own fault. And I don't even really care. Before you came along, there was only one person whose opinion I cared about."

"Who?" she asked him.

He looked at her. "My father."

"I thought you couldn't care less about what he thought."

"No. That's what I wanted *him* to think. I was so afraid I'd try and I still wouldn't be good enough that I decided not to try at all. You, on the other hand, had the courage to go out there and try to do something. To try to make your father proud of you."

"Didn't work," she said.

"But you did it anyway. Both our fathers said to us, you're no damn good. I decided to go out and prove that mine was right. That's the easy way out. You tried to go out and prove yours wrong. The more hopeless the task, the more courage it takes to keep at it."

She'd never thought of it that way. Even as she was searching for a reason why he was wrong, she felt a small glow, a kernel of something that might grow into a sense of peace.

"You showed me that," Nicolas said. "And since then, I've discovered some other things about myself that I'm not proud of. Like I always pitied those ordinary guys going to work, eating their brown-bag lunches at their desks, going home to watch TV with their kids, maybe having sex with their wives before they fall asleep, only to wake up the next morning to do it all over again. When did they ever get that crazy exhilaration from knowing you almost died but there you were, still alive? But now . . . now I almost envy those ordinary guys. I realized that what they've got, they aren't willing to risk for a cheap thrill. I've spent my life trying to avoid anything like that—that was a risk I was too scared to take."

Ellie was picking at the blanket, pulling out stiff threads of wool.

"Do you understand what I'm trying to say?"

"Yes," Ellie said. "I understand." She didn't think she'd ever understood anyone so well before—because though he had been talking about himself, he could have been describing her. They'd made different choices along the way, but underneath they were the same.

The worst part was that, while she was listening to him speak, that comforting, bracing hate had disappeared. Ellie discovered that it was hard to hate someone when you understood them.

"Anyway, I was thinking, after this thing is over, I might try my hand at a job," he said.

"A job? What kind of job?"

"I couldn't do a desk job or anything like that. What do you say to me as a rescue swimmer?"

"I think you'd be great," she told him.

 Sam lifted off the tarmac and headed south, following the coastline and the dark, spiky silhouettes of the high pines. He could see the moonlight pick up the ripples in the water beneath them.

"Beautiful night," the copilot said.

"It is," Sam agreed.

"Don't get many of these this time of year. Wind's picking up a bit, though."

Sam checked. Patrick was right. The wind was rising.

"You think we might have a problem bringing the buoy in?" Patrick asked.

"You know," Sam said, "I wouldn't be surprised."

■

Nicolas and Ellie were sitting silently, their backs against the cabin, when the radio crackled.

"I'll get it." Nicolas let the blanket fall off his shoulders as he got up.

Ellie knew she should follow him inside to listen, but she didn't move. She just sat there and marveled at the sharpness of the moon shadows.

A moment later, Nicolas came back out and stepped to the rail, looking out north over the water. He said, "They should be here soon."

■

"There," Teddy called from the jump seat. "I see them."

The boat was bobbing gently, anchored just off the shore of one of the thousands of islands that dotted the Inside Passage.

"I think you're right." Sam banked the helo in a turn.

Patrick was peering out from the copilot's seat. "Someone is waving at us from the deck," he said.

"But where's the buoy?" Rusty asked from the back. He was the rescue swimmer, and it was his job to go down and rig the buoy for the sling haul.

Sam pulled back into a hover, not far from the boat.

"I'm trying to raise them on the radio," Patrick said. "But I'm not getting any response. We might need to send Rusty down to find out what happened to the buoy."

"You can drop me right down on that deck, can't you, sir?" Rusty said.

Here we go, Sam thought, but he said, "We could do that."

"He's coming down," Nicolas called to where Ellie stood, just inside the door of the cabin. "Better put your mask on. We don't want anyone recognizing you."

Ellie tightened her ponytail and pulled the ski hood over her face. Nicolas glanced over and smiled. "You look like a bank robber from the movies."

"I feel ridiculous."

"You can see well enough to fly, can't you?"

"See? Yes, I can see."

"I got my props too." Nicolas lifted his shirt and showed her the butt of a gun sticking from his waistband.

"Jesus, Nicki," she started from the cabin.

"Get back inside," Nicolas hissed, flapping at her with his hand.

But she tugged the mask off and took another step forward.

"You said no one was going to get hurt." She had to raise her voice to be heard as the helo dropped lower over the boat and the wash from the main rotor whipped and tugged at Nicolas's clothes.

"How did you think I was going to get them to give me the helo?" he yelled back. "You think all I had to do was ask real nice? Come on, don't you trust me?"

She hesitated. She tried to read his face, but his eyes were in shadow.

"It's not loaded, silly," he said. "Now will you get back inside? We've got company coming."

"Hold, hold, hold," Teddy chanted, and Sam maintained a steady hover while Rusty was lowered out the open door down to the deck of the boat below.

"He made it," Teddy said. "Rusty's on deck."

"And the guy on the boat?" Sam asked. "Can you see him?"

"I can see him well enough," and from Teddy's voice Sam knew that it was Nicolas.

"What are they doing?"

"Talking," Teddy said. "Hold on, they're going into the cabin."

Sam backed off a ways from the boat, but maintained the helo in the low hover, the wash ruffling the water, waiting for an update. Finally he asked, "You see anything?"

"Not yet," Teddy said. "They're still in the cabin."

"Tell me when they come out, all right?"

"As soon as he pokes his nose beyond the doorway, you'll know about it."

"What are you two so worked up about?" Patrick said. "I'm sure they're talking about how we're going to rig the buoy. By the way, have you spotted it? You think it might have washed up on the rocks?"

"No. I'm sure the buoy's fine." It was probably still anchored in its proper position, Sam thought. Nicolas wouldn't have gone to the trouble of really cutting one loose. All he would've had to do was interfere with the transponder that allowed its position to be tracked.

"I can see Rusty," Teddy reported. "He's in the doorway. Now he's signaling."

"What's he saying?"

"Wait a sec. He's saying to bring this guy up."

"I'll bet he is," Sam muttered.

"Bring him up?" Patrick said. "Why would we bring him up?"

"What do you want me to do, sir?" Teddy asked Sam, ignoring Patrick's comment.

Sam didn't hesitate. "Do it," he said. "Bring him up."

 Ellie watched the basket—with Nicolas squeezed inside— as it was drawn up to the open door and maneuvered inside. When it disappeared, she glanced uneasily over her shoulder. Rusty was there in the corner of the cabin, his wrists and ankles bound together in front of him with duct tape, his knees awkwardly jutting up near his shoulders. He had a blindfold covering his eyes, but Ellie still felt strange, standing that close to him.

She looked away, and her gaze fell on the console. After that final call, Nicolas had done a thorough job making sure that no one would be going anywhere anytime soon in the *Taku Queen*. The radio and all the controls were smashed and any wires he could find, he had cut. A couple of blows to the engine itself, and the boat was just a big, fancy dinghy.

She glanced up and saw that the basket was on its way back down. This time it was for her.

It descended, barely swinging at the end of the cable, and Ellie had to admire the steady hover of the pilot. Sam, she thought. Sam was the only person she knew that could keep a helo as still as if it were sitting on the tarmac. At least now he was the only one. She had been able to, once.

When the basket reached shoulder height, she grabbed it and guided it to the deck. Then she climbed in and felt the line tighten as she lifted off the ground. She had never ridden in the basket before. Now she knew what it felt like to be the one rising slowly toward the belly of the helo. At this moment, the people they rescued usually felt their panic giving way to relief—but her panic was just beginning.

■

A minute later, Ellie stood beside Nicolas in the back of the helo. They both had their masks over their faces, and Nicolas held the gun almost casually at hip level.

Ellie had to fight down the urge to laugh. It was like a bad sitcom. She was wearing a ski mask so Teddy wouldn't recognize her, and Teddy was trying to pretend he didn't know exactly who she was.

"Tell the copilot to climb out of his seat and get back here." Nicolas had to yell to be heard above the noise of the rotor, but Teddy nodded to signify he heard and obediently relayed the command.

Over the headset Patrick said, "Did you hear that, Sam? What should we do?"

"Go on, do what he says," Sam replied. "It'll be fine."

Patrick unhooked his headset, unbelted himself, and squirmed with difficulty back between the seats.

"Go ahead," Nicolas said to Ellie, jerking his chin toward the vacated seat.

"I need his helmet," Ellie shouted, pointing at Patrick.

Nicolas oversaw the transfer of the helmet, then he turned back to Teddy and Patrick. "Now, which one of you can rig a big object for a sling haul? 'Cause the other guy's going down to join your buddy."

Ellie managed to climb into the copilot's seat. Then she strapped in and plugged into the ICS.

How many times had she done that? A thousand? Two? But in all those times, had she ever felt this way? No, not even on her first flight. She had been excited, a little nervous, but never scared. Not like this.

"Hey, Ellie," Sam's voice spoke into her ear.

"Hi, Sam," she murmured, as if afraid that Nicolas could hear her.

"Everything going all right?"

"So far," she said. "You still with us, Teddy?"

"Still here," Teddy responded. "We're about to lower Patrick down into the boat. Bring us back ten. We've drifted a bit. Back five. Okay, hold."

Ellie didn't speak, letting Sam concentrate on the flying while Patrick was descending to the deck.

"Patrick's safe on deck and the basket's back in. This guy wants me to tell you . . . well, it looks like he's going to tell you himself. He's putting on Rusty's helmet."

And then it was Nicolas's voice in her ear, saying, "Time to switch drivers."

"Is your colleague capable of flying a Jayhawk?" Sam said.

Sam didn't know that it was the exact question Ellie was asking herself.

"Of course my colleague can fly it. Now shut up and do what I tell you, or your friend gets a hole in his head."

"Ready to start the transfer procedure?" Sam asked Ellie.

Ellie curled her hands around the cyclic and collective. Then she rested her feet on the pedals. "Ready." As I'll ever be, she added silently to herself. Then she started the standard procedure that had been developed so that there was never any confusion as to who was flying the aircraft. Ellie took a deep breath and said, "I've got control." Sam responded, "You've got control," tapping the glare shield to prove it. Sure enough, she could feel the helo in her hands. She was tense and all her movements were jerky and abrupt when she needed to be smooth and subtle. It was like she was a beginner all over again.

She tried to steady her hands. Somewhere in her brain she had hoped, prayed, that it would just come back. The skill. The confidence. The feel.

It hadn't.

There had been a time, not so long ago, when being anything less than the best had seemed like tragedy. Now here she was, barely keeping the helo in the air, but it didn't seem to matter. They hadn't fallen out of the sky. For now, that was enough.

C H A P T E R 5 9

When she turned the helo out to sea, Ellie was worried that they might have to expend extra fuel searching for the container ship, but they found it almost before they started looking. From a distance, the container ship looked like a tall, awkward, slow-rolling block of a vessel. It was only as they approached that Ellie started to grasp the scale of the thing. It was as if a hundred-story skyscraper had been laid on its side and set afloat. There were so many containers stacked on the deck, and they stretched so far into the distance, that it was impossible to count them.

Teddy voiced the question that was in her mind. "Christ, how many are there?" It was a rhetorical question, but Nicolas answered him.

"About eight thousand."

Ellie looked again, but even with the sight in front of her, it was hard to believe that number.

"And you want to sling haul one of those off the ship?" Teddy said. "How are you gonna find the one you want? How do you know it's not buried on the bottom?"

"Everything is done by computer—we've got advanced tracking systems for loading and unloading," Nicolas told him. "At any given moment you can pinpoint the location of any one of those eight thousand containers. The one we're looking for is at the forward end, first row, fourth from starboard. I've got a man on board who has already disengaged the container. All we have to do is attach the cables to lift it. You do that right, and your pilot doesn't get hurt."

"Someone needs to position the helo as I'm going down," Teddy said.

"Okay, so you," Nicolas said, meaning Sam, "climb back here."

"I can't go back there," Sam protested. "This helo isn't rated for one pilot. Only in extreme situations would you have one pilot at the controls."

"Guess what," Nicolas said. "This qualifies."

It was Sam's turn to climb into the back. As they approached the front of the ship, Sam coached Ellie over the headset while Teddy stood in the doorway, waiting to launch.

"Forward ten. Forward five. Too much. Back five. No. Too much. Okay, deep breath. We need to go forward five and left five. Easy on the stick," Sam guided her over the ICS.

Ellie couldn't maintain her position over the container. The wind had picked up out on the Pacific, and it was blowing from the west. At the same time, the ship was plowing steadily south. Ellie had chosen to face into the wind and to maintain a sideways creep to match the ship's speed, but she couldn't seem to keep pace.

"Come on, we need to get this done," Nicolas said.

"I know," Ellie snapped.

She wanted to leave the damn container where it was. She figured that if she flew back now, at least Nicolas wouldn't get away scot-free. They'd have him on whatever charges came along with stealing a Coast Guard helicopter. The sticking point was that they had nothing concrete to tie him to the drug running. But if they had the container . . .

"Everyone just calm down," Sam said. "Let's try it again." And they started all over again. This time around, she managed to stop overcorrecting, and a minute later, Sam said, "Good, yes, hold. Can you maintain your position at this speed?"

She wasn't sure if she could, but she knew it was now or never.

"Send him," Ellie ordered, and then Teddy was on his way down.

"Back ten," Sam said.

She groaned. That meant Teddy was dangling over the water in front of the boat. She eased back on the throttle.

"Not too much."

Then she heard Nicolas say, "Oh no."

"What? What happened? Is he okay?"

"He's fine," Sam said. "Almost . . . almost. Yes. He's down."

"What is it then?"

"It looks like there are crew members coming out from the bridge," Nicolas said. "So he'd better work fast."

The ship was a quarter of a mile long, and the bridge was at the opposite end. There was a walkway along the side, but to reach Teddy they'd have to climb up to the top of the containers. Even so, the two crewmen were only a single container-length away and climbing when Nicolas yelled into the headset, "He's got it. We're hooked up and ready to go."

"What's Teddy waving about down there?" Sam said. "What does he think, we're going to leave him or something?"

"We are," Nicolas told him. "We don't have time to bring him back up. Signal for him to get off the container."

"But—"

"Get him off."

"I'm trying, but he doesn't seem to like it. He's pointing down at the ship and waving like he doesn't want to get left."

"The crew is almost there," Nicolas said.

"He's seen them now," Sam reported. "Stand by. Okay, we're clear."

Surprisingly, Nicolas said, "Hold on."

"What's wrong?" Ellie demanded. "What's going on?"

"Are you sure you can do this?" Nicolas asked her. "I want you to tell me if you don't think you can do this."

"It's a hell of a time to be asking me," Ellie said.

"Well, this is the time to tell me if you can't."

A cloud passed over the moon, throwing a shadow on the water. The rotor's heavy throb beat outside. It was quiet inside the craft.

"Of course she can," Sam answered for her. "Ellie's one of the best. Maintaining speed and position over the bow of this ship is a lot harder than lifting off with the container."

"Is that true?" Nicolas asked her.

"If I can lift it clear without creating a swing, then yes."

"All right," Nicolas said. "Then let's go."

CHAPTER 60

 Maintaining the sideways creep, Ellie raised the collective, bringing the helo up slowly and evenly. She felt when the cable tightened, and she heard the throttle rev higher as the engine strained.

"Forward ten," Sam said into her ear. "Stay over the center."

Ellie made the adjustment.

"A little more juice," Sam encouraged her. "We're almost there."

Then Ellie could feel the weight of the container in the sudden sluggishness of the controls. She needed a bigger movement with the cyclic and the collective to pull the helo up, and free the container from its snug fit.

"Tell me when we're free of the ship," Ellie said.

"Almost, almost, almost," Sam chanted. "You got it."

And she felt it. The container must have started a slight swing because the helo yawed right, then, as she corrected, it swung hard left.

She started to panic, her hands tightened on the controls, and she felt the rotor dip to the side.

"Slight swing in the container. No problem. Just hold her still."

Sam's calm assurance did the trick. Ellie forced herself to breathe, her hands and feet made the delicate adjustments, and the helo steadied.

"All clear," Sam said, as if it were the most natural thing in the world.

"Everything's okay?" Nicolas asked.

"Perfect," Sam answered him. "Now if you'll let me return to the cockpit, I'll be able to plot our course back."

"I don't think we'll need your help with that."

Ellie would have liked Sam in the seat next to her, but she didn't want to protest. She didn't want to draw any attention to the fact that she had started a wide, almost imperceptible turn that would bring them around on course to the air station.

She couldn't have imagined a better return—flying in with the man responsible for what had happened to her and a container with enough evidence to put him away until he was his father's age. This was what she'd wanted—exactly what she wanted. She was sternly reminding herself of this fact when she heard Nicolas's voice over the ICS, addressing Sam.

Nicolas said, in sudden discovery, "You called her Ellie."

"What?" Sam said.

"You called her Ellie," Nicolas repeated. "You said, 'Ellie's one of the best.'"

Ellie felt her stomach dip, as if the helo had suddenly gone into free fall.

"I . . ." Sam faltered then tried to recover. "I recognized her voice."

There was a short silence from the back. Then Nicolas remarked, "Did you hear that, Ellie? He says he recognized your voice."

She wasn't sure how to respond, but it turned out she didn't have to. He answered his own unspoken question.

"I don't believe he did recognize your voice," Nicolas said. "I think he knew who you were all along."

Ellie thought that his voice sounded strange. If the ICS had been clearer, she might even have said that he sounded sad.

"We're not headed to the location I gave you, are we?" he said.

There was no point in lying anymore. So she told him. "No."

Ellie waited for his reply, but he didn't respond.

"Sam?" she called uncertainly.

"I'm here," Sam's voice assured her.

"What are you worried about, Ellie?" Nicolas said. "What do you think I'm going to do? You think I'm going to point this gun at your friend's head and tell you to turn around?"

She understood that Nicolas was describing the scene in the back, and that he had raised the gun and was pointing it at Sam. In her mind, she imagined the barrel of the pistol pressing into Sam's forehead.

"You just keep flying, Ellie," Sam said. "He's bluffing. He's not going to shoot me. Where would it get him? And he can't shoot you. He needs you to fly the helo."

"That all sounds reasonable," Nicolas agreed. "But Ellie, can you risk it?"

He'd done it again. Why hadn't she made him show her that the gun had no bullets? It was because, despite all he'd done to her, she had still wanted to trust him. Deep down, she had wanted some small part of the last few weeks to be true, to be real. She should have known. He had outplayed her again in this final move.

"I'm sorry, Sam. He's right. I can't risk it." She eased them around, respectful of the heavy weight dangling from the helo.

When they were back on course for the location he'd given her, she said, "Okay, Nicki, we're doing it your way. No one gets hurt, right?"

She meant to leave it at that, but the bitterness, the disappointment found words for itself. "That's what we said, isn't it? No one was going to get hurt. That's what you *swore*."

At last she stung him into a reply.

"That's what we said, Ellie, but it seems we both lied a little."

"I lied? *I* lied? Oh, that's rich." The anger flushed through her, and she had to consciously stop herself from gripping the controls as if they were his throat. "Who sabotaged the helo I was flying? And then, what was it you were doing when you showed up at that store and 'saved' me from the store alarm? I'd lost one of my closest friends, my job, lost my whole life—"

"I didn't mean for any of that to happen," Nicolas protested. "I didn't intend for anyone to get hurt or for you to resign. I just wanted a distraction so I could make sure the boat got through. That's it."

"Maybe not, but when it did happen, you used it to your advantage. You needed a pilot, and I was an easy mark. What was it you were doing then, if not lying?"

"Keep your concentration," Sam reminded her. "Let's keep this helo in the air."

"I can concentrate better if I get an answer. How about it, Nicki?"

"Yes, I came back because I needed your help, but it wasn't all as cold-blooded as you make it sound. I didn't have much time, and I'd read about what happened to you after . . . after your helo went down, and I thought . . . well, I thought it was worth a try. But it wasn't only about that. I mean . . . we had *fun*, didn't we?"

"Fun?" Ellie echoed. "Do you think it's fun being used? Do you think it's fun being set up? Do you think it was fun when I found out the truth about what you were doing?"

Nicolas didn't respond immediately. When he spoke, he didn't answer her question but asked one of his own. "How *did* you find out?"

"A friend told me."

"Teddy?"

"No, not Teddy. He helped, but you're looking at the guy I have to thank. Let me introduce you. Nicolas, meet Sam. He's a stiff, righteous son of a bitch, and he's so by-the-book you'd think he might have it tattooed on his ass, but he's a better man than you could ever be. When no one else believed in me, when my best friend thought I'd fucked up, he went to bat for me. He was the one who got the helo raised, and that's how they found out about your little piece of sabotage. Then he risked his job to find me and warn me about you. He didn't even argue when I said I wanted to stay so I could make sure you went down for this. He just told me he'd help however he could.

"But you—you've never done a single thing for anyone else. I think you'd do just about anything to get what you want. I thought I could beat you at your own game, but I can't compete against someone like you. I'm not in the same league. I'm such a sucker I even bought your last lie. What was it you said? I think it was, 'It's not loaded. Don't you trust me?' And I did trust you. Even knowing everything you'd done."

When she finished, she waited for a response, but there was only blank silence.

"Sam?" she called. "Sam, you okay?"

"I'm fine."

"What's going on back there?"

This time it was Nicolas who answered her. "You're wrong," he told her. "You weren't a sucker for believing me. I wasn't lying . . . the gun's not loaded."

Ellie's hands jerked in surprise. The weight-clumsy helo responded, and she felt the container below start to swing in reaction.

"Steady," Sam said.

"Watch it," Nicolas barked at the same time.

"I've got it," she said, slowing their speed. "I've got it. Everything's fine." The helo was fine, but she wasn't.

"Sam, why don't you go back up and help out," Nicolas said, his voice subdued. "It's better with two pilots."

Sam carefully eased himself back through the seats. While he was unplugged from the mike, Ellie said, "Nicki?"

There was no answer.

She called his name again, "Nicki? Are you there?"

And then Sam was in the right-hand seat, plugging back into the ICS.

"Sam, is Nicki okay? He's not answering me."

"Because he can't hear you. He took the helmet off."

"What's he doing? Can you see?"

Sam twisted around to look. "He's sitting in the corner."

"Just . . . sitting there?"

"Yes. Just sitting there."

This was probably another stunt, she thought, though she couldn't imagine how he could possibly benefit from it.

"Could you give me a route to Sitka?" she said. "We should make it fine, but I'd like the most direct way back. We don't want to push the fuel supply."

Sam entered the fly-to point on the computer, and Ellie adjusted her course. Then all she had to do was fly straight, but for the first time since she'd been back in the pilot's seat, she regretted not having her hands full.

"I'm sorry for getting you mixed up in this, Sam," she said abruptly.

"Don't be. It was my choice." Sam glanced over his shoulder into the back again.

Ellie waited a minute, then couldn't resist asking, "What's he doing now?"

"Same thing. He hasn't moved."

She nodded, as if this was just another piece of information.

"I almost feel sorry for him," Sam ventured.

"How can you, after everything?"

"I don't know. I guess I can't. Not when I think of Dave."

"But that was my fault," Ellie said. "If I had been flying responsibly, things would have been different."

"You can't know that for certain. It might have been worse if you'd been flying higher."

"You can't know *anything* for certain. That's part of the problem. Something I do . . . or don't do, could end up killing someone else. I was petrified when I got back in this seat," she confessed.

"You seem to be doing fine now."

"You know what they say about appearances." She paused, but she figured since she had gone this far, she might as well admit it all. "I don't know if I'll be able to come back to the Coast Guard, Sam. I'm not sure I can handle it anymore—not when all I can think about is what could go wrong."

"That shouldn't make you quit. Thinking like that doesn't make you worse, it makes you better. To me, that means you're finally a pilot. The thing is, flying with fear is harder—it's a lot harder. As to whether or not you want to stick with it, well, that's a decision you'll have to make for yourself."

"I know," she acknowledged.

She was thinking that there was another decision she had to make as well—a decision about Nicolas. There had been no reason for him to admit that the gun wasn't loaded. He'd done it, knowing that he was giving up his leverage. Knowing that she was planning on turning him in. Knowing that he would be going to jail as a result. But he'd done it anyway. Just to prove to her that it hadn't been all lies. How could she hand him over after that? As soon as she asked herself the question, she knew there was only one answer. She couldn't.

"Sam," she said hesitantly. "Sam, I . . . I don't think I can do it. I don't think I can turn Nicolas in. Especially with the mandatory minimum sentencing. He could get life. But I can't deliver his drugs either. I don't know what to do."

She half expected a lecture, but Sam said, "Who says it's a choice between turning him in or delivering the drugs? I was thinking . . . sometimes, when there's a drug bust at sea, instead of bringing it back into port, they dump it over the side."

"Just dump it?"

"Why not? It's not as if you'll be letting him off completely. The Mishap Board is onto him. They may be able to tie him to the other incident, they might not, but that's not in your hands."

"Why are you suggesting this?"

"What? You mean because it's not in the book I have tattooed on my ass?" he said.

"I'm sorry. I didn't mean . . ."

"I know what you meant. It's all right. I'm saying it because there are some things that fall outside the rules."

"You're a good guy, you know that?"

"Great. The kiss of death. I'm the nice guy."

"I didn't say you were nice. Most of the time you're a son of a bitch, but you're still a good guy."

"Are we gonna dump this container or what?"

"Yes, sir." She maneuvered into a hover.

"Ease it down into the water, and then let it go."

"All right. Going down." She lowered the helo toward the water.

"Nice and easy. That's it."

She felt when the container touched the water.

"What the hell are you doing?" Nicolas's voice burst over the ICS.

"I'm giving you that second chance," she told him, her heart suddenly as light as the helo. Then she said to Sam, "I think it's down. Hit the release."

"Wait—NO!" Nicolas yelled, his voice crackling over the microphone, nearly splitting their eardrums, but Sam released the hook beneath the helo and the container was set loose on the ocean.

"Please, Ellie, please don't tell me you let the container go," Nicolas begged. "Please don't tell me that."

Ellie felt a stab of bitter disappointment. "I just gave you your life back, and all you can think of is your drugs."

"Oh God, Ellie. It's not drugs," Nicolas said.

Ellie felt the sudden stillness. She was falling again. Falling without movement.

"I was smuggling people," Nicolas cried out. "There are people in there."

CHAPTER 62

"Don't do anything," Sam ordered. "Just hold on. I'm coming back there to help. Just hold on."

"I've got to get the door of the container open before it sinks," Nicolas said.

"Low as you can, Ellie," Sam said. Then, urgently, to the back, "Nicolas, how many people? How many people inside?"

"They told me eight people. Two families. There are kids. I've got to get the door open."

"Wait. You'll be able to help them better if you put on a survival suit. In water that cold, you might only have fifteen minutes before losing consciousness."

There was no response.

"Nicolas?" Sam called. He twisted around.

"Damn. He's gone in," Sam said. "I've got to get back there."

Ellie opened her mouth to tell him to take over the controls and let her go and help from the back, but he had unplugged from the ICS before she could speak.

The fear she'd felt before seemed trivial now. As long as she didn't impact the water, there had been no real threat except to her vanity. Now if she took too long to position the helo in the hover, or if she drifted, or overcorrected, it might mean the difference of a life. Or two. Or eight.

■

Nicolas could hear them screaming. As soon as he managed to get away from the helo, out of the rough water from the rotor wash, he could make out the echoing boom of fists pounding against the steel sides and the muffled sounds of screams.

He swam harder. The container was now listing sharply to one end; he could see the dark bulk jutting out above the water. He blinked, and suddenly the container was illuminated in a tight circle of brilliant light. From twenty yards away, it looked like a stage set, the action picked out by a spotlight.

Now he could see that the end that rose from the water was the back end. All the people inside must have rushed to the door when the water started seeping in, weighting it down on that side.

They hadn't been thinking. That door opened outward. With the pressure of the water, it would be as immovable as if it had been solid welded steel, but he'd had the container specially made to accommodate people. One of the features he'd installed was a window at the opposite end. He just hoped it was large enough for them to fit through.

When he reached the container, he realized he had a problem he hadn't anticipated. With the weight of all the people at one end, the container rose out of the water at a sharp angle. He tried scaling the side, but it was too steep to climb. All the while he could hear the people inside—not screaming now but sobbing and calling out in hysterical voices. They spoke in Russian so he didn't understand the words, but he had no doubt of their meaning. They were prayers.

■

"He's trying to climb on top of the container," Sam reported. "But it's still too far out of the water."

"Is he trying to get to the doors?" Ellie asked.

"No. The doors must be underneath, but it looks like there's some kind of opening on this end."

"Then let's get over there and help him."

Ellie nudged the helo forward, and she found that without the dead weight hanging from the belly, it felt light and responsive. She sensed a glimmering of her old feel, the way her palm curved around the cyclic, the way she rested her feet on the pedals.

"Conn me in," she called.

"Forward ten. Easy right. Perfect. Hold it right there."

■

Nicolas tried digging his fingers into the steel corrugations to get a purchase, but as much as he willed it, he only got a few feet out of the water before sliding back in. His teeth were chattering, and his arms and legs already felt sluggish.

He couldn't see beyond the sharp edge of the spotlight, so he wasn't aware of the approach of the helo until he noticed water scudding up the sides of the container. Then he could barely see, the force of the rotor wash sending the water spraying into his eyes and up his nose, making him choke and gag.

He looked up to try to wave them away, but then he saw the basket, coming from the light as if from the sun itself.

■

"He's on top," Sam said. "I'm reeling in the basket and detaching it so he can use the cable to keep his balance up there. Hold it as steady as you can, Ellie." But holding it steady was a misnomer. The swells were just big enough that she had to follow the motion of the water. To some extent, Sam could make up the difference with the hoist controls, but she also needed to judge the drift because if she didn't remain centered over the container, she could very well pull Nicolas off into the water.

"He's trying to force the opening," Sam said. "It won't be long . . . it can't be." Sam didn't need to tell her—too long, and the container would sink from beneath his feet.

■

Nicolas hung grimly onto the cable so that he could stand on the slanting top of the container and hammer on the opening with his heel— over and over and over. Every blow sent pain shooting up his leg, but he thought he could see the edges of the window starting to buckle.

■

"Talk to me, Sam. What's going on down there?" Ellie said.

"He's doing his best. Maybe if the water inside the container gets high enough, they'll be able to open it from the inside."

"The container will get sucked under before they get close enough to open it themselves," she said.

Sam had no answer to that.

■

When Nicolas first started pounding, the whole container sounded like a gong being struck. As the seconds ticked by, he noticed that the sound was changing. It was deadening, losing the booming resonance. He knew what that meant. The water was filling the container, pulling it deeper into the ocean.

He had an image of the steel husk being sucked under with a swirl of water and disappearing beneath the waves, falling slowly, the temperature dropping—until an edge struck the sandy bottom, and there it would settle with the eight bodies suspended in the dark water.

The image might have given him the extra desperation he needed. With the next blow of his heel the window gave, and the light spilled through the opening onto the upturned faces.

■

"He's through. He's got it," Sam cried. Then, calmer, "Now, Ellie, are you ready to bring it low?"

"What do you mean bring it low?" she demanded. "We already are low. We don't need to be any lower to bring them up in the basket."

Sam explained, "We need to get them out of that container fast. The basket won't fit through the opening, so I figure the best way is to drop the line down inside so they can use that to climb out. But once we get them out, they won't all fit on the top, and we can't drop them in the ocean. If we do that, there's a good chance we'll lose some, what with the water temperature and the current. We don't even know if they can swim."

"So what are you planning on doing?"

"It's what you're going to do," Sam told her. "You're going to bring us low enough so I can pull them right in."

■

Nicolas sat perched atop the bobbing container. His wet clothes were flapping madly, snapping in rotor wash from the helo. His hair tossed in his face, and the wind seemed to beat at him, as if it were trying to push him off. When he looked up he saw the reason.

The belly of the helo was right above him. It was so close that if he had been standing, he could have touched it.

Inside the helo, Ellie focused grimly on her task. Now there was no room for error. Sam couldn't take up the slack with the hoist. She needed to maintain a constant altitude over the bobbing container. Too high and someone could slip from Sam's grasp. Too low and she would crush anyone on the top of the container. This was the situation she had been dreading. One mistake from her could mean someone's life.

Nicolas was quick to grasp the situation. He had to get the people on top of the container so that Sam could pull them in. The water level inside must be rising, but it hadn't reached anywhere near high enough for them to be able to climb out themselves. Then Nicolas realized he was still hanging on to the cable. He guided it through the dark opening.

It helped that the container was listing to one side. The people inside didn't have to climb up the cable—they used it to walk up the steel wall until they were close enough for Nicolas to lean in, grab them, and haul them up.

Nicolas felt like he had enough adrenaline to haul a linebacker up through the window, but the first hand Nicolas grasped turned out to be a young boy's. He came up as if he weighed nothing, and Nicolas saw that his lips were deep purple with the cold. Then Sam was there, leaning down over the edge of the doorway, grasping the boy's raised arms, lifting him up into the helo. Next there was a teenage girl, her face still round with baby fat, then a thick, matronly woman, who made his arms pull in their sockets, but who clung to his hands with a fierce will.

The process seemed agonizingly slow. Nicolas could sense the water seeping in faster as the container settled lower.

Another woman, thin, gray-haired, with the tendons on her thin forearms standing out like ropes, was pulled up to safety. A young man followed her, then an older one, coat-hanger thin underneath his wet shirt, who tried to smile as Nicolas hauled him through the window. Following him was another man, beefy and hard-muscled, who half lifted himself.

And then . . . Nicolas looked down and saw that there was no one else gripping the cable, though only seven had passed by. As the last man was reaching up for Sam's hands, Nicolas grabbed his sleeve. "Where's the other one?" he shouted, trying to raise his voice above the noise of the helo. "Where's the last person?"

The man shouted something back as Sam hauled him up, but Nicolas couldn't make it out. He peered down into the container; the inside was pitch-black. He thought he saw the glimmer of water, but couldn't make out anything else. Eight people. His contact had definitely said eight. That meant there was someone still down there.

Nicolas glanced up at the open door. In a moment Sam would be leaning out for him.

Nicolas grabbed the cable and started climbing—down.

■

"How many do we have?" Ellie called.

Sam grunted then said, "We've got six in. Hold on," and Ellie heard a groan of effort. "Seven," Sam said, after he'd pulled the bulky man inside. "There's no one else coming through. It's just Nicolas on the container now."

"But there were eight. Nicolas said eight."

"Just a minute. I'll ask."

Sam turned away from the door to yell, "Aren't there eight of you?"

They all looked at him with blank expressions.

The young man said, "No good English."

"How many?" Sam said, pointing at them. "How many are there? Are there eight?" Sam held up his fingers to illustrate.

The young man's face lightened with understanding. He shook his head vigorously and, holding up eight fingers, said, "Nyet, ne vosem." Not eight. He folded one finger under and said, "Sem."

Seven.

"What's going on?" Ellie demanded. "Do we have everyone?"

"We got 'em all," Sam said, giving the young man the thumbs-up.

Then he turned back to the door to beckon Nicolas up, but all he saw was the cable trailing gently in the water.

 It was one of the rare, sunny days in Sitka. The air station personnel were lined up inside the hangar in military rows alongside the Jayhawks. The windows of the hangar glowed like bright rectangles of light, and the helos looked freshly scrubbed, paint shining.

Commander Traub stood at a podium, and Ellie, in her dress uniform, stood on his right, facing her colleagues. The CO read in a solemn, measured voice from the sheet in front of him. "Citation to accompany the award of the Distinguished Flying Cross to Lieutenant Commander Eleanor R. Somers, United States Coast Guard."

Ellie had pulled her brimmed, gold braided cap low over her eyes. She stared at the floor, feeling as if everyone was looking at her, and when she glanced up, she found they were. The only thing that bolstered her courage was the sight of Teddy's covert thumbs-up and Sam smiling lopsidedly at her.

Traub read on. "Lieutenant Commander Somers is cited for conduct above and beyond the call of duty, as well as extraordinary achievement while participating in aerial flight."

How many years, she thought to herself, had she dreamed about getting the Distinguished Flying Cross? Almost before she ever knew it existed. And here she was, living her dream—and it felt nothing like she had imagined it would.

"It was due to Lieutenant Commander Somers's skill and ability that seven people didn't perish when a sling load was inadvertently released into the ocean."

That part of the story had been Sam's doing—he claimed to have forgotten to toggle the switch for the cargo hook to the safe position, so when he accidentally hit the button on the cyclic, the container was released. He had forbidden her to correct the lie, though otherwise he probably would have received the DFC as well. When she pointed this out, he brushed her off, saying, "I've already got one hunk of metal sitting in my dresser drawer. I don't need another."

"It was her ability," Traub continued, "to maintain a hover right above the sinking container, at night and without a copilot, that allowed all seven people traveling inside to climb to safety. Only one individual was lost, an alleged saboteur, who of his own accord climbed back down into the container just before it was pulled under."

The saboteur . . . Nicolas . . . the person who jumped into the freezing water to pull seven people out of that steel coffin—who had gone back down inside to get the eighth. The nonexistent eighth. And here they were, calling him a saboteur, as if that somehow made it okay that he was dead—as if that constituted a happy ending. He was the one who should have been getting the medal, Ellie thought, but then Nicolas wouldn't have cared about a medal any more than Sam did.

"Lieutenant Commander Somers's courage, judgment, and devotion to duty are most highly commended and are in keeping with the highest traditions of the United Stated Coast Guard."

Traub turned to Ellie and pinned the medal to the lapel of her uniform. She could see the bright flash of a camera. Traub shook her hand and said, "Congratulations, you've earned it. Glad to have you with us again." He took a step back and saluted.

She returned the salute, and then, instead of dropping her hand to her side, she touched the surface of the medal. It felt cold under her fingers.

CHAPTER 64

Ellie stepped through the airport doors, leaving the protection of the air-conditioning. The Nevada air was thick with heat. It hadn't been long since she had flown out from this airport with Nicolas, but she discovered that she had already forgotten the intensity of the climate. Her memory had whitewashed the temperature. What else had she distorted, Ellie wondered. She still couldn't figure out if it had been the best time of her life or the worst, and the only answer she could come up with was—it had been both.

"Excuse me, miss," a voice said at her elbow.

Ellie turned and found herself looking down on a thin, stooped old man incongruously dressed in a black suit despite the heat. That face, the suit—both were familiar.

"Anthony?" she said.

"You remember." He seemed pleased.

"Of course I remember. You picked us up at the hotel and brought us out to that party. You helped Nicki with his father."

"I don't know if I helped, but I tried. I tried . . . usually without much success."

"I'm sure they didn't make it easy for you," Ellie said.

"Stubborn as mules—both of them," he agreed. "Together, a nightmare, but separately, both wonderful men in their way. Mr. Andreakis was honored by your request to attend the service, and he asked me to come meet your plane and escort you to the church."

The Greek Orthodox Church was located west of the Strip, in a part of the city Ellie hadn't seen. They drove through wide, vacant streets, lined with suburban houses. There were no outrageous buildings, no flashing neon lights, no crowds—this was not the fantasyland of castles and pyramids and Venetian palaces.

However, the church itself was striking, with its large dome, red tile roof, and tan stucco walls. There were no spaces in the church parking lot, so they had to use the one across the street. They entered the church just as the service was starting and slipped into a pew at the back. It was clear to Ellie in the first few minutes that this service was not going to be what she had hoped.

At the air station, everyone had looked on her return as an unmitigated success. They had seen Nicolas's death as justice for Dave's, and they couldn't understand why—now that she was back—she wasn't her old self again. Sam was the only one who came close to understanding, and though she knew he would have been willing to listen to her talk about Nicolas, she didn't try. She thought it would hurt him, and she found that she very much did not want to hurt him.

So she had come down to the service in the hopes of hearing people who had known Nicolas get up and talk about him, tell funny anecdotes, and maybe break down and cry as they tried to go on with their speech. She wanted to be around people who felt like she was feeling, but she quickly discovered that it wasn't that type of funeral. It was a formal religious service, with selections from the psalms, Bible readings, and a few hymns. The clergyman was the only one who spoke, and none of what he said had anything to do with Nicolas. Instead of feeling closer to Nicolas, as she had hoped, she felt he was slipping further away. She couldn't even summon up the image of his face.

When the service was over, Anthony had her sit and wait while most of the people drifted out the doors. "It will be easier for us to slip out without anyone noticing," he explained.

She thought he must be exaggerating the need for caution, but as they left the church, she saw a crowd of reporters surrounding one side of the entrance, and at the center of the crowd, a step higher and a head taller than the rest, was Nicolas's father.

He was presiding over them like a king holding court. Ellie slowed automatically, and at that moment Alexi lifted his gaze over the heads of his audience and looked straight at her. Their eyes locked. Alexi gave a solemn nod— almost a little bow—then turned back to the group.

And that was it.

Anthony had her arm and was pulling gently, trying to get her to keep moving. "Let's go," he murmured.

But one of the reporters had noticed the direction of Alexi's gaze, and he followed them, calling, "Miss. Excuse me, miss." He caught up with them as they were about to cross the street. "What's your name? Miss? How do you know Mr. Andreakis?"

Ellie tried to keep her face averted but the reporter circled around. "Hey, I recognize you. You're . . ." he paused, groping in his memory. "You're the pilot. You're Ellie Somers, aren't you?"

Anthony pulled her out into the street, surprisingly quick on his feet, and they darted between the lanes of traffic. The reporter was left on the curb, staring after them.

They climbed into the stuffy heat of the car and, once they were under way, she asked, "What did all those reporters want? What is there left to write about?"

"Didn't you hear? Alexi has turned Nicolas into a martyr." Anthony chuckled. "He's turned it into his latest cause. At the moment, he's fighting the deportation of the Russians that were in the container. He's having a grand old time, talking about how this country used to be open to immigrants, and now people are forced to pay thousands and endure potentially lethal conditions for a chance at a life here. In the industry of smuggling people, Nicolas was a rather strange exception to the rule. I'm sure you've read about how he spent time searching out the most deserving cases, and that he brought them over at no charge. He even had a special container designed to make the journey as comfortable as possible."

"I read about it," Ellie said. "It didn't surprise me. Nicolas didn't do anything for the money. But do you know why he did it?"

"Alexi had the same question. He tracked down Nicolas's partner over in Russia—the man who helped find the people and set things up from that end. Apparently Nicolas told his partner that he wanted to give other people the chance his father had, though he hoped their children would turn out a little better."

"That sounds like something Nicki might say," Ellie said, smiling a little. "At least the second part." She turned to study Anthony's profile. "Do you believe it?"

"His father does. Alexi repeats that story at least ten times a day."

"So his father's finally proud of him," Ellie said.

"It's easier to be proud of a dead martyr than a living son."

"Especially one like Nicolas," Ellie agreed.

She glanced out her window and caught a glimpse of the Strip in the distance. "Anthony," she said. "I have some time before my flight back. Do you think you could take me down the Strip? For old times' sake? Maybe tell me some stories about Nicolas and the crazy things he did when he was growing up."

"It'd be my pleasure," Anthony replied.

CHAPTER 6 5

It was raining.

Ellie sat at her desk, listening to the soft, steady beat of it on the roof while she worked through the pile of papers in front of her. It was only four o'clock, but the December days were short and it was pitch-black outside.

She had been at her desk since seven that morning. She had vowed to herself that she would get through the stack today, no matter how long she had to sit there, but when she heard the knock on her door, she felt a distinct sense of relief.

"Come in," she called, leaning back in her chair and stretching her arms above her head.

Sam stepped into her office.

"Hey," Ellie said, brightening. "Have you come to rescue me from death by paperwork?"

He shut the door behind him and turned back to her.

"Yes, but the cure may be worse than the ailment. There's a reporter outside who wants to talk to you."

"Oh no, I thought all that was over. It's been almost six months now. You'd think they'd let it go."

She had let it go—almost. At odd times, she would remember Nicki's lazy, wicked grin. Or she'd see him stretched out in the suite at Caesars, with his narrow bony feet propped on the end of the couch. Or she'd recall his dark eyes, watching her from across the casino floor. The difference was that now she could think of him without that sharp, stabbing sense of loss, just as she could think of Dave without the devastating guilt.

The sadness—that didn't go away—but it was a more peaceful kind . . . the kind she could live with.

"This reporter, he says you know him," Sam said. "His name's Whalen, and he says he was up here to do a profile on you the night you . . . the night it all started."

He meant the night she had been called out on the SAR and had rescued Nicolas.

"So why is he back now?"

"He says that his magazine never printed the piece because of what happened, but apparently they want to run it now, and he's here to get the update."

"Remind me why I need to do this?" she said.

"For the team," Sam told her, mimicking the CO's voice. Then, switching back to his own, he said, "You want me to get rid of him?"

"No," Ellie sighed. "If he came all the way up here, I'd better see him."

"I'll give him ten minutes, and then I'll invent an emergency," Sam said. "Oh, and I meant to ask you. Do you want me to pick up a bottle of wine for tonight, or do you think we should bring over some food, like a cake or something?"

"Tonight?"

"Alex and his wife have invited us over for dinner. You didn't forget, did you?"

"Right. Yeah, of course." She had forgotten, but she covered quickly. "Alex could be flying tomorrow, so a cake might be better. I'll pick it up. I have some errands to run anyway."

"And I told Teddy we'd meet him afterward," Sam added. "He says we're neglecting him."

They *were* doing more things with the other couples on base. At first she'd gone reluctantly, suspecting that the invitations were due to Sam's efforts, but she had been surprised at how well it went—how much she had liked the wives of her colleagues, and even more unexpectedly, how much they seemed to like her. Now she thought she might be invited even without Sam.

"We went out with Teddy day before yesterday," Ellie reminded him. "You're such a sucker. He wouldn't be so anxious to see us if you didn't pick up the tab all the time. I swear I should take lessons from Teddy. He's got you wrapped around his little finger."

"You don't need lessons from him," Sam said, taking a step around the desk and bending down to kiss her.

After a minute, she pushed him away, laughing. "No more of that. What would happen if someone walked in and saw us?"

"If they had any manners they'd say 'Excuse me,' and get the hell out," Sam said, starting to bend down again, but Ellie warded him off. "I want to get this reporter thing over with. Go on. Go," and she made shooing motions with her hands.

Sam reluctantly obeyed, backing toward the door.

"Ten minutes, tops," she said. "I want you to promise."

Whalen sat in the chair on the other side of Ellie's desk, his writing pad balanced on his knee, tapping his pen on the paper impatiently. He had asked if he could record the conversation, but this time she had declined.

Ellie let the silence ride and tried to check her watch surreptitiously. Surely it had been at least ten minutes.

Whalen had tried to take her back through the events of the preceding months, and her responses had been as brief as she could make them. It was strange to remember how easily she had talked to this man only a few months ago. Now she found that she had very little to say.

After the short silence, Whalen abruptly gave up trying to ask about the incident which had brought her so much attention and asked instead about how it was to be back.

"It's good," she said simply.

He waited for her to elaborate, and when she didn't, he looked at her for a long moment. "You've changed," he said, almost accusingly. "You used to love it."

Yes, she thought to herself, she *had* loved it. She remembered that feeling—the rush, the leap of excitement—when the whoopee sounded. Now, instead of excitement, a small charge of fear shot through her. She didn't love it anymore. Not in the same way. Every time she went up, she thought about the Coast Guard's unofficial motto, "You have to go out, but you don't have to come back." She'd said it often, but she hadn't understood it the way she did now.

"Have you been out on a SAR since you've been back?" he asked.

Ellie smiled. He was certainly asking the pertinent questions.

"Yes. A few weeks ago."

"What happened?"

She remembered the blinding mix of rain, sleet, and snow. It had been "zero zero" weather—zero ceiling and zero visibility—and she'd had to fight vertigo the whole way, keeping a close eye on her instruments to reassure herself that she wasn't rolling upside down or flying straight into the ground. It had been a nerve-wracking, exhausting flight, and she had never been happier to step out of the helo and back onto the solid tarmac. Before, she might have welcomed the opportunity to recount the rescue in detail. Not anymore. Instead of describing the difficulty of the conditions, or how it had taken every ounce of skill and courage she had to make it back, she reported the only thing she cared about now.

She said, "We saved three."